Her lips opened—enough that he caught a flash of glistening, sharp, white teeth.

"I'm not going to hurt you," he said. "Not unless you make me."

Her gaze dropped to his mouth, then to his throat and the part of his chest that was exposed. Her heart thudded against her ribs and she shivered just a little against him.

The scent of her flesh—her blood—called to him. She spoke to some deep primal part of him that longed for home.

He could kill her for that—promising something he could never have.

But as she stared at him, stormy eyes wide, cheeks flushed, pulse fluttering, obviously as tempted by him as he was by her, Temple decided to kiss her instead.

"I want to taste you, sweet Vivian," he murmured. As her eyes widened, he continued, "But a kiss will have to do."

Other **Avon Romances**

THE ABDUCTION OF JULIA *by Karen Hawkins*
A BRIDE FOR HIS CONVENIENCE *by Edith Layton*
THE BRIDE PRICE *by Anne Mallory*
HER SECRET LOVER *by Sara Bennett*
THE HIGHLAND GROOM *by Sarah Gabriel*
A VIEW TO A KISS *by Caroline Linden*
WILD *by Margo Maguire*

Coming Soon

LOVE WITH THE PERFECT SCOUNDREL *by Sophia Nash*
NEVER RESIST TEMPTATION *by Miranda Neville*

And Don't Miss These
ROMANTIC TREASURES
from Avon Books

BETWEEN THE DEVIL AND DESIRE *by Lorraine Heath*
NEVER DARE A DUKE *by Gayle Callen*
WHEN A STRANGER LOVES ME *by Julianne MacLean*

Night After Night

BROTHERHOOD OF THE BLOOD

KATHRYN SMITH

AVON

An Imprint of HarperCollinsPublishers

AVON BOOKS
An Imprint of HarperCollins*Publishers*
10 East 53rd Street
New York, New York 10022-5299

Copyright © 2009 by Kathryn Smith
ISBN 978-0-06-163270-9
www.avonromance.com

First Avon Books paperback printing: February 2009

Avon Trademark Reg. U.S. Pat. Off. and in Other Countries, Marca Registrada, Hecho en U.S.A.
HarperCollins® is a registered trademark of HarperCollins Publishers.

Printed in the U.S.A.

10 9 8 7 6 5 4 3 2 1

For Amie, Amanda, Min, and Heather, the girls who keep me sane, and make me get away from the desk and out into the "real world" every once in a while. And to Jesse and Adele, who listen to me ramble on about plot and never complain. Extra thanks to Jesse for reading this book in its early stages.

I'd also like to dedicate this book to all the readers who took the time to let me know how much they enjoyed this series, especially Andrea W, who has buoyed my ego more times than I can count, and Joe F., my favorite former marine drill sergeant.

And to Steve, as always. Who loves ya, baby?

Night After Night

Chapter 1

Somewhere in Europe, 1899

He should kill her. Whether or not he could wasn't the question that plagued him; it was why hadn't he done so already?

Lying on a narrow cot in a cool, dank cell, Temple listened to the footsteps on the floor above. Long, determined strides carried his visitor toward the door that led down into the cellar where they'd sequestered him for . . . he had no idea how long. He knew that stride almost as well as his own now. It came out of the fog they'd kept him in—the fog that had been steadily clearing for days, though he never once let on that their drugs no longer worked.

Yes, now that he had regained much of his strength, he was very tempted to kill his sweet-smelling captor.

He was tempted to do all kinds of things to her.

When they had first taken him, they used some kind of drug—a poison—on him. It deadened his nerves and rendered him unconscious. They kept him that way for much of the journey. And when they finally arrived at their destination—wherever the hell that was—they switched from their poison to opium, great amounts of it, given to him by the one person trusted to deal with him. The one person who his captors obviously believed could handle him if the need arose.

Vivian.

Her heart rate almost doubled whenever she came near him. Temple knew this because he could hear it. Lying on his bed, in his prison of silver, he could hear her approach and the muffled *woomp-woomp-woomp* beneath her ribs.

Being a vampire had its advantages, and one of them was knowing when a woman was sexually attracted to him. Vivian was. She also feared him with equal or superior passion. It wasn't personal. It was because he was a vampire. But regardless of how wary she was of him, that wasn't the sole reason her heart kicked up a fuss whenever she came near him.

Thank God she couldn't hear how *his* heart reacted to her.

He could smell the delicate ginger-peach scent of her skin as she came down the cellar steps. He didn't put his bare feet on the floor—three days of painful, oozing blisters after he tried to escape the first time broke him of that. The floor had flecks of silver in the paint that burned his soles. And every hour another guard came and sprayed a fine mist of holy water through the bars—just in case blisters—and opium—proved not to be deterrent enough.

Still, even the thought of blisters wasn't enough to sour the sight of her. And his vision had cleared enough that he could fully appreciate her. Oh, he could kill her on the sheer premise that she was one of *them*, but there was no denying the woman was a ripe piece of heaven personified.

She had to be at least six feet tall. It was difficult to tell as he'd never had the honor of standing next to her. Clad as she was in a shirt, trousers, waistcoat, and boots, there was never any chance of her being mistaken for a man. Her thighs were far too shapely, her hips too round, her waist too small, and her breasts . . . Well they were abundant handfuls, and Temple had big hands.

And that was only the beginning of her charms: skin the color and smoothness of rich cream, cheeks and lips naturally burnished like a succulent peach. Her eyes were the same shade as a storm-swept sea—he'd always harbored affection for inclement weather. But it was her hair that drew the eye. Nature rarely bestowed a red so vibrant on any human head, nor gloss or thickness.

And she was strong too. Fast. More so than a woman should be. What other special abilities did she have that Villiers put her in charge of the big bad vampire?

She was a member of the Order of the Silver Palm, that much he had long ago deduced. The man she answered to—Rupert Villiers was obviously high in the organization's ranks, if not its heart and soul. Vivian hadn't been with them when a group of them found his lair in Cornwall, poisoned him and took him captive, but she had been a daily torment ever since with her sweet-smelling skin and flaming hair.

Yes, he should kill her. He could do it now. Draw strength from the vein in her long slender throat, and make his escape. He should.

He should.

"Are you awake?" she asked in an English accent as rich and crisp as a gingersnap.

Temple made a low groaning sound, slowly turning his head toward the cell door as he heard the key clank against it. He didn't open his eyes very far, so she couldn't see the clarity in his gaze and realize that his body had adapted to the opium—it was no more effective than a glass of wine now.

That Vivian and her boss didn't know that his body worked that well was an unexpected boon, because they obviously knew enough not to starve him and allow him to become feral.

A slippery bunch, this Order of the Silver Palm. They'd started growing in number the last couple of decades, their interest in vampires—particularly Temple and his friends—increasing as well. He didn't know what they wanted from him, and his own curiosity had led to his being taken prisoner. He should have put up more of a fight, but he wanted to know what they were up to.

And he had grossly underestimated their abilities. He'd only killed a couple of them before the others overpowered him with their poison.

"Dinner time," Vivian murmured as she closed the cell door behind her, pocketing the key. She was carrying a bottle of what had to be blood, and a washbasin. "Time for a bath as well."

A bath? He had vague memories of someone washing him. That was her? Did she always talk to him? That was lost in the fog as well.

His gums itched at the sight of her standing there, ripe and flushed. She would be aged whiskey on his tongue—mellow and smoky, with a heat that would flood his veins and muddle his brain.

This was why he hadn't killed her. She called to him like a siren. It was more than physical; it was literally as though she cast some kind of spell over him. A witch, that's what she was.

Each step she took toward him was careful. Her gaze never left him as she approached. She wasn't stupid, and she was properly wary. How had she ended up with Villiers? In another time and place he would have approached her, wooed her, and made her his own. He'd avoided such romantic attachments for many reasons—Lucinda being the first and foremost. The second was the strange attachment he formed after taking a person's blood. It grew stronger with every feeding, until it was like that person was part of him. The rest of his brethren didn't seem to share this affliction, a fact that bothered Temple more than he wanted to admit.

But right now, he was tempted to use that "gift" on Vivian, see if he could uncover her heart, her soul. As if she wasn't under his skin enough already.

She approached from the head of the cot. Temple stayed perfectly still as she snapped a manacle over his left wrist and then his right. These shackles had no doubt held him before, when he was weak and drugged, but now . . . Now he could snap them with little effort.

He'd always been different from the others—a little stronger, a little faster. Brownie said he had something magic in his blood that made him the perfect vampire. He used to deny it because the others already looked at him as a leader, but right now he was glad for it.

Once she had him locked up, Vivian sat down on the side of the cot. The scent of her overwhelmed his senses, making him dizzier than the opium ever had. She smelled like hope and freedom and everything that was right and good with the world. That didn't make sense.

Temple's gums began to ache as she lifted his head and put the cool mouth of the bottle against his. Blood. It was laced with opium, but that didn't matter now. He swallowed as she poured the rich, warm liquid into his mouth, and tried not to sigh in pleasure as strength seeped into his muscles, and a strange peace settled over his soul.

That peace turned into something else entirely when she opened his shirt. When they took him, he'd been wearing a simple tunic held close with a sash. He was wearing it still, though it was obviously worse for wear. Luckily, vampires didn't sweat like humans, so he wasn't as ripe as a mortal man would be. Odd as it was, he didn't want her to wrinkle that lovely little nose at him.

Cool air met his skin as she opened the light garment. Through narrow lids, Temple watched as Vivian studied his naked chest. Her fingers hovered in hesitation before settling gently on his sternum. Her other hand traced an old scar along the side of his ribs. Her touch was light, delicate, and so unexpectedly sweet it made his throat tight.

"I know you're a monster," she said in a voice that was more of a whisper than anything else. "But you don't look like one to me." Then she laughed bitterly. "I wonder if you'd say the same about me."

Temple had to keep from frowning. He kept his face as relaxed as possible so she wouldn't know he was awake. Her words didn't quite make sense. Did she see herself as some kind of monster?

She dipped a cloth in the washbasin, wringing it out before running it over his chest and sides, under his arms and over his stomach. For a moment, while she bathed him, he could almost believe she gave a damn about him.

Almost.

Afterward, she dried his skin with a rough towel, but rather than refasten his shirt, she set her long hands on him once more, as though the feel of his flesh fascinated her. Temple stayed as still as he could until her palm cupped his cheek. That was too tender—too much.

He grabbed her wrist and lifted her hand from his face. He didn't want to hurt her, but he couldn't stand the torture she was putting him through any longer.

She gasped. Was it the sudden movement, or the contact that elevated her heart rate to the frantic thumping it had become? But she didn't struggle, and that was good. She didn't move at all, like a frightened deer.

Or another predator that knew when to be wary.

Vivian's gaze met his, and Temple swore to himself when her eyes widened. There could be no doubt that she had seen his clear gaze, his distended fangs. He could smell a faint trace of fear—she wasn't stupid—but more than that he could smell aroused woman, the sweetness of blood-warmed flesh and juices that would engulf him like a hot bath.

She looked at him with longing in her tempestuous gaze. Her chest rose and fell with every shallow breath, the buttons on her waistcoat straining against the push of her breasts. He could tear those buttons apart like wrapping paper.

Temple couldn't remember the last time he'd lain with a woman, the last time nipples had pebbled against his palms and pliant thighs wrapped around his hips. It had been too long.

"You don't look like a monster to me," he murmured, mocking yet sincere as he held her stare.

She jerked against his hold with surprising strength. Obviously he'd struck a nerve. "Let me go."

So commanding! So very strong for a human, especially a female. Temple tightened his grip, tugging her closer. "What kind of monster are you?" he asked, placing her hand against his cheek once more. He resisted the urge to rub his face against her palm like a needy cat.

Her eyes weren't so wide anymore. Her heart wasn't quite so frantic. "The kind that scares grown men."

Temple smiled at the bravado in her voice. In another life he could truly like this woman. "We have something in common, then."

Her gaze dropped to his mouth, and his cock swelled in response. Had she no idea just how tempting she was? He didn't think so.

"Not quite," she told him. For a second he thought she had read his thoughts. "I don't eat the men who fear me."

Temple returned the grin, forgetting that he was shackled and dirty, forgetting that she had played a part in all of that. "You can take a bite of me if you want."

Her eyes darkened and that was the end of his control. Turning his head, he held her wrist to his mouth. He traced the vein there with his tongue, feeling her shiver at the contact. And then, he opened his mouth, revealing his fangs. They slid into her flesh like hot knives through butter. Vivian cried out—but not in pain. Her free hand slapped the mattress beside his head as her body fell forward, her torso pressing against his.

Temple could feel her hair against his forehead, her breath against his cheek as he pulled his fangs from her and let her hot sweetness fill his mouth. The first swallow arched his spine. It was like fine cognac after a lifetime of cheap gin. The next swallow was even more sublime. Chocolate, sensual pleasure, a hot bath—all of this was in Vivian's blood.

She tasted like . . . hope.

Tears filled Temple's eyes as he jerked his head away, unable to take anymore. He couldn't even lick the wound to close it—he was too tempted to drink more of her, even though his body was already tingling. He pushed her away, fighting for control, thankful for the shackles, however flimsy they were.

"What are you?" His voice was like gravel as his heart twisted and writhed in his chest. Sweet Jesus, had she killed him?

Pain contorted her features, clouded her amazing eyes. Holding her bleeding wrist, she turned and bolted, fumbling with the lock before leaving him alone in his cell once more.

She ran up the stairs, leaving him with the taste of her on his lips and the thrill of her in his veins. Licking his lips, he gasped for air.

Did she know how lucky she was that he couldn't chase?

Vivian ran outside, just as she always did whenever she'd been inside Temple's cell. She hated cages—hated anything that made her feel like an animal on display.

What are you? The question had stung twice as sharp coming from him. Some part of her had expected him to understand—to have some sympathy. Instead, he'd looked at her like everyone else had.

It hurt—even worse than the others, because he had tasted it in her blood. Whatever made her this way was *in* her.

She sat on the bench on the back terrace and eased the grip she'd kept on her injured wrist. Tentatively, she peeked at her punctured flesh. Her hold on the wound and keeping it elevated had slowed the bleeding, and her natural "unnaturalness" had it clotting already. She'd be completely healed in no time, without so much as a scar to prove it had ever happened.

She'd been bitten by a vampire. Not just any vampire, but Temple. And she had liked it.

Shame, thick and heavy, washed over her. Though she hadn't invited the bite, she'd allowed her attraction to Temple to cloud her wits and her judgment. She should have noticed that the opium no longer held him. How was that possible? She'd given him the drugged blood herself, every day. Had just given him some moments before he bit her.

And the feel of his fangs in her flesh! God above, she hung her head as sensations flooded her. She had been fascinated by Temple since they first captured him. Rupert allowed her to tend to him because she was stronger than any of the men who worked for him. For years she'd been taught to respect and fear vampires. She'd fought them, thought of them as monsters—anything but human.

Being close to Temple challenged that belief. He'd never hurt her, just looked at her with cloudy pale eyes. Tonight, seeing that gaze so sharp and so fixed on her had unsettled her. For a second, she'd been tempted to give herself over. Hadn't even fought when he grabbed her.

She had betrayed Rupert in that moment.

And Rupert Villiers had always treated her like a princess, unlike her real father, who had tried to sell her to a traveling freak show when she was fourteen. Were it not for Rupert's kindness, God only knew where she might be right now. He rescued her from the traveling show—rescued her from her father. And then he brought her to live on an estate the likes of which she had never seen before, having grown up in one of the poorer areas of London.

He ensured that she wanted for nothing, and in return she learned whatever he saw fit for her to learn. And when he urged her to hone those traits—such as her strength and speed—which made her ashamed and embarrassed, she did so without fuss. After all, he had saved her and Vivian would do anything for him. Even die.

So when the French doors leading into the house opened, Vivian fixed her sleeve so that it covered her wrist and positioned her arm behind her back.

Rupert walked out, gifting her with a smile that always brought a rush of affection and gratitude to her chest. "Hello, Pet."

She smiled, thought about rushing to him for a hug, and then remembered her manners. He might allow her to walk around in trousers and carry a dagger, but he expected her to act like the lady he taught her to be.

His bright blue eyes sparkled at the sight of her, crinkling at the corners so that fingers of fine lines fanned down his cheeks. At forty-eight he was a fine figure of a man in the prime of his life—handsome, wealthy, confident, and comfortable in his own skin. His thick, dark hair was graying at the temples, adding a distinguished air to his otherwise youthful countenance.

If it weren't for him, she wouldn't know what the word *countenance* meant. She owed him so much—her very life perhaps, and yet . . .

An image of Temple captured her mind. Clearly, she could see his long, dark tangled hair, strong, stubbled jaw and unyielding mouth. From the tanned, chiseled planes of his face, piercing green eyes peered into the very core of her, stripped her bare and laid open all her secrets. It was as though he knew her—knew what was in her heart. All the weeks they'd held him captive and he'd never once said an unkind word to her—until tonight.

He was a big man—bigger than her own six feet. He had a way of making her feel delicate, even stretched out on his back on a rickety cot. When he grabbed her earlier, he hadn't hurt her though he easily could have. He'd held her gently, and when he touched his tongue to her skin, it had been too much to take.

Perhaps that was why she found him so dangerously tempting. Other than Rupert, she hadn't known much understanding or patience in her life, and it was rare that a man made her feel remotely small, or even feminine. When she was near Temple, Vivian was acutely aware of just how much of a woman she was.

Her guardian—her friend—regarded her silently for a moment. "You've been to the cellar, haven't you?"

"I have." Her gaze locked with his, frank and unflinching though she wanted to look away. "Tell me again why he's here, Rupert."

"Because he's useful to me." His eyes narrowed slightly. "Did he try to talk to you? Did he touch you? He's a dangerous creature, Vivian."

"No," she lied, keeping her arm behind her back. "Would you let me anywhere near him if he was that dangerous?"

He smiled kindly, almost patronizingly—another word he'd taught her. "You are strong, my dear, but not as strong as Temple. I let you tend him because I believe his honor would keep him from doing you harm."

"You talk as though you respect him, yet you keep him as your prisoner."

He frowned at the challenge in her tone, but as quickly as it came, the ire was gone. Damn him for not giving her the fight her tense and confused body sought. Temple's bite had left her unfulfilled, empty and wanting. A fight would be just the cure, but it seemed no man would satisfy her this night.

"I do respect him. He is an amazing creature, capable of many things—one of which is ripping out our throats with his pinky. Would you have me invite him up here for tea?"

Vivian had no doubt that Temple was capable of doing just what Rupert claimed. "You're not going to tell me what you want with him, are you?" For the first time, she felt as though she didn't know Rupert—that maybe he thought her just as "dangerous" and untrustworthy as the vampire below ground.

The kind smile returned, with little brackets of lost patience around his eyes. "He will bring the others of his kind to us."

Vivian stiffened with surprise. She hadn't actually expected him to tell her. "How?"

"Because he is their leader. They will go wherever he is. In fact, I've heard that most of them are already en route to Italy. There, does that ease your troubled mind?"

How could it? She clenched her fist behind her back, the tenderness in her wrist a reminder to be strong. "What do you want with them?"

She knew the story he told—that years ago a vampire had taken the woman he loved and planned to marry, but that didn't explain revenge on this scale—not when Temple wasn't that vampire.

"That, I'm not prepared to share, my dear. Not even with you. But trust me when I say that it will benefit you almost as much as it does me."

That cut deeper than she would have thought possible. "How can I trust you when you don't trust me?"

He placed a gentle hand upon her shoulder. "Have I ever given you reason to question me?"

"No." Shame claimed her once more. Rupert had never been anything but good to her.

He sat down on the bench beside her, his smile still patient, and placed his arm around her shoulders. "I know you feel that I do not trust you because I haven't told you what I have planned, but the less you know the better. Believe me, my dear, when the time comes I will tell you everything. Until then, know that I trust you with my very life."

Vivian nodded. Their heads were so close that it was oddly intimate sitting with him like this. All the years she had lived with him she'd never felt that he saw her as a woman, and sometimes she wasn't certain he did now, but there were moments like this when she was uncomfortably positive that Rupert was attracted to her.

When he'd first rescued her she'd developed a terrible infatuation for him, but he had treated her as he would a daughter. Now that she thought of him not only as a father but a friend, this new awareness was like a giant spider crawling down her spine.

"You know how dearly important you are to me, don't you, Vivian?" Rupert's fingers massaged her shoulder through the thin lawn of her shirt. "My life would be empty without you in it."

"Without you I might not be alive now," she murmured, admitting what they both knew but rarely discussed.

Was it her imagination, or had he inched even closer? What was that light in his hooded gaze?

He was going to kiss her. She knew it as true as she knew her own face. And all she could think of was Temple. Would Temple know if Rupert claimed her mouth with his own?

Yes. Somehow he would know. Why that should matter made no sense, but it did.

"I have to go." She rose and moved back, away from her mentor's touch, and the promise of his kiss. This was wrong—not only because he had raised her, but because he was not the man whose lips she wanted on her own. Rupert was not the man whose body she wanted to hold, whose hands she wanted to feel upon her skin. He was not the one who haunted her dreams or made her heart pound.

Temple was.

Chapter 2

He heard every word they said.

Temple lay on his cot and stared up at the peeling paint on the ceiling of his cell and smiled. There was only one explanation—Vivian's blood. He could still feel her sweeping through his veins, filling him with strength and a sense of well-being he hadn't felt in a long time.

It was like coming home.

But it had heightened his senses as well. His vision was already better than a cat's, and now it was even keener. His skin felt every brush of fabric. He could taste Vivian clearly on his lips— and her voice in his ears. It hadn't been loud, but he had heard them as though he'd had his ear to a door. They had been outside where he normally wouldn't have heard them, but tonight he'd heard the crunch of gravel beneath Vivian's feet as she walked away from Villiers.

Vivian spoke to Villiers as though the man was her father. How long would it be before Villiers decided he didn't want to be her "papa" anymore? How long before he tried to press himself between those strong—and no doubt supple—thighs and claim what he believed to be rightfully his?

She was his enemy. He shouldn't care what Villiers wanted with her—or if she would welcome his advances. He shouldn't desire her as he did. He should hate her.

And part of him did—a little. He didn't trust her and he despised what she stood for, but he couldn't shake the feeling that she was just another pawn in this game. Villiers wouldn't have her around if she wasn't useful.

But that wasn't what he should be thinking about right now. Villiers had said that he was using Temple to bait the others—Chapel, Bishop, Saint, and Reign. His friends—his brothers—were in danger because of him. He'd had no idea when he melted down the Blood Grail and sent a piece of it to each vampire, along with instructions to meet in Italy that he'd played right into the Order's plans. He was sending his friends into a trap.

The time to escape was now. There was no time to waste. He could only hope that he could send word quick enough to keep the others from reaching his villa, and direct them elsewhere. Once they were reunited they could best plot how to fight the Order—and perhaps figure out just what the Silver Palm wanted with them.

Sitting up, Temple gave a quick jerk on the

shackles that bound him. They snapped like twine, falling back against stone with heavy clanks. God, he felt invincible. Flexing his fingers, he looked around for the best escape.

The wall was too thick and ran against solid ground, so there was no escape through it. He could try the bars, but his feet would be badly burned and smashing against the bars would shake the house itself. He'd be set upon before he even reached the top of the stairs. No, he had to be fast and he had to surprise them if he was going to get away. His strength and speed might be far above the realm of normal human capacity, but the men upstairs knew what he was, and knew how to combat him. He didn't know how many there were, but if Villiers was as intelligent as he seemed, there would be enough to bring Temple to his knees.

And there was Vivian, who would no doubt lead the charge.

His gaze went once again to the ceiling. It creaked as someone walked the floor above him.

He knew the way out.

He sat up, rolling into a crouch on the mattress. Tucking his head and shoulders down he rocked up onto his toes and then . . . sprang.

Wood splintered against the force of his body. Tile cracked and popped as he burst through the ceiling of his cell into the ground floor of the house.

Of course there was no muffling the sound. He was shaking dust and debris from his hair and back when he heard the first door whip open, the first surprised footfalls running in his direction.

Temple didn't waste time noting the ruined elegance of his surroundings. He saw only that he was in a large front hall, lined on three sides by tall, narrow windows. He ran toward the closest one and dove through it, sending shards of glass spraying through the air like sharp pellets of icy rain. He could have gone for the door—that would have been the civilized way, but the window faced away from the street, where his escape route would be well lit and easily discerned. And he rather liked the idea of Villiers having so much mess to clean up.

The night air hit him like the warm embrace of a freshly bathed woman. His knees buckled at the sheer sweetness of it, so fresh and clean. A thousand wonderful scents and sounds bewildered his senses, jangling for dominance as the moon shone down, igniting the world in a blaze of silver-blue fire.

Instinct drove him toward the back of the house, where the scent of flowers and grass was the strongest. There was a garden there that bordered on a small expanse of forest. It would be dark there and hard to track him unless they had dogs. Once he was safely embraced by the trees he could fly—but only when the risk of being shot down was no longer a concern.

The ground blurred beneath his feet as he ran. The wind whipped at his hair and stung his eyes as he leaped over a hedge as tall as his waist. Freedom was upon him, so sharp he could taste it.

And then he caught a flash of red and his heels dug into the earth so suddenly he nearly fell flat on his face.

Vivian stood by a fountain made of cavorting stone nymphs—as shocked to see him as he was to see her. She also looked terrified—of him—but that didn't stop her from reaching for the pistol strapped to one full hip.

Why hadn't she reached for that weapon in his cell?

One quick movement and he had her hands pinned behind her back, bowing her torso so that her chest pressed against his. Her breasts were so soft, and the heart beneath them pounded so hard each pump seemed to echo in his ears.

She didn't move, his Amazon. Didn't struggle, but Temple didn't let himself believe for one second that she wasn't a threat.

A threat he was admittedly loath to leave behind.

"If you're going to kill me," she rasped, "just do it."

"Kill you?" he repeated dumbly. "It would be an affront to the artistry of nature to destroy a creature such as you."

• Vivian blinked. Her lips opened—enough that

he caught a flash of glistening, sharp, white teeth. A small frown creased her brow, as though she didn't quite understand what he was all about. He didn't blame her. He didn't quite understand himself.

"I'm not going to hurt you." Then he qualified, "Not unless you make me."

Her frown didn't ease, but her gaze dropped from his mouth to his throat and the part of his chest that was exposed by his ruined shirt. Her heart thudded harder against her ribs and she shivered just a little against him.

God, she smelled so good—so clean. He craved another taste of her. The scent of her flesh—her blood—called to him with memories of his grandmother's house and the scent of hot buttered bread, autumn evenings, and frost-kissed hay. She spoke to some deep primal part of him that longed for home and boyhood simplicity.

He could kill her for that—promising something he could never have.

But as she stared at him, stormy eyes wide, cheeks flushed, pulse fluttering, obviously as tempted by him as he was by her, Temple decided to kiss her instead.

Behind them the entire house was in a clamor, and soon even this little piece of paradise would be overrun with guards, but for this moment, there was only the two of them beneath the moon, surrounded by the warm caress of darkness.

"I want to taste you again, sweet Vivian," he

murmured. As her eyes widened even further, he continued, "But a kiss will have to do."

Before she could protest—by God, why hadn't she screamed before this?—Temple seized her mouth with his. Her lips parted easily for him, her full form supple and limber in his arms. There was no fight in her, no fear—not at this moment. She wasn't afraid of him. The realization of that brought with it an overwhelming rush of need— of want—so thick and hot his head spun.

She moaned. He felt the sound reverberate through her as her shoulders pressed against his chest. A slow ache began to build in his tightening gums as his fangs eased from their sheaths. Temple let himself savor the tangy sweetness of her mouth, the damp heat that drew his tongue inside. He breathed her fresh scent deep inside, allowing it to muddle his brain with welcome anticipation of what might come next had they the time to let nature plough her course.

In his arms, Vivian shivered despite the warm summer night that sang all around them. Temple smiled, lips curving against hers. Knowing that she wanted him as much as he wanted her was all the satisfaction this night would bring. It would be all he could ever have from her. If he didn't take some pleasure from that he would have to defend the strange heaviness in his heart, and he would accept no explanation for it save that her blood had been the sweetest he ever tasted.

Were it not for her—and the preparedness of his enemy—he'd kill Villiers and save himself from having to face the bastard in the future. And he would face him again. Men like Villiers didn't just give up or back down. They kept fighting until they either won or died.

Temple had no intention of accepting defeat.

It was that realization that made him break the kiss and pull away from the heaven of Vivian's mouth. If he did not make his escape now he might not make it at all. Shouts rang out in the night, growing closer. And they had dogs—damn them.

Despite the loss of precious time, he took a few seconds to gaze into Vivian's heavy-lidded, bewildered gaze. Her face was a memory he would carry with him for years to come, but he knew that it would one day fade. After five hundred years, every memory eventually did.

"Good-bye, sweet Vivian," he murmured, still holding her hands behind her back. She may have submitted to his kiss, but he wasn't foolhardy enough to release her just yet. She was abnormally strong for a human, and while she may be no match for his superior strength and agility, she could still do more damage than he was willing to risk. And he was unwilling to risk harming her as well.

"He'll find you," she replied flatly, hoarsely.

Temple's smile turned sad, but not for himself. "If you care for him, my dear, pray that he doesn't."

With that advice, he released her wrists and stepped back at the same time. His estimation of her had not been wrong; as soon as she was free, she moved to attack, but he was already in the air when she lunged.

He hovered there as two men armed with rifles rushed toward the garden. They would be upon them in seconds. Slowly, he willed himself higher into the sky.

Vivian stared up at him, growing ever smaller as Temple moved closer and closer toward the stars. He blew her a kiss as one of the men on the ground fired off a shot. It whizzed past his shoulder. He laughed as he turned and propelled himself higher—faster. No other shots followed him.

He was free.

"Where would he go?" Vivian demanded as she hurried toward the stables. For once she was glad for her long legs as each quick stride took her closer and closer to her goal. "Who would hide him?"

This was all her fault. If she had told Rupert about the bite, about the opium not doing its job . . . but she willfully kept the first from him, and now it was too late to remember the second.

If her guardian had trouble keeping up with her he didn't show any signs of it. Rupert's normally pleasant face was a harsh mask of frustration and fury. "Ireland," he replied in a voice that was little more than a growl. "He'll go to Clare."

"Clare?" If the woman's name irked her it was only because she was already in a bad temper, no other reason. "Who is she?"

Rupert shot her a narrow, sideways glance, as though he could somehow read her mind and saw the truth there. "It is a where, not a who. The island of Clare is off the western coast of Ireland. A tiny little place—very remote."

Strangely giddy that Clare was a place and not a person, Vivian tried to keep her mind on more important matters as she entered the stables. "Why would he go there? It shouldn't be hard to find him in such a small location."

"He has friends there. He'll know we're coming before we ever set foot on the island."

Vivian pulled a saddle off the wall and started toward the stall where her gelding waited. "If that's true, why are you smiling?" If that was true, what was the point of chasing after him?

This time he faced her fully, his countenance restored to its usual pleasantness. "Because I have friends there as well."

Her temper darkened as she hoisted the supple leather saddle on top of the blanket on her mount's back. She paused in her work long enough to turn to the man who had been both her friend and father, mentor and master.

"Friends? Then why am I to chase after him?" Bad enough she had let him get away in the first place, but to pursue Temple after that kiss . . . Her mouth still tingled with the taste of his. Going after him made her feel too much like a jilted lover, without enough pride to let him go and say good riddance.

Rupert regarded her as though he thought she had lost her mind. Thinking of Temple as her lover, perhaps she had, but it wasn't the first time she'd harbored such thoughts about the vampire.

"My friends haven't the strength nor the knowledge of Temple's kind to contain him. You do."

Unease rose in Vivian's stomach. She'd almost forgotten how odd she was. For those brief moments in Temple's arms she'd been nothing more than a woman embraced by a man—not a mockery of all that was feminine. Most of the world didn't even know vampires existed and not only did she know how to fight them, but she had helped hold one prisoner for weeks.

And she'd let him escape because he rendered her stupid and weak with nothing more than a kiss.

Anger replaced unease, and with her saddle in place she swung herself up and into it. She would find Temple and she would bring him back, or die trying.

Rupert handed her a coat and she slipped it on as he secured the leather pouches that served as saddlebags. She had packed a change of clothes and the necessary toiletries. The other bag had some food and water. Her knife was strapped to her thigh. Another was tucked into her boot. And inside a secret pocket in the front of her corset was more than enough money to purchase anything else she might need on the journey—such as passage to Ireland.

"Make him believe you've left me," Rupert instructed. Vivian shifted in the saddle. He made it sound as though they were lovers. "Share my secrets with him, make him believe you're on his side."

She stared at him, mouth agape. "How will I know what not to tell him?"

"I haven't told you anything you cannot share."

Of course he hadn't. On one hand it made his closed-mouthed attitude suddenly make sense. On the other, it made her feel like she'd never had his trust at all, and that made her blood run cold.

Her mentor continued, not noticing the sudden stiffness of her spine, or the dejection that must surely reflect in her eyes. "Once he takes you into his confidence you will report to me." He patted her thigh. "I'm counting on you, Pet. You're the only one I trust to do this."

It was the best thing he could have said. How could she have doubted him? Of course he trusted her. He wasn't throwing her to the wolves, he honestly believed she was the only person who could track Temple and fool him into thinking her loyalties had changed. Everything rested on her being able to do this. On her going alone to Clare.

She had never traveled alone before. Rupert had always been with her, ever since rescuing her from the sideshow. One glance at her mentor and she tucked her fear away.

"I'll find him," she vowed. And she meant it. She would find Temple. She would do whatever necessary to ingratiate herself into his life and his trust. The why of it didn't matter. All that mattered was that she do it, and repay Rupert for all he had done for her.

Shrewd, pale eyes bore into hers. "Do whatever necessary to make him believe you."

Vivian sucked in a sharp breath. Was he asking her to do what she thought he was? "You want me to be a vampire whore, sir?" She had heard of woman who gave their blood and bodies to vampires. In fact, she'd heard that there was an entire brothel in London owned by one of Temple's friends. No matter how . . . *stirring* the idea of intimacy with Temple might be, she knew how Rupert and his counterparts looked upon such women—with a mixture of awe and loathing that no one deserved.

And Rupert had always taught her regardless of her special talents and abilities, that her virtue was her most prized possession, to be held on to at any cost.

Her mentor's cheeks reddened in the lamplight, but he did not look away. "Of course not. But Temple is a man, and a devious one at that.

Your best weapon against him is your feminine charms."

"He's not a man," she retorted harshly, reminding him needlessly of what he already knew far better than she as she steered her horse out of the stall.

"And you needn't worry," she continued, tightening her hold on the reins just enough to keep the horse from bolting. "I can be devious as well."

With that said, she leaned forward and let the gelding lunge into the night, away from the man who had made her into what she was. And after the one who might very well prove to be her undoing.

Unexpected rain forced her to stop just a few miles shy of the French border. It was a summer thunder storm that spooked Vivian's horse and soaked her to the skin. Wrapping her long cloak around her to hide her unusual garb, she exited the stables where her horse would be groomed and fed, and walked across the little courtyard to the inn where she hoped to find a hot bath and a hot meal.

The innkeeper claimed to have seen a man matching Temple's description a little earlier, but that was all the information he could—or would—offer. He did, however, have a room for her. Dawn wasn't far on the horizon and she was exhausted. Wherever Temple was he would be forced to soon take shelter if he hadn't already, and since she had a good idea of his final destination she didn't feel time slipping through her fingers as she might were the situation different.

"And send up some wine with bread and cheese, please," she instructed the little man, whose head barely reached her chin.

He nodded and handed her a shiny key from a slot on the wall behind him.

Vivian didn't have to suffer in her wet clothes for long. The food arrived moments after she let herself into the small, but comfortable room. She'd paid extra for a private bath, and while it wasn't anything fancy, the promise of a hot soak had her drawing water as she bit hungrily into the crusty, heavily buttered bread.

She hung her wet clothes over a dressing screen with red roses painted on it and climbed into the narrow tub with a glass of wine in one hand and a piece of cheese in the other.

Groaning as the hot water washed over her, easing the chill from her bones, Vivian leaned her head back against the wall, took a sip of wine and shivered in pleasure. Finishing the piece of cheese, she took another deep swallow from her glass and let her body relax.

Tomorrow she would board a train that would take her to Bordeaux and from there she would take passage to Ireland. Once there she would have to secure transportation to Clare and find Temple.

The thought of him brought goose bumps to her wet skin, a flush of anger and desire to her blood. Her feelings were a betrayal of her loyalty to Rupert, something she'd vowed would never happen. It was wrong to miss Temple—wrong and twisted. Her mind had formed a bond between them based on the respect of one monster for another—a bond that didn't exist.

She was disappointed that Temple had escaped. Disappointed not only in herself for allowing it, but in him as well. What had she expected? That he would stay and allow Rupert to do whatever it was he planned to do? Were the situation reversed, Vivian would have done exactly what he had—she would take advantage of her guard, and escape the first chance she had. It was only her pride hurt by Temple's successful run at freedom, nothing more.

She would not allow it to be anything more.

Firm, rough warmth pressed against her forehead, directly between her brows. "You shouldn't frown so, sweet thing."

Vivian's eyes flew open as she lurched upright. She knew that growl of a voice. Water sloshed over the sides of the tub, but before she could rise, strong fingers gripped her shoulders and she found herself staring into all too familiar green eyes.

Temple. He squatted beside the tub.

"You might want to think twice before rising,"

he murmured with enough humor to bring her blood to a simmer. She was naked, weaponless, and almost entirely defenseless. Damn it all. How long had he been watching? Waiting?

"What do you want?" she demanded, more or less hoping he might tell her why he had chosen to sneak up on her rather than increase the distance between them. He'd obviously been watching or tracking her. Why? Why not run immediately to Clare?

His gaze drifted over her, warming her damp flesh where the night air had chilled it. Her entire chest was out of the water, naked to his appraisal and frank appreciation. Her nipples, already tight, puckered even more. It was debasing, to be so vulnerable—and to take pleasure in it.

"There are so many answers I could give you." The fingers gripping her shoulders kneaded ever so gently, easing the tension she fought to retain from her muscles. She did not want to relax. She did not want to notice that somewhere between kissing her in the garden and accosting her now he had managed to find clean clothes, albeit slightly ill-fitting ones. He was still in want of a shave and a haircut, but that scruffy shagginess only added to the dangerous appeal that clung to him like salt to the shore.

"Choose one," she replied, daring to meet his gaze. "I assume I'd already be dead if you wanted to kill me?"

He grinned, baring those fascinatingly big white teeth. "Such bravado. I admire that in a woman—defiance in the face of fear."

Vivian's chin lifted. "I'm not afraid of you."

"No." It was said much too quietly. "Not as you should be."

Not at all, she wanted to protest, but knew there was no point. He could smell the truth. No doubt he could smell her body's other reactions to him as well, such as the steady thrumming between her thighs. Why, of all men, did it have to be this one who made her tingle so wantonly? How dare he make her feel *something* for him, something that made her question the man who had been like a father to her.

They were alone, face-to-face with no bars between them or guards to hear them. She was naked, and his clothes could be discarded in a matter of seconds. She could feel his strong, hard body against hers. She could take him inside and have him unravel all the mysteries of lust for her. She knew she could have all of this and more— his teeth at her throat—for the simple price of asking.

Pride declared it much too high a cost. She could never live with the guilt. Although, Rupert had told her to do whatever necessary to win his trust . . .

Sweet God. "Why are you not far away from here by now?" She deliberately avoided mentioning Ireland. No need to reveal what Rupert suspected.

"I had to see you." He released one of her shoulders as he spoke, but moved before she could raise her hand in defense, wrapping his arm around her chest, so that her breasts were flattened beneath his forearm, her side pressed against his torso. She could feel his breath on her neck, and oh, it was warm.

"See me?" Vivian laughed harshly, despite the startled pounding of her heart. She wanted to lean into his embrace and give in to the foolish notion that he could protect her from the world, instead of her always protecting everyone else. "You couldn't wait to escape me earlier."

"Escaping capture is not the same as escaping you, Viv."

She closed her eyes at the pet name, the warm brush of it against her skin. Behind her, she heard him dip something in the water. "You should be more leery of me than any of the men who guarded you." It wasn't bravado that made her speak this time, but sheer belief. It was obvious that he felt some attraction for her as well. Did he not realize how easy it would be for her to take advantage of that? How much she wanted to take advantage of it?

Was she the same woman who just a few hours earlier accused her mentor of asking her to make a whore of herself? Now she contemplated doing it willingly.

"I know." A wet, soapy cloth slid over her upper back and shoulders, drawing a shudder of sensation. "You are quite possibly the most dangerous person I have ever met."

"What do you mean?" She couldn't move save but to turn her head, and she did so with a narrow gaze. "Do you mock me, vampire?"

"No." He continued to wash her back, denying her the satisfaction of even the barest glance. "And I doubt you would believe me if I bothered to explain myself further."

"You have yet to explain why you are here." Why he was washing her as though she was a child, or some fragile creature in need of tender ministrations. She was neither, and the urge to burrow herself against his chest and fall asleep in the safety of his arms was one she resented greatly.

"I want you to let me go."

At first she wasn't certain she'd heard him correctly. Let him go? He was the one who had come to her. He must know that she intended to pursue him, hunt him. "I can't do that."

"For your own safety, you must."

She wrapped her fingers around the thick muscle of his forearm. He was so hard and warm, so strong. "You cannot threaten me, Temple. If you wanted to hurt me you would have by now." There was some smugness in that—knowing that the all-powerful vampire couldn't harm her.

It also made her wonder why Rupert kept such a creature in a cage, like a wild animal.

And then she felt the sting of fangs scraping her shoulder and she remembered that he *was* wild. Unpredictable. Dangerous. She gasped as his lips brushed her skin, pressed against her. The moist heat of his mouth touched her, arching her back as he gently sucked where his teeth had broken the skin. That sob—did it come from her?

Sweet Jesus, it felt as though he had crawled beneath her skin, like he was becoming an extension of her, or she of him. It felt good—too good.

Too *right*.

And then it was gone, swept away in a hot, wet stroke of his tongue that made her jerk against his arm.

"I want you to run away," he rasped, the stubble of his jaw scratching her spine. "Forget about me, forget about Villiers and start a new life for yourself far away from here."

Weakly, Vivian turned her head. All she could see was the thick column of his throat where it met his shoulder beneath the open neck of his shirt. Would that she could bite him there and incite the same emotions within him as he did within her. "You would have me betray him?"

Temple lifted his head, and his gaze locked with hers once more. There was no denying the sincerity there—or the desire. "Before he betrays you, yes."

Vivian's mouth opened. She didn't know what to say. His hold on her had loosened and she lifted her hand to his cheek. It was the perfect opportunity to strike him. He'd never see it coming, but there was no way she'd manage to get dressed and haul him out to her horse with no one seeing. No way she'd get anywhere with him this close to dawn.

She caressed him instead. Leaned toward him. Brushed her lips against the damp curve of his and tasted the faint coppery tang of herself there. It should disgust her, but it didn't. In fact, the realization was disturbingly exciting.

He pulled away before she could explore his mouth or soak the front of his shirt any further by pressing her body against his. Vivian fell back into the tub with a splash as Temple rose to his feet.

"You are a part of me now," he informed her forcefully as he backed toward the window. "You are *mine*. Come after me and I just might decide to stake my claim."

There was something almost sinister yet strangely ironic about a vampire using the term *stake*, but Vivian could hardly respond to the humor in it. She was too busy fighting the yearning that made her want to throw herself at his feet and beg for him to bite her again. She was trembling.

Trembling.

She was also alone. There was nothing but the gentle flutter of the curtains in front of the open window and the fading sting in her shoulder to prove that he'd even been there.

Oh, and the taste of her own blood in her mouth. She touched her fingers to her lips, shivering in the cooling water as she fought to calm the fire raging inside her.

"Come after me and I just might decide to stake my claim."

He left her no choice, she told herself that was the unfortunate truth. She had her loyalty and her duty. Come tomorrow she would fulfill both. But that wasn't it, not really. She would fulfill her duty to Rupert of course, but if she was honest with herself, she had to admit that she looked forward to what would happen when her path crossed Temple's once again.

She was going after him. And if Temple claimed her as he promised, then she was going to have to do her best to claim him in return.

Chapter 3

A few nights later . . .

The woman had a rifle aimed at his head.

It didn't waver, didn't tremble in the slightest, despite the fact that she was a tiny little thing clad only in a dressing gown. The hands that held it were dry and steady—sure of purpose and not in the least hesitant. She would shoot him without so much as a question if she believed him a threat to her little haven.

Slowly, Temple turned and smiled down the length of the shiny barrel, revealing his features to the bright moonlight spilling across the balcony. "You wouldn't shoot an old friend would you, Brownie?"

Kimberly Cooper-Brown—"Brownie"—uttered a sharp cry of exasperation, and the rifle dropped a fraction of an inch. "Jesus, Mary! I could have killed you, you blooming idiot!"

Laughing, Temple nudged the rifle away with

the tip of one finger. "But you didn't—and unless you've got silver in there I doubt it would have done me much harm."

His companion snorted as she tossed a lock of curly strawberry blond hair out of her eyes. "Not with a skull as thick as yours." She lowered the rifle to stand at her side. "Give us a hug then, you hulking brute."

He did as she bade, embracing her tiny slender form tightly, his arms almost wrapping double around her. Little his Brownie might be, but she was as fierce as any warrior he had ever known— and twice as sly.

He trusted her with his life, his secrets and his friends. That was why he was there.

"There" was the island of Clare—a lovely jewel just off the coast of Ireland. A small, craggy island that was difficult to reach—or escape—unless one could fly as Temple could, or had access to a boat. There was only one ferry service that ran between the island and the mainland, and Brownie knew everyone on the island. No one would set foot on the beach without his knowing, not without help.

Brownie lived here in the school. The Garden Academy for Young Ladies was operated entirely by women—the Sisterhood of Lilith, a group who revered the first wife of Adam, and the mother of all vampires. The same woman whose blood ran in Temple's veins. He had no way of knowing six hundred years ago when he drank from the same silver chalice as his friends and brothers that it was the blood of a goddess he drank, that it would make him immortal.

That blood made him something of a deity to these women, a fortunate coincidence he didn't mind taking advantage of given the circumstances.

"You're not here on a social call." Her pretty, pale face was serious as she gazed up at him, her expression as blunt as her tone. "What's happened?"

It was long after midnight and he was tired and hungry, needs that would have to wait. Explanations—preparations—wouldn't.

"We need your help, my friend." He didn't have to explain who "we" were. Her spine stiffened as soon as he said it, snapping into a posture as rigid and resolute as steel. "Can we count on you for assistance?"

She looked offended that he would even ask. "Of course you can!" Linking her arm through his, she steered him through the heavy French doors into her bedroom without the slightest hesitation. Her loyalty was obvious in the fact that she didn't bother to ask about the situation.

Temple stepped out of the night into the spacious, yet cozy chamber. It hadn't changed much over the years. Still decorated in rich, eastern hues, it reminded him of a harem's sanctuary with lush fabrics and thick, soft pillows strewn about.

The bed was large, heavy and ornate. He remembered many nights in that bed, buried in the wet warmth of Brownie's welcoming body. There hadn't been any love between them, but she offered a solace he needed, and she thought of sex with him as a pleasurable way to worship her deity. He slept with others in the sisterhood during that stay, quickly accepting the notion that his body was some kind of altar to these women. And his natural arrogance liked that they treated sex with him as a religious experience.

He was a man, after all.

Several paintings adorned the walls, all of them depicting Lilith in various poses, including the one painted by Collier a few years ago, showing the nude Lilith in the Garden, with a serpent wrapped around her pale body.

One of the paintings was terribly old—much older than Temple himself. Despite its age it was still a copy of the original—perhaps even a copy of a copy. In it a curvaceous, ivory-skinned woman draped in crimson robes that matched the richness of her hair, sat on a stool, a beautiful cherub of a child at her feet.

Some referred to her as Madonna. Some mistakenly thought of her as Eve, but Temple knew who she was. It was Lilith—the real Lilith, and not just some artist's interpretation of her. The image of her called to him, awoken something in his blood that could only be described as love. It was impossible, of course, as he had never met the woman, but the emotion she invoked was unmistakable.

She was his mother.

The sensation was stronger now, more acute. There was more than a familial longing in his chest as he stared at the striking features of the woman in the painting. Realization prickled the back of his mind, pinched sharply at his heart.

It all made sense now, and it scared him.

He was shaken from his stillness by a tiny hand on his bicep. Turning, he found his old friend staring up at him with carnal interest. "Will you share my bed, my lord?"

Inside he flinched. He hated when she talked as though he was better than she—and when she acted as his servant rather than his friend. And yet, the release she offered was tempting. It had been so long since he'd felt a woman's softness, a woman's strength.

But the taste of another lingered on his tongue, and he knew that even Brownie's erotic knowledge couldn't wash away Vivian's earthiness. Nothing could. The woman was under his skin; and even though he'd warned her away, a part of him hoped she gave chase, despite the danger her presence would bring down upon Brownie and this place.

If she came it wouldn't solely be because Villiers sent her, although he didn't question her loyalty to the bastard for an instant. She would come because she couldn't let him go, just as he had gone to her at the inn. It had taken all his resolve not to carry her to the bed and let their bodies melt together into one. There was something between them, something that had started when they first met and had grown even stronger now that her blood ran in his veins.

God love his dear Brownie, but there was no way she could ever compare to that kind of connection. That kind of *need*.

"Thank you, my friend," he replied, touching her cheek with the tips of his fingers. She didn't lean into the touch, but simply smiled. "But what I need right now is blood and a bath—in that order."

She wasn't offended in the least, he could tell. That in itself only proved how right his decision to refuse her was. "May I offer myself as sustenance if not pleasure, then?"

Yes, he thought as she tilted her head, baring her slim throat to his gaze. Gums constricted. Contracted, as fangs slid down. Saliva flooded his mouth, sharp with hunger.

"No." He took a step back. He could no more drink from her than he could bury himself inside her. There was no explanation for it that pleased him, but he just couldn't. "It's late. I want to retire, and you need to return to your bed." He softened the rejection by kissing her on the forehead before bidding her good night.

As was customary for his kind, Temple had apartments in the cellar of the school. A subbasement, actually. At one time it was believed the rooms, with their access to the cliffs and the beach below, had been used by smugglers or pirates. Now they provided him with protection from the sun, access to the school, and a convenient escape route—the same features he'd used to choose his hiding spot in England years earlier. That one had worked out well until that Ryland girl decided to go digging for treasure and the Silver Palm found him.

What did they want? The question occurred to him not for the first time as he navigated down the rough stone steps into the cool blackness below. What part did he and the others play in their plans? How could he have left without trying to find out? Why hadn't he questioned Vivian at the inn when he had the chance? He'd been too busy trying not to stare at her breasts to ask the right questions. Damn him for a fool. He should have killed Villiers when he had the chance. Now Christ only knew what the bastard had planned, or how much Temple's actions had helped him.

There was no time for regret now, he realized as he lifted the heavy bolt on the door to his hideaway. There would be plenty of time for it later. There always was, in his experience.

There was no electricity down here in the dark, but the lamp and matches were exactly where

they should be and so he struck a match on the
doorframe and lit the wick. Soon, warm golden
light spread across part of the room.

It was dusty and cold, but a fire and a little clean-
ing would fix that. For now, all he needed was the
bed and the bath. He ran the water to clear out
any debris or insects and pulled the dustcovers
off the bed while the tub filled.

In the bath, he scrubbed at himself until he felt
the grime of travel and the weeks spent in Villiers's prison leave his skin and hair. He knew
the "dirt" was more in his head than actually on
his person, but the bath made him feel better all
the same. He shaved as well, sighing as the blade
whisked the itchy stubble from his jaw.

Once done with the bath he tossed the clothes
he'd purchased in London on the floor to be laun-
dered later and set out a fresh set for the next evening. He also put coals from the fire into the bed
warmer and slipped the ancient relic between the
covers on the bed.

Then, sitting naked by the fire with a mirror
propped on a chair, he cut his hair with clippers
and a sharp pair of scissors he'd found on the
dresser. Like many vampire safe houses, this one
was kept up to date just in case one of them happened to appear. It was a privilege most of them
took for granted.

Finally, clean, shaven, and shorn, he emptied
the bed warmer and slipped between the heated

sheets, unable to stop the sigh that escaped his lips at the soft, enveloping comfort. He'd lived— and been kept—in sparse accommodations for far too long.

It was then, as Temple lay alone in the dark, that his thoughts turned to Vivian and how she had looked when last he saw her. Her skin glowed in the lamplight, all ivory and gold, her nipples tight and pink. God, she had lovely breasts—high and round. His cock stirred at the memory, at the thought of them in his hands, how they might taste in his mouth.

He shouldn't think of her. He shouldn't mourn the loss of her. Even if she weren't in league with his enemy—as though that weren't enough—she was mortal and he wasn't, and he knew better than to play at that game again.

Still, his mind refused to let go, and plagued him further with thoughts of Vivian's lush body, strong thighs and undoubtedly tight cunny. He could almost smell the beckoning bouquet of her warm flesh, flushed with blood, and the heady musk of arousal. She would be so wet, so hot . . .

With a groan, he brought his hand down to the cock-stand tenting the blankets, demanding to be relieved. He threw back the covers with such force the entire four layers were ripped completely off the bed.

He was ruthless, jerking his fist up and down roughly as thoughts of Vivian rushed through his mind. Vivian on top of him. Vivian beneath him. Vivian's mouth engulfing him with the same intensity as his own hand did now. It was that thought—of her full lips wrapped so sweetly around his cock, her tongue gliding over his hard flesh—that made him come with a violence that tore a harsh gasp from his throat and made stars dance behind his eyes.

He lay there for a long time, letting the darkness ease the tempest within him. Finally, the cool stickiness on his belly demanded that he get up and clean himself once more. Only then was he able to climb into bed, pull the covers over him and entertain the notion of sleep. His lust reasonably satisfied, his body lax and replete, he was able to roll onto his stomach as he felt the approaching dawn, and will himself toward slumber.

But the last image he saw in his mind's eye before sleep claimed him was of Vivian and her stormy gaze, and he knew, unlike his body, that some needs would not be so easily satisfied.

Vivian's sullen mood worsened over the days following her bathtub encounter with Temple, and being only a few miles away from the island of Clare didn't help it any, as she thought it might.

In fact, as the ferry she'd hired to take her the short distance to the island neared the rocky shore, she wanted nothing more than to tell the pilot to turn around and return her to the main land.

She didn't want to fight Temple. At that moment, she didn't want to turn him over to whatever fate Rupert had in mind for him either. In fact, she wanted very much to take the advice Temple had given her and run away from not only him, but her mentor as well. It only made matters worse that more than wanting to run away, she wanted to see Temple again.

She wanted to test whether or not he would follow through with his threat to claim her for his own. God help her, but she wanted to be claimed, even though what little sense she had left screamed that it would be a mistake. That it would be a sin.

Rupert preached to her relentlessly over the years the value of a woman's virtue, and yet she'd gladly give herself to Temple and damn the consequences. What did that say about her? Was there something wrong with her? Or was this a natural reaction of a healthy woman to an attractive man?

Only Temple wasn't a man. Perhaps that was the attraction. Temple defied nature, and in that she found a kindred spirit. After all, hadn't she been the only fourteen-year-old—male or female—in their village as strong or stronger than a full-grown man in his prime? Hadn't she been able to run almost as fast as a horse could gallop?

Her father had profited from it; and now, in his way, Rupert as well. She had no illusions that her guardian had taken her in purely out of the kindness of his heart, but it had been a kindness and for that he deserved her loyalty.

She didn't intend to let him down. Rupert's disappointment was not something she wanted to face, not after all he had done for her.

So she would not think of how it felt to have Temple's arms around her, or the rush of pleasure the feel of his mouth against her skin had wrought. She would think only of the mission she was charged with, and as soon as she managed to locate Temple, she'd send word to Rupert, or capture the vampire herself. She could do it if she was careful.

Telling herself that this was the right course of action, that duty was more important than whatever feelings she might *think* she harbored for Temple, put a straightness to her spine and shoulders as she stood on the deck of the boat. The water was calm—like floating on a pool of ink in the moonlight. The air smelled of coming rain, and the breeze held a touch of salty dampness that spoke to some deep melancholy inside her. There was something beautiful about the sea at night, something almost wild.

The little island grew closer. She could see houses with light shining from the windows, so warm and cozy—like something out of a painting. A touch of woodsmoke and fresh grass clung to the breeze in a scent she could almost taste it was so sweet.

She'd never been to Ireland in her life, despite her mother being from that very country, yet there was a familiarity to this place. Her heart was lighter, her mind clearer. A sense of peace filled her, despite the peril she floated toward.

And part of her worried that it was the man she'd followed here that gave her that feeling rather than the place itself.

"Here you are, miss," the ferryman remarked jovially as the boat was maneuvered into the dock. "Safe as a babe in arms, just like I promised."

Vivian flashed him a grateful smile as she gathered her things. She slipped some coins into his palm and asked, "Do you know if there's an inn on the island?"

He looked as though he was caught between a laugh and a gasp. "Nay, there's not. Mostly locals only on the island, not much call for an inn or anything so fancy." He squinted at her. "Do you mean to say, miss, that you haven't a place to stay?"

Her smile tightened. "That's exactly what I mean to say, yes. I don't suppose you know of anyone who might accept a lodger for a night or two?"

"There's the Garden Academy on the west side of the island. Missus Cooper-Brown's sure to have a room you can have."

"Academy?" Vivian frowned as her gaze surveyed the island. "There's a school?"

"Aye. A fine establishment for young ladies."

This was delivered with more than a touch of pride. "A right saintly lass is Missus Cooper-Brown."

It was all Vivian could do not to make a face. Such a paragon would hardly approve of a young woman traveling alone and dressed in men's clothing, but there was nothing she could do to remedy that now. Were she better prepared she could have thought to pack a gown or two, but she hadn't thought of such fripperies.

She hadn't been able to think of much after Temple's kiss and daring escape.

"Thank you," she said to the weathered old man, and smiled when he offered his hand to help her onto the deck. She didn't need his assistance. In fact, she probably could have tossed him over her shoulder and still made the transition on her own, but she accepted the gesture and stepped onto dry land once more.

"You're amongst good people on Clare, miss," he replied with a gap-toothed grin. "You just follow the main road up the hill and you'll see the signs for the academy. Can't miss it."

Vivian thanked him again and set out on foot in the direction of the road. It was a bit of a climb up from the beach, but there was a well-worn track to guide her and she followed it as the old man had instructed.

There was enough of a moon despite the increasing cloud that she could see her way with relative ease. Hopefully she would reach the academy before the rain hit. Fortunately, the island was small enough that it shouldn't be too long a hike.

What the devil was she doing here? Why had Rupert sent her on this errand and not a group of his men? Oh, she knew all the reasons he had given her, and at the time she'd been so ashamed of having let Temple escape that she had wanted to chase him, but now . . .

Now that she was in a strange place, with no friends, nothing that usually brought her comfort, she couldn't help but think that this was a foolish plan. And part of her suspected that Rupert hadn't been entirely truthful with her. What kind of man allowed his ward to chase a vampire across Europe? Wasn't he the least bit concerned for her safety?

No, he wasn't. And that told her that either his confidence in her abilities was grossly exaggerated, or that he simply didn't care what happened to her. She found both difficult to believe.

Or perhaps she was simply a diversion while he formed his "real" plan for recapturing Temple.

Regardless, perhaps Temple would give her some clue as to why Rupert wanted him so badly in the first place. Maybe she would be able to get useful information out of him as she revealed to him what little she knew of Rupert's plans. At least that knowledge would make some of this journey worthwhile.

Since there was nothing else to occupy her

time, she sang to herself as she walked—not loud enough to disturb the occupants of the few houses she passed, but just loud enough to entertain herself and keep her mind busy. Otherwise, she'd start thinking about Temple again, and not in a productive manner.

A dog barked as she walked by a small farmhouse and she shushed it softly, smiling when the barking stopped. Her singing interrupted, her thoughts once again returned to Temple, and this time she had neither the energy nor the inclination to stop them.

God, she hoped she reached the academy soon so she could go to bed and stop these senseless ponderings! That was her great flaw—too much idle time and her mind went off in all sorts of unsavory directions, entertaining notions better left alone.

The road to the school was uphill, and she was breathing a little heavy by the time she was halfway. She could see the looming shadow of the academy not even a quarter mile in the distance now. Thank God she hadn't packed more than she had, or she'd be ready to lie down under the closest tree. She was strong, but she wasn't accustomed to this much foot travel, and she was tired and hungry as well. The fact that she was making excuses for herself was a sure sign that she needed food and rest. Not to mention her mind's constant fretting over Temple exhausted her. The thought of their next meeting exhilarated her, and not just because she looked upon him as a worthy adversary.

At the top of the hill she stopped to rest for a bit. Just ahead, past the tall gate, the Garden Academy beckoned like a new friend. It was an old manor house from three or four centuries past, but it was solid and inviting, with light glowing in several of the lead-paned windows.

The gate wasn't locked, merely latched, and it creaked on its hinges as she pushed it open. Here the night seemed just a little quieter, even more still. She was suddenly very aware of how much noise her boots made on the finely crushed gravel, the rush of her breath in the darkness. A voice in her head cautioned her to be stealthy, even though there was obviously movement within the school—its inhabitants were not yet abed.

She had just raised her hand to pull the bell when she was seized from behind. A warm, slightly calloused hand clamped over her mouth, stifling her cry, as a muscled arm snaked around her, pinning her arms to her sides. Not even her legs were left for defense, as they were caught between a longer, stronger set. A hard chest pressed against her back, hot breath fanned her cheek, and yet Vivian felt no fear, only excitement. She knew who her captor was, and she was almost as thrilled at being caught as she knew he was at having caught her.

"Hello, sweet thing."

Chapter 4

She bit his hand.

It wasn't the pain that made Temple jerk back, easing his hold on her. It was the pleasure of it. Her sharp teeth gripped the flesh of his palm and dug in—not enough to draw blood, but enough that he wanted to demand she do it harder.

Vivian took advantage of his surprise, and as he ripped his hand away, she smashed her head back into his face. She missed his nose, else she probably would have broken it, but the blow was hard enough that it made his teeth snap together. It actually hurt, which surprised him more than it should have.

But when she broke free of his grasp and whirled around to confront him, he was ready for her. Almost.

She didn't fight like a woman. For that matter she didn't fight like most Englishmen. Her first attack was an arcing high kick that was definitely Oriental in origin. Temple dodged it, but not the fist she slammed into his throat. Instinct took over and he struck back. His fist caught her in the jaw, snapping her head back. He didn't even have time to feel guilty for it as she quickly recovered and launched herself at him once more.

Her fists struck his cheek, his belly, and when he grabbed her arms, she brought her knee up with alarming swiftness. Fortunately, he was faster and blocked the blow, sweeping her legs out from under her with one of his own and taking her down to the soft, cool grass. He landed on top of her, pinning her between the ground and his body.

Vivian grunted at the impact. He felt the rush of breath brush his face as it was knocked from her lungs. And then she was still, save for the rise and fall of her chest as she fought to regain her breath.

Temple gazed down at her flushed face. She would have a bruise where he struck her, but other than that, she looked no worse for wear. In fact, she looked magnificent, with her color high and her lips parted, her eyes glittering with blood lust and . . . desire as she stared back at him.

Damn, she felt good. Her full hips cushioned him. Firm thighs cradled his, nestling his pelvis against hers. She was all heat, strength and softness and he was hard already. He adjusted his hips for a better fit and was rewarded with a little gasp from the woman beneath him. Her legs clenched his.

He should subdue her and lock her up in the academy. He should listen to that voice in his head telling him not to kiss her, touch her.

He was never very good at listening.

She stiffened when his mouth came down on hers. Her fingers dug into his biceps, but he had her arms pinned between his elbows and her body—immobile and useless.

Raindrops pitter-pattered on his back as Vivian's lips parted. Warm water splattered on the grass, ran down the back of his neck. She tasted sweeter than the rain, sweeter than the storm building above them. And when he breached the inside of her mouth with his tongue, she didn't fight him. Why fight what they both wanted—needed?

They had been moving toward this since the first time they met. She had been his captor then, and he the captive. Now the roles had reversed, but he was every bit in her power now as he had been then. Helpless to fight against the demands of his body even though he knew taking her would only add more complications to an already precarious situation.

Vivian's tongue moved against his, tasting him, not tentative in the least. Her hips arched, pressing the soft heat of her pelvis against the aching hardness between his legs. He would know no peace until he was buried to the hilt inside her, drenched in her juices.

Wrenching his mouth free of hers, he stared

down at her, as rain darkened her hair to the color of blood in the faint light. "Tell me you want this."

Vivian heard the rough-edged question through the haze in her mind, the beat of rain on the grass by her head. She should tell him no. She should deny it, but there was no way she could. It was wrong—went against everything she had been taught, but if she didn't have him now—if she didn't give in to the demands of her body she would never know peace. Perhaps once the demands of this obsession with him had been met she would be able to think clearly once more. Perhaps she would be free of the violence that seemed to take hold whenever he was near.

She told herself this would help the cause, that she would be in a better position to learn his secrets and help Rupert, but Rupert wasn't a consideration at this moment. Neither was loyalty or duty or any of those things.

God help her, just this once she was going to do what she wanted, rather than what was expected of her—damn the consequences.

And there would be consequences.

Her arms were no longer pinned. Temple had raised himself up on his hands, pressing the iron-hard ridge of his erection against her. It hurt. It felt good. But he didn't move—scarcely breathed—as he waited for her reply. He was going to make her say it.

"I want it," she replied, hardly recognizing that husky rasp as her own voice.

Above them lightning lit up the sky, illuminating the feral pleasure in his expression. How could he be even more beautiful than she remembered? He'd cut his hair and the dark, wet waves clung to his head, obscuring none of the bold planes and angles of his face.

Fierce, that's what he was, as his long fingers opened her waistcoat and shirt—made short work of the laces of her corset. He straddled her hips, thighs as unyielding as steel. She could barely make out the deep set of his eyes, the high jut of his cheekbones. Thank God she couldn't see the vague mocking in his gaze. It had to be there—it always was, mixed with arrogance and just enough integrity that she felt as though he was a better person than she ever could be.

Slightly rough palms ran over her ribs as he slid her corset open. The rain—heavier now, like lying beneath a shower-bath—struck her bare skin, cool against her heat. Vivian gasped. The water and the night air was a sensual shock, drawing a shudder from her that had her writhing beneath him, breasts tingling as her nipples puckered into hard peaks.

"Why," Temple demanded, as he came down on her, "do you have to be so beautiful?" And then he took one of her nipples into his mouth and sucked it—hard.

Vivian arched upward with a cry—in response to both his touch and his words. He thought she was beautiful.

She tried to grab his shoulders, but her clothes were tangled around her arms. Desperately, she yanked herself free. Her fingers dove into his hair, pulling at the wet strands. She wanted him to stop. She didn't want him to stop.

The pressure on her breast eased, and the ferocity of his embrace was replaced with an almost gentle lapping of his tongue that was even more difficult to bear. An awful, wonderful ache blossomed and grew between her thighs, spreading deep inside, so deep she didn't think it could ever been assuaged.

"I want to feel you," she told him, hands now sliding down the shirt plastered to his back.

Temple lifted his head, but kept his gaze locked on hers as he peeled the thin linen from his shoulders and torso. Vivian watched, dry-mouthed in anticipation as another flash lit up the sky, and illuminated the breadth of his chest, heavily muscled and dusted with dark hair. Thunder drowned out the pounding of her heart as her hands came up to caress his stomach.

His skin was hot to her touch, slippery with rain. It was as though the heavens had opened up in an effort to cool their blood. The heavens failed.

Nimble fingers unfastened her trousers and drew them down over her hips. She arched, digging her heels into the softening ground, making it easier for him to strip her bare. He even removed her boots, as though he thought she might yet run away.

She wasn't going anywhere. Not yet. She was going to see this through, because she wanted it. Wanted it more than she had ever wanted anything before. Wanted him. Tomorrow could bring what it would, but tonight they were nothing more than a man and a woman giving in to the attraction between them.

She wasn't a total innocent. She had been fortunate that no one in the traveling show had taken it upon himself to relieve her of her virginity, but her child's view of the world hadn't lasted long. They slept three or four to a wagon, or room if they were lucky. One of the women always had a lover in, and though Vivian pretended to be asleep just like the others, she learned quickly what happened between a man and a woman.

So when Temple had her naked on the grass, she spread her thighs in invitation.

He stood. Did he plan to leave her there? Humiliate her completely? The thought was sharp and sobering.

Her fear was short lived. He stood over her, water running over him, godlike in the thin light from the school. Anyone could stumble upon them and she didn't care. Temple was removing his trousers, and it would take nothing short of being struck by lightning to convince her to move now.

Naked and hard, he came to her once again, positioning himself between her splayed legs. Legs that trembled with need.

"Next time," he said, his voice a murmur against the pounding rain, "I'm going to take you slowly, but I can't wait any longer."

Next time. She might have panicked were she not so far gone. As it was, her body thrilled at the thought that he would not be content to have her just once.

Sitting back on his heels, he drew her upward with an arm behind her back, so that she straddled his lap. His other hand went between them and brought the thick head of his erection to the damp entrance of her body.

Vivian pushed down, forcing him into her, drawing a gasp from both of them. Between Temple's lips she saw the glint of fangs and shivered, remembering how it felt when he bit her just a few nights ago at the inn.

His arm hooked around her waist and pushed, shoving her down so that he was buried inside her. A burning sensation tore through her. It hurt, but it felt good too, and when she cried out she didn't know if it was from pleasure or pain.

Temple's gaze locked with hers, wide with surprise. He hadn't suspected she might be a virgin and she didn't blame him for that. Why would he?

She moved against him, and pleasure began to overwhelm whatever discomfort remained.

"You've claimed me," she told him, reminding them both of the threat he had made. "Don't you dare stop now." Her voice shook and she knew the rest of her did as well.

He might have chuckled, but it sounded more like a growl low in his throat. "I'm not going to stop."

She knew he referred to far more than what was happening between them at this moment and she didn't care. She was single-minded and not afraid to admit it. Selfish, even. She wanted him and she had him and there were no excuses or apologies that could change that.

He moved easily, almost gently at first. Tears pricked at her eyes at the thought of him restraining himself out of concern for her. Tenderness was not what she wanted from him. Didn't want to think of him as sweet or considerate, not when she was here to triumph over him. He was her prey, not her lover.

"If I wanted to be made love to I would have chosen someone else for the job," she snarled, digging her nails into his shoulders just before she leaned in and bit his bottom lip. She didn't draw blood—she didn't know what effect his blood would have on her—but she bit hard enough that his fingers dug into her hips and he surged upward, plunging deep into her with one powerful motion.

She sobbed and moaned against his mouth,

shoving her body down on his. Oh Sweet God, the feeling of having him inside, stretching, pushing. She planted her feet flat on the soggy grass and pushed into each of his thrusts, each slick movement building the coil of tension within her. Nothing had ever felt like this. Never had made her ever feel so alive.

Temple's mouth broke free of hers, his teeth scraping her lips, her chin, and jaw as he worked his way down to her throat. He wrapped her thick braid around his hand, tugging her head back. She didn't fight him. Even if she wanted to, she was well aware that she couldn't stop him, not when he was intent on having his way.

And she wanted to give it to him.

Again there was that strange sweet sting as his fangs broke the fragile barrier of her neck. Vivian moaned as Temple sucked fiercely on the wound. What would it feel like if he bit her on the breast? The thigh? What would those teeth feel like scraping her most intimate flesh? The thought was enough to send her spiraling even further out of control and she thrashed against him, impaling herself on his hardness over and over again until his arm tightened around her and her head began to swim with loss of blood and control. Climax struck with a flash of lightning—as though the tempest was controlled by their passion rather than nature. Thunder drowned out their cries as Temple stiffened beneath her, holding her so tightly she thought her ribs might crack and didn't care.

His shoulders were bleeding where she had dug her nails in. The rain washed the blood away and she watched as the tiny wounds became almost imperceptible and then disappeared completely. He healed faster than she ever thought possible. Or was it just her imagination? Her mind was swimming . . .

"This doesn't change anything," she informed him, hearing the words slur as she spoke them. She pulled free of his hold and he let her go. Her vision went blurry as she stood. Too fast.

Cool green eyes locked with hers, but she couldn't focus. He had her blood on his lips. How much had he taken? "It changes everything."

Vivian opened her mouth to protest, but then the world tipped and everything went black.

He shouldn't have taken so much blood, Temple thought as he carried Vivian and their clothes down the steps that led to the cellar and eventually his apartments. Thank God many of the students were home for the summer or he might accidentally mentally scar a young woman for life by walking around naked as a babe in the middle of a thunderstorm. Never mind that he was carrying an equally naked woman.

A woman whom he had no idea what to do with.

A woman who had been a virgin until he violated her.

No, he wasn't going to go down that road. He wasn't going to assume guilt or blame for what happened on the lawn. It might yet prove to have been a hellish mistake, but for now it was one of the most incredible experiences of his long, long life.

The most incredible lover he had ever known was the puppet of a man who would see him and his kind destroyed. And destruction had to be what Villiers had on his mind, no other explanation made sense.

Why had Villiers sent her—to distract him? Had her mentor ordered her to play the seductress? No. He heard the lust in the bastard's voice when he spoke to Vivian—he wouldn't send her willingly to another's embrace.

Temple grinned as he balanced Vivian's weight with one arm, opening the door to his chambers. Wouldn't he like to see the look on Villiers's face if the son of a bitch discovered Temple had gotten into the feisty Amazon first.

Sweet Christ, but she was something. He had given her practically nothing in the manner of foreplay and she hadn't seemed to need or want it. Her body had been tight and wet and ready for him. Everything he gave she took and gave back tenfold. Would she approach all of life with the same blunt defiance she used toward sex? If so, she was a more formidable opponent than he ever would have thought. That concept of her was as arousing as it was admirable.

But no matter how much he wanted her or admired her, he didn't trust her at all. Their intimacy might have changed things, but not that.

For that reason, after he placed her in his bed and pulled the blankets over her, he went through the contents of her meager baggage—nothing threatening there. Of course, the woman was a weapon by herself, so why bother with guns?

Then he found the knife sheathed inside her boot and smiled. Such a warrior.

Temple slipped into a dressing gown he found in the armoire and left the room with their clothes and Vivian's belongings. The clothes he took to the laundry. The bag, he hid.

Then, he returned to his apartments and pulled the cord that rang a small bell in Brownie's room.

He was glad when his old friend arrived eleven minutes later. He had spent the time waiting for her sitting in a chair watching Vivian sleep. She looked so pale and peaceful, so much a fallen angel that his heart pinched uncomfortably at the sight of her.

Attachment was not something he could afford, and certainly not something he courted—not with this woman, not if he was smart.

"What is it?" Brownie asked, stifling a yawn as he opened the door to her. "Is something . . . Temple, there's a woman in your bed."

Closing the door to seal them inside, lest the walls have ears, Temple smiled at Brownie's bewildered expression. That was it—no jealously or pique, just curiosity.

"Sent by the man I told you about."

The little woman made a scoffing noise as she tossed him a disbelieving glance. "He sent a mere woman to deal with you?"

"She's no mere woman." And if he were mortal he'd have the wounds to prove it.

It was that cryptic remark that got him a fine brow arched in his direction before she tiptoed toward the bed, as though afraid of waking the slumbering princess within.

Temple watched his friend closely, taking in every nuance of her expression, waiting for the realization . . .

Brownie's eyes widened. Her lips parted on a gasp as color bloomed in her cheeks. She pressed her fingers to her mouth as she turned to him, clearly shocked.

"Temple, she's—" She stopped, clearly unable to form the words.

He nodded, pleased to have his own suspicion confirmed. "I think so. It makes sense, and it concerns me, given the man who commands her loyalty."

The petite Irishwoman turned her attention back to the bed, her gaze falling on Vivian's impossibly crimson hair. "What are you going to do? And why is she naked?"

A chuckle escaped him despite the situation. "I'm going to send for the others, and she's naked because she can't run away if she hasn't any clothes."

Brownie nodded, obviously still stupefied. "I'd like to talk to her."

Of course. He knew she would. "Later. She's not to be trusted, my dear."

"But, she—"

"Could have no idea of what she is. You can't tell her, Brownie. Promise me you won't."

She practically rolled her eyes at him, but in the end she gave her word. "What do you need me to do?"

"Help me earn her trust."

"Help you keep her prisoner, you mean."

Temple flashed a half grin. "Semantics."

His friend's delicate countenance took on a worried expression. "Temple, you don't mean to use her for revenge, do you?"

"I hadn't thought of it," he admitted but now that he did, it certainly gave him a degree of power having Villiers's ward in his possession.

"*Temple.*" There was genuine warning in her tone and he bristled at it. What kind of monster did she think he was? Did she think that he would hurt an innocent woman?

An innocent one, no. But Vivian wasn't innocent, and he didn't know if she was conflicted in her feelings for him, or if she'd kill him as quick as Villiers gave the word.

"Revenge, no." He kept his gaze fastened on the woman in his bed. "But that doesn't mean I can't use her to my advantage."

Chapter 5

Vivian knew there would be consequences. What she hadn't suspected was that they'd jump up and bite her on the backside quite so soon.

She woke up late the next day, sore but strangely replete, to find Temple slumbering beside her. Naked.

As much as she wanted to explore him, study every inch of him, she wasn't foolish enough to indulge. He hadn't chained her or bound her in any way. The door wasn't even locked. Surely he wasn't so foolish as to let her walk around freely. Was he? Or if he was, it had to be because he had complete confidence in her inability to escape. Or maybe he believed after one night with him she wouldn't want to. He wouldn't be far from wrong with that one. It was very tempting to snuggle against his warm body, wake him up and let him claim her once more.

She had given her virtue to a vampire—her

enemy. That realization didn't bother her half as much as it should have. She had enjoyed every minute of it. In fact, what bothered her was her lack of guilt. She was winning Temple's trust, she told herself. That was why she didn't feel badly. Yes, that was it.

Now she had to find a way to get word to Rupert. He had told her he had friends on Clare as well. Would one of them manage to find her? To be sure it would be much more difficult for her to find them.

Still, she didn't have time to laze around. The more information she could glean the better. She was at a disadvantage here, and Temple had all the power. Not a balance she was comfortable with.

Vivian slipped out from between the soft, warm sheets and began searching for her clothes. They weren't in any of the dresser drawers, nor were they in the armoire—that housed a small amount of Temple's clothing, she could tell from the simple lines and the smell of vanilla and cloves that clung to them. He smelled good enough to eat.

My God. She paused, leaning against the door of the armoire for support. *What have I done?*

Her gaze drifted to the man slumbering on the crisp white sheets. She had done whatever was necessary—she could tell herself that. Truth of it was she could have put up more of a fight. She hadn't wanted to. A moment of weakness and she gave in so easily, wanting to experience what his body promised. It might prove to have been a colossal mistake, but it was also one of the most amazing experiences of her life. Never had she felt such abandon, such sensations.

Such completion. She had expected to feel some pleasure, but not the other emotions. Not a connection.

She was tender inside, and a little sore. The blow Temple landed on her jaw had hurt more. Absently, she rubbed the bruise just to the left of her mouth. Any marks she'd given him had long disappeared. It must be wonderful to heal so quickly.

He could have killed her. Why hadn't he? Obviously he has uses for her, just as she planned to use him.

"You're staring."

Vivian actually screeched. Damn him all to hell for turning her into a stupid, easily frightened female. She ducked behind the armoire door to hide herself from those mocking green eyes. He not only made her stupid, but modest as well. She peeked around the edge of the oak.

He was sitting up on the bed, covers bunched around his hips, baring his upper body to her curious gaze. He was so big and strong, scarred from century-past battles and tanned from a sun long ago set.

She wasn't sure what she thought of his hair. She liked it long, but the shorter style made his rugged features all the more prominent. He wasn't her wild vampire anymore. It had been easier to think of him as dangerous when he looked the part.

Now he simply *felt* dangerous.

His thick, muscled chest wasn't as hairy as a beast, nor was it as a smooth as a boy's. But there was enough of the dark, springy stuff that she itched to run her palms over it, just to feel the heat of silky skin beneath.

Her gaze moved over wide shoulders, up a broad neck, to a strong stubbled jaw. His slim mouth curved into a crooked smile that matched the glint in his pale eyes.

"Staring," he reminded her.

Vivian blushed. Damn him again. She expected him to treat her with mockery, derision even, not amusement. He wasn't even malicious about it.

"Where are my clothes?" she demanded in her haughtiest tone.

"Would you like a bath?" he countered, tossing back the blankets and swinging his long legs over the side of the bed.

Vivian knew she should look away—and she did, but not before she got a good look at the part of him that had been inside her the night before. The part that looked ready to have a go at her again now.

"What did you do with my clothes?" she demanded, her gaze fixed on his face, where it was relatively safe.

He flashed a grin as he walked by. She pulled the door closer, stepping back until she was forced to either stop or climb into the wardrobe. "I'll start the water."

"I don't want a bath."

Another smile, this one over his shoulder. Lord, but he had a lovely backside! "I don't care. You *need* one."

No wonder his backside was nice. She jerked her gaze back to his. "You're an arse."

Temple chuckled, and Vivian glanced away as he bent over to turn the taps of the tub. "Be nice, or you'll never get your clothes back."

What stung more? The fact that he had her so easily where he wanted her, or the fact that she wasn't nearly as angry as she should be? He had been expecting her. Obviously he had been watching for her, and that took some of the hurt out of the fact that he had left her in the first place.

Left her? Where the devil had that come from? He hadn't left her, he had escaped. She had nothing to do with it. But it had hurt, and she couldn't escape the truth of that now that it had revealed itself in such an unwelcome manner. Better to be angry instead. Angry was easier to face.

Temple made an idiot out of her—and that made her angry, not only at him but at herself. Whatever situation she was in now was of her own making.

"So, what happens now?" she demanded with more hauteur than she felt. "Do you use me to have your revenge?"

Straightening, Temple turned to face her in all his naked glory as the tub filled behind him. "That wouldn't be very sporting of me, would it?"

Vivian kept her gaze focused on his face. She wanted to hit him, but she wanted to kiss him too. Wanted to take him inside and ride him hard until he promised her anything she wanted—until he was under her control. "That hardly answers my question."

"If I was going to hurt you, I would have by now." His head tilted thoughtfully. "I hurt you last night, didn't I?"

Did he mean the fist to her jaw, or taking her virginity? "I'll heal. But you still haven't told me if I'm to an instrument of revenge."

He smiled, and not happily. "Instrument. Makes you sound like you are an object to be played or manipulated."

Her fingers tightened on the armoire door, the only thing protecting her from him, even then she knew he could snap it like a twig. An object to be manipulated. Wasn't that how Rupert saw him? How she saw him as well? "I was your jailor." Why on earth was she reminding him of that fact? "I would think you would hate me."

He turned around to dip his fingers in the tub, then adjusted one of the taps. He moved leisurely, as though she weren't any threat at all. And yet, she sensed a tension in him that was entirely natural. He was relaxed, but always on guard.

Where as she never seemed to be on guard enough.

Muscles rippled as he moved. Flesh pulled over his ribs and flanks. He was comfortable with his nudity—and her regard.

He made her wait until he had the water to his liking before straightening and replying, "I feel a great number of conflicting emotions where you are concerned, Vivian. Hate is relatively low on the list."

Her heart skipped a beat. "What could you possibly feel for me?"

Temple shook his head with a rueful grin. "You don't honestly think I'm going to make it that easy for you, do you?"

"I don't know what you mean." And she didn't—not really.

Another adjustment of the taps. "I warned you what would happen if you came after me, yet you did anyway. You either really wanted me, or Villiers sent you." He smiled, looking at her as though he could actually peer inside her soul. "Or both. Either way, I'm not going to give you what you want so easily."

He spoke so nonchalantly, his words so close to the truth, the base of Vivian's spine tingled with unease. She looked away from him, her gaze falling on the clock on the dresser. It was a little after twelve.

"What time of day is it?"

He chuckled, no doubt amused at how easily she gave up pursuing the topic of feelings. "Shortly after noon." The water shut off as he bent over the tub once more.

This time Vivian kept her eyes on his smooth back and wide shoulders. "Shouldn't you be asleep?"

"I can be awake during the day—I just can't be out in it." He held out his hand. "Now, if you're done asking me questions, your bath is ready."

He stood there, unashamed of his body, and not seeming the least bit interested in hers. Vivian hesitated. There had to be a trap somewhere, but for the life of her she couldn't see it. And he was right, she did need a bath. Worse, she wanted one.

Tentatively, she stepped out from behind the door, her arms stiff at her sides. Trying to hide herself would just make her all the more foolish, and give him even more power.

He surprised her by keeping his attention focused on her face rather than ogling her body as she had done to him. That he treated her with such respect was unsettling to say the least—and shaming. She crossed the carpet to the stone section where the tub sat, ignored the hand he offered, and stepped into the tub.

The water was hot, but not painfully so, and she sank into its blissful embrace with a sigh. Remembering her manners, she glanced up at Temple. "Thank you." Despite the reversal of roles, he had never been rude to her and she would do her best to return the favor. More flies with honey, or whatever the saying was.

"Lean forward," he instructed. "I'll wash your back."

"There's no need . . ."

"Do it."

And she did. There was something in that commanding tone that had her pressing her chest to her raised knees so fast she hadn't even realized she'd moved. She could feel the pounding of her heart against her thigh.

Temple knelt. He wet a sponge and generously lathered it with sandalwood-scented soap. Then he began scrubbing her back—and not in a gentle, seductive manner either.

"Trying to wash me to death?" she asked drily. It didn't hurt, but it wasn't exactly pleasurable either.

"You have dirt and grass stains on your back," he replied with a smile, in that low accent that was neither French nor British, but something in between. "I imagine your ass looks much the same. Shall I wash it as well?"

"No!"

He chuckled and leaned forward, so that his

breath was hot against her ear like that night at the inn. "You can't stop me."

This time when she looked at him, Vivian felt the first inkling of real fear. He was right. She couldn't stop him. He could do whatever he liked to her. Oh, she could put up a good fight, but in the end he would win.

What the hell had Rupert been thinking sending her after him? What had she been thinking saying she'd go?

He'd been thinking that she would find a way to control Temple. Her mentor believed she was the only person who could stand against the vampire at all, who could gain any power over Temple. She would not disappoint him.

She kept herself stiff and still. "I thought you weren't going to hurt me."

Soft, but firm lips brushed the slick skin of her shoulder, and beneath those, sharp teeth nipped. "A little pain can sometimes feel good."

Fire shot through Vivian's veins. She'd never known any kind of pain to ever feel good, except for that which Temple offered. He made her feel as though drawing breath was exquisite agony.

"If I were to exact any manner of revenge upon you, Vivian," he growled, abrading the skin of her chin with his own as he rubbed his face against hers. "It would be to spend the next few days making you want me as badly as I've wanted you all these weeks."

She turned her head, feeling the solid warmth of his cheekbone against her own. The soap he used on her smelled like him, except for that elusive sweetness that clung to his skin. It muddled her brain, made her feel loose and wanton, beautiful and desirous.

"How could you want me when I was one of those who kept you locked in a cage?" Like an animal. Like a freak.

"I don't know." Turning his face, Temple brought his mouth within a whisper of hers. "How could you want me?"

"I didn't." Even as she lied, little shivers raced down her spine, raised tiny bumps of anticipation on her skin.

He chuckled, warm, surprisingly sweet breath fanning her cheek. "Liar."

And then he kissed her, parting his lips and claiming her mouth with the bold intrusion of his tongue. One arm came around her, holding her shoulder against the unyielding wall of his chest, the other slipped into the water between her thighs, cupping her where she was still tender, yet wanted him again.

Her hands gripped the sides of the tub as his fingers parted her. She couldn't bring herself to touch him. It was too dangerous. He already sensed too much and putting her hands on him, letting them explore him—worship him—as she wanted would reveal more weakness than any words ever could. So she dug her heels into the smooth bottom of the bath and tried not to arch against his hand when his blunt yet gentle finger stroked her sweet spot.

"Promise me you won't try to escape," he murmured against her mouth.

Vivian's eyes opened, locking her gaze with his. He leaned back a bit so they could see each other clearly, but his finger continued its deliberate and delicious torment.

"No." Her voice was low and hoarse to her own ears—a weakling's voice and it shamed her even as she spread her thighs wider. It wasn't that she couldn't say the words—she could easily lie—it was that she wouldn't say them just so he would give her what she wanted. She wasn't going to give him that power.

A slow smile curved his lips. There was no mockery in his countenance, only determination. The tempo of his strokes slowed to a maddening degree. "Promise."

Gritting her teeth in frustration, Vivian shook her head. "No."

Temple tried another tactic. The motion of his finger increased once more and then increased again, winding her tighter and tighter until release loomed.

"Promise me, and I'll do this with my tongue."

Damn him. Reason flew away as pleasure built, and Vivian knew if she refused he would stop and not give her what she so desperately wanted. She wouldn't try to escape, it was too important that she stay there—with him. Telling him what he wanted to hear would only help her.

"I promise," she cried out as orgasm struck with a vengeance—not giving a damn about her mission or anything else. "Oh God, I promise!"

And as the bathwater sloshed onto the floor, she thought she heard Temple laughing.

In another lifetime Temple might have lost his heart to such a woman.

Then again, he reflected as he tucked his shirt into the waist of his trousers, in another lifetime he might have simply had her for breakfast and moved on to the next tempting morsel. He hadn't always stopped to consider the sanctity of life in the past.

In the old days he would have killed her for being his enemy. It would have been a matter of self-preservation back then. Now . . . well, perhaps she was something of a threat to his existence, but she could also provide information that might save them all.

Between escape and arriving on Clare, he had managed to garner a little information from some of his sources. Rupert Villiers had tangled with a vampire before. About twenty years ago, he'd lost his fiancée to a vampire named Payen Carr. After that, Villiers had made a career out of climbing the ranks of the Order of the Silver Palm.

If Temple was correct in his suspicions about Vivian, then she was worth more to Villiers than anyone could imagine. And if Villiers had sent her after him, then there was more afoot than simple revenge against vampires.

That was why he let it be known he was looking for Payen Carr. If the vampire was still alive, word would reach him.

He glanced at his prisoner. Dry and clad in an old dressing gown, Vivian looked every bit as fetching as she had naked in the tub, her luminescent flesh flushed with desire. He knew the dangers of entering into a sexual relationship with her. He also knew better than to trust her. She was playing with him, just as he was playing with her—both of them intent to be the victor. It was going to be one hell of a game.

"Are you hungry?" he asked, watching her cinch the belt on the blue paisley gown. Many would want her weakened, at their mercy, but he wanted her strong and at her best. A fair fight. Christ, he looked forward to doing battle with her.

She shot him a gaze that was as thankful as it was distrusting. He could practically smell her desire to defeat him mixing with her attraction to him. "Yes."

Yes, he wanted her strong. "I'll have some food sent down, then."

"And my clothes?"

He grinned at her, knowing full well she hated it. "I rather like you without them."

She flushed, her cheeks blossoming like spring roses. He was hungry too, he realized, hearing the increased rhythm of her heart.

"I'll give them back," he assured her, crossing the carpet to pull the cord for a servant. "Don't fret."

"I never fret," she retorted, twisting her glorious hair into a damp braid.

"Never?" Christ she amused him. "I suppose you never lie either."

If the glare she shot him had been made of silver he'd be dead.

Vivian climbed onto the bed, and pulled the quilt over her lower body, but not before unwittingly flashing him a length of firm, pale leg. The woman was the closest thing to perfection he'd seen in a long time.

What would the rest of his brethren think of her? Would his former comrades, his brothers, find her as enticing as he, or would they revile her?

And how much of their reaction to her would be their choice? Temple didn't know how much of his attraction to her was because of her, or because of twice taking her blood. Her sweet, unnaturally potent blood.

He should be careful of feeding from her just in case, at least not until he discovered the effects.

"You're staring," she remarked.

"I like the look of you."

She flushed again. She really wasn't very good at being coquettish, which he appreciated. Every reaction he drew from her was real, but she was smart enough to know to use that to her advantage, just as he would use it to his.

He moved to sit at the foot of the bed—not so close as to make her wary, but close enough to force some intimacy upon the situation. "What is your relationship with Villiers?"

Vivian stiffened—even her face tightened. "That is none of your concern."

Temple arched a brow. "Beg pardon, but the man is trying to kill me." He didn't sound half as sardonic as he should. "I think it is my business."

"He doesn't want to kill you." She didn't sound convinced. And judging from her expression she regretted speaking so quickly.

"Then, what does he want?"

She looked away, and he realized something. It wasn't that she wouldn't tell him, but that she *couldn't*. She didn't know what Villiers was up to any more than he did. Shit.

"He's a crafty bastard," he muttered around a bitter chuckle.

"He is *not* a bastard." True belief lit her eyes and heightened her color. Her round chin lifted defiantly. "He is a good man."

Both brows went up this time. "A good man who keeps other men in cages."

"He only keeps vampires in cages," she shot back. Ah, there was that expression of regret again. And something else. That blood intuition of his raised its head. What cage had someone put Vivian in?

Temple smiled. "My mistake. Tell me, then, what is it that makes Mr. Villiers such a paragon in your estimation?"

Stormy eyes narrowed. "You mock me."

"Most assuredly. But, I would honestly like to know why he has your unswerving devotion."

Vivian glanced down at her hands, bunched in the quilt, her brow knitting. "He saved me."

Before Temple could ask from what, there was a knock on the door. He practically leaped off the bed and across the room to answer it, not wanting to give Vivian time to guard her words. It was a servant and he asked her to bring them whatever food was available. Then he returned to his former perch at his captive's feet.

"Saved you from what?"

Any uncertainty in her countenance was wiped away by the return of defiance. But it wasn't feeling for Villiers that had her stiffening her spine. He didn't know how he knew it, but he would have bet his immortality on it. She defied him to think poorly of her—to see her as less than the amazing creature she was.

"From a traveling show that showcased oddities."

He would accuse her of lying were it not for the stark truth in her eyes. "A circus?"

Her nostrils flared slightly as she drew a sharp breath. "A freak show."

Having her suddenly burst into flames would have been less of a shock. "How did you end up in one of those?" And for what? More importantly, who put her there?

Long, strong arms folded across her chest, lifting her breasts against the dark fabric of the robe. She looked away, as if holding his gaze had become too much to bear. "My father sold me for fourteen pounds and a side of salt-pork. They advertised me as Boadicea, the warrior queen of Briton."

For the first time in a very long time, Temple didn't choose silence, he was forced into it by the simple fact that he had no bloody idea of what to say.

"Villiers took me in. He treated me like his own daughter—better than my own father ever treated me. I owe him my life."

Temple cocked his head to one side. "What did he want in return?"

Anger flared, brightening her entire face. "Why would he want anything?"

He shrugged. "Obviously he didn't want your virginity." He ignored the increased flush of her cheeks, the smell of shame on her skin.

She didn't speak and so he pressed on, "What is it about you that makes you a freak?"

Vivian winced, but she didn't back down. The fact that she shared this obviously painful part of her past with him humbled him, and he had to remind himself that she was just as capable of playing on his weaknesses as he was on hers. "Surely you've noticed I'm stronger and faster than most women? Most men for that matter. I was beating up boys twice my size by the time I was nine."

He had. In fact, he thought he knew why. The question was, did Villiers? It seemed awfully coincidental given Villiers's interest in vampires.

"I've noticed." He rubbed a hand over his hair, surprised to find it short even though he had cut it himself. "I suppose your father didn't fancy his daughter beating up the local lads?"

"My father would have sold me to one of them if any had wanted me. I was an embarrassment."

Temple watched her closely, watched her arms straighten and her hands clench and relax. Then, she folded them again. Twitchy, she was.

"What happened?" he asked, feeling suddenly very insightful. "Did your papa hit you, only to be hit back?"

She didn't have to answer, he saw the truth in the ruddiness of her burning cheeks. "Yes," she replied, her voice small and hoarse. "I knocked him through the barn door in front of a neighbor. It was the last time he ever struck me. Three days later the traveling show came into town and he sold me."

At that moment, Temple would have hugged her if he thought she'd allow it. She was either sincere, or a very good liar. He didn't think she was lying. "I'm sorry I hit you."

Her eyes widened, and her fingers went to the discolored patch on her jaw. "I attacked you. I would have done the same thing."

"But I'm not human."

Vivian smiled, and for some reason Temple thought of the last sunrise he had seen. The memory of it paled next to that smile, however sad it might have been. "Sometimes I don't think I am either."

A knock on the door kept him from replying, which was just as well. It was Brownie, carrying a tray laden with food and a pot of richly fragrant coffee with two cups.

"You didn't have to bring it yourself," Temple softly chastised his old friend as he took the heavy burden from her.

Brownie flashed him a look that might have been contrite were it not for the impishness of it. "And miss out on an introduction?" she whispered. "My dear Temple, you know me better than that."

"Good morning," the older woman said as she swept into the room. Vivian eyed her warily. "I'm Kimberly Cooper-Brown. Welcome to the Garden Academy."

Two finely arched russet brows rose high on

Vivian's smooth forehead. Temple could almost read her thoughts. She questioned Brownie's welcome, when it should be obvious that she was there as a prisoner.

"I'm Vivian," came the reply, and Temple realized that he didn't even know her last name. Then again, he did well to remember his own; it had been so long since he used it.

He had forgotten more than most people would ever learn.

Not one to indulge in self-pity, unlike Chapel or occasionally Saint, two of his oldest friends, Temple shook off the melancholy thought and took the tray to the bed, placing it over Vivian's lap. She shot him a foul look, as though she thought him treating her like an invalid. He was only trying to be kind. Perhaps he wasn't very good at it.

Brownie was smiling like a baptized whore seeing the light of God. "Please let me know if you need anything at all, Miss Vivian."

"I'd like some clothes," came the quick reply. Temple choked back laughter. He admired her spirit, damn her pretty hide.

His friend didn't even glance at him. "I believe your belongings are in the laundry. Anything else?"

"We'll let you know," Temple replied before Vivian could speak. Brownie was going to make Vivian suspicious with all this bowing and scraping. "Thank you for breakfast."

Vivian murmured her thanks as well, and Temple took Brownie by the arm, steering her toward the door so quickly she had to run to keep up.

"Try not to treat her like the second coming," he growled as he practically shoved her out of the room.

Brownie wasn't the least bit sorry. "You cannot expect me to treat her like any other person."

He scowled. "You treat me like any other person."

She waved a dismissive hand. "You are."

He bared his fangs, reminding her rather dramatically of just how wrong she was. His reward was seeing her press a hand against her throat as her heart pounded like a scared rabbit's. Now he had frightened his only ally.

"Please, Brownie," he said softly, taking her chilled hand in his. "I need you to show some restraint. At least for a little while. I don't think Vivian knows what she is, and I don't want to tell her until I know for certain the part she's to play."

Brownie sighed. "I understand. Please don't hiss at me like that again."

Temple squeezed her fingers. "I won't." He released her hand. "I need a favor. Can you send these telegrams for me?" He handed her the small stack of papers sitting on the table beside him.

They were messages to various acquaintances around Europe—people he knew his friends would go to.

By now Chapel would have discovered his former hideaway in England. He had been taken before he could speak to the other vampire, but there was plenty of evidence left behind. Chapel had to know something bad had happened. He would alert the others. By now at least one of them had to have received the medallions he had sent.

They would come. They wouldn't walk into whatever trap Villiers set for them in Italy. Together, the five of them would plan and launch their own attack against the Silver Palm. This was going to end. Temple tried not to think about what would happen to Vivian when that final battle came.

To her credit, the little woman didn't even glance at the letters. "Of course. I need to send out some correspondence myself later on this afternoon."

Temple thanked her, told her he would talk to her later, and closed the door. When he turned, it was to find Vivian watching him closely as she broke apart a flaky croissant and stuffed the chunks into her mouth. For a moment he was somewhat saddened, knowing this time alone with her would soon end.

"So," she said, tearing off another piece of pastry, "are you going to have something to eat?"

He thought of her thigh and how delicious it looked earlier. And then he flashed her a broad grin, full of fang.

"Yes," he replied, slipping the deadbolt into place. "I believe I will."

Chapter 6

No word from Vivian.

Rupert Villiers fingered the length of one of his own perfectly groomed sideburns as he sat behind the massive desk of his London town home and stared out the window at the West End evening traffic as it clattered by.

Almost a week had passed since her telegram informing him of her arrival in Ireland, and her preparations to journey to Clare. His own contacts had confirmed not only that Temple was on the island, and Vivian should be as well. So why had she not contacted him?

Surely he would know if she were dead. Surely someone would have contacted him by now with the awful news. He wouldn't have sent her if he thought Temple would kill her. She was far too important to him. He couldn't have misjudged the appeal she would hold for Temple.

No, she could not be dead. She was simply too important to his plans for him to believe her gone so easily. There had to be another explanation for her lack of communication. One that had her alive. More than likely she was already warming the vampire's bed. The idea soured his stomach, but he knew it was a necessary component of manipulating Temple into conforming to his plans. The more sexual experience Vivian had, the better it would be when everything came together and she was finally his.

After twenty years of planning, he was so close to the fulfillment of all his dreams. It had taken almost a decade to rise in the ranks of the Order, to make them see the possibilities of his plan—the certainty of it. His discovery of Vivian had done much to win them over. Another five years of experiments on lesser vampires, of showing them what Vivian could do. They had seen how the young vampires reacted to her, and even though Vivian herself hadn't understood, the Order did. His climb started then, and he hadn't looked back. Now he was the most powerful man in the organization. His only competition for the position had died in an unfortunate accident several months earlier.

And soon, he would be the most powerful man in the world. A far cry from the stupid boy who had lost his fiancée to a vampire. Of course, he owed Payen Carr so very much now that fate had worked her magic. If Payen hadn't interfered, hadn't shown him the true purpose of the Order, he might not be where he was today.

And most certainly Violet would have started to lose her looks by now. Of course, the fact that she was now a vampire kept that from happening. She had become the vampire's whore without so much as a blink, turning her back on the promise she had made Rupert. At least Vivian had an excuse. She really couldn't help herself. Attracting and being attracted to vampires was in her blood.

Staring out the window, he caught sight of a familiar face beneath the lamp across the street. A face that had him bolting upright in his chair for a better view.

Was it he? The man stood on the walk, a beaver hat pulled low over his forehead, but Villiers saw enough to want to press his fist against his mouth in fear.

Payen Carr.

Twenty years ago—had it really been so long?—on the eve of his wedding to the lovely Violet Wynston-Jones, he saw that face for the first time. Payen had interrupted a party, barging in like some kind of mad man, demanding that Violet not be allowed to marry Rupert.

But the last time he saw Carr, Villiers accidently shot Violet. If that was Carr across the street, then the vampire was in London for one reason and one reason only.

To kill him.

A knock on the door called him back to the

here and now. He cast a glance that was both fearful and defiant toward the window, only to find the man gone. Perhaps he hadn't been there after all. An old ghost kicked up by the memories that haunted him. Memories that drove him.

"Come in," he called, settling back in his chair. He'd reacted like a scared little boy, damn it all. He was a match for Payen or any vampire now. And he had the silver bullets and safeguards to prove it.

It was his housekeeper. "A telegram just arrived for you, sir."

Villiers rose from his desk, ashamed to find that his legs were shaking a little. "Give it here, then."

The woman did as he bade. Then with a curtsey she took her leave.

Another glance out the window, but he could see nothing but the reflection of his own lamps. Damn his mind for playing such tricks when he needed his thoughts clear.

He pulled the drapes closed and sat behind his desk once more. The telegram was from his contact in Ireland. Vivian had indeed made it to Clare, and was now a resident of the Garden Academy, as was Temple. It appeared that she was Temple's prisoner, but suffered no ill treatment save for a rather nasty bruise. He kept her in his apartments and she was treated like a guest. More news would be sent when it was had.

A gusty sigh escaped him as Villiers slumped in his chair. Vivian was fine, but it was no wonder she hadn't been able to send him a message. If Temple kept her segregated from the others at the school, then she would have yet to meet the person who could get messages to him.

Instinct had told him that Temple wouldn't hurt her. Now his beautiful protégé could work on earning the vampire's trust, make him believe she wasn't dangerous. Distract him. Seduce him into believing she was his salvation rather than his destruction.

He took a drink from the snifter of brandy on the desk, smiling now, all fear and uncertainty fading away like smoke rising from a chimney.

They were so close. So very close to achieving all he had worked toward the last two decades. Soon he would be the most powerful man in all the world. Being First Master of the Order of the Silver Palm already made him powerful and wealthy beyond all expectations, but when he had the five vampires in his possession, had their blood at his disposal . . .

Knowing what destiny held for him was very satisfying.

In the morning he would meet with his secretary and make plans to leave for Ireland as soon as possible. All of the equipment was already on its way, as well as his men. They would have to work quickly. According to the telegram in his hand, Temple had sent messages to various contacts around Europe, calling the other vampires to him. Soon they would assemble, and it was important that Villiers catch them off guard. If they launched a united front against him, he would not be able to stand.

But the vampires were not as smart as they were strong. Yes, they would avoid his plans to intercept them in Italy, but he could work around that. For months he had proven his intellect superior to theirs, staying at least one stride ahead. Never had he needed his mind sharper than he did right now. He would succeed. He must.

And then it wouldn't matter if Payen Carr came for blood. Villiers would be ready.

And Villiers would have the power to literally tear Carr—and any other vampire—limb from limb.

The women made Vivian uncomfortable. During the past two days since Temple had decided to give her back her clothes and allow her to wander around the academy she had spent most of her time suffering through stares and whispers.

It reminded her far too much of her youth to be pleasant.

And so an unpleasant situation became even more so.

Not that being with Temple was unpleasant—it was rather the opposite, at least physically. The

man played her body like she had been created
for his hand. That wasn't the issue. What plagued
her were these feelings of guilt.

She should not enjoy the vampire's touch. She
should not revel in his attentions when it was obvious he was simply trying to distract her from
her mission. And she did revel in them. In fact,
she craved them. It was almost painful to be away
from him for long. What was the flaw in her that
made her want him so?

Let him think he had succeeded in distracting
her. Let him think he held all the power. She could
play at that game as well. In fact, she knew he
was as drawn to her as she to him. She had some
power as well, and she had to remember that. She
had to remain clear and remember her loyalty to
Rupert. What Temple made her feel wasn't real. It
was lust and nothing more.

Today was the first day he slept rather than
ramble through the academy with her. So long as
the heavy drapes were closed he could go wherever
he wanted, untouched by the sun's dangerous rays.

It was good to know that even he had to rest
sometime.

He trusted her not to run away while he slept.
He hadn't said it, but it was there unspoken between them. There was nothing he could do if she
decided to run. He'd be powerless to stop her in
the full light of day. Shunned from God's sight, as
the legend said, the sun would burn him with ex-

cruciating ease, eventually reducing him to nothing but ash.

She shuddered just thinking about it. It seemed a little excessive. Yet surely, that was proof of how dangerous vampires were. How evil they must be if they were denied God's acknowledgment. And that made her attraction to Temple all the more deplorable, did it not?

If not for her duty to Rupert, she would consider running. Of course, once she reached the beach, she would be powerless. Unless there was someone there with a boat, or someone with whom she had made prior arrangements, there was no way off the island. Unless she wanted to swim to the mainland. Unfortunately, she wasn't that good a swimmer.

Standing in the parlor, gazing out the window at the lush greenery, steep cliff, and wild ocean, Vivian's thoughts were little but turmoil. She knew what she had to do. She knew what was right, and yet a voice inside her insisted that this was wrong. Just plain wrong. That there had to be some way to end this so no one had to suffer.

That she thought these things filled her with even more shame. She owed Rupert her very life, and how did she repay him? With doubt. How foolish was she to dare think there could be some kind of peaceful outcome? Either Rupert or Temple would fail, and she would have played a hand in that outcome.

She knew what side her mind was on, but her heart? Her heart asked far too many questions—most of them about Rupert and the Silver Palm.

It would be so much simpler if Temple would just be the villain Rupert said he was. But he had been nothing but tender to her. Of course he was arrogant, and lorded himself over her, but there was none of the violence she expected. He was nothing like she believed he should be.

Perhaps he was waiting for the right moment to reveal himself, her mind suggested. Or, perhaps Villiers was wrong, said her heart.

Or perhaps both men saw her as a pawn in the war between them. Without her, what did either of them have? Rupert claimed that she was "very important" to his plans, that he needed her by his side when it all came together, but beyond that he trusted her with little information. Temple kept her prisoner because he knew that she was close to Rupert. He knew of their relationship now as well, because she had so stupidly confided her darkest secret to him.

If she ran away, neither of them would be able to use her. Maybe then she would be able to find out exactly what part she played in this game.

Maybe the women would stop whispering about her.

"May I join you?"

Vivian turned to discover Miss Cooper-Brown standing just inside the door, a tea tray in her hands. This woman knew Temple well—perhaps better than Vivian wanted to know. She would also know why the women watched her so.

"Of course," Vivian replied. Truth be told, she was happy for the company.

"Brownie" as Temple called her, entered the room with a swish of delicate skirts and the scent of roses. She was so little, so very dainty. Her hair was perfectly dressed, her blue gown impeccably ironed and turned out. Not a wrinkle anywhere—not even on her face.

Vivian ran her palms over the front of her trousers, feeling the fullness of her thighs as she did so. Next to this woman, this lady, she was a hulking giant of a woman with no taste, no manners, and no grace.

And yet, Miss Cooper-Brown looked at her as though Vivian was a wonder—something fascinating and lovely.

Quickly, Vivian sat down on one of the little high-backed chairs near the tea table. It was stronger than it looked, not even groaning beneath her weight. And it made her a better height to socialize with the other woman, made her more comfortable. She wasn't used to this. Rupert had taught her the niceties, but she'd rarely had a chance to practice them. And she was accustomed to using her stature to intimidate. She did not like feeling like she was the one being intimidated, especially not by a woman almost half her size.

Miss Cooper-Brown sat as well, to Vivian's right. Smiling serenely, she poured steaming tea into two gilt-edged china cups. "Honey?" she asked.

Vivian nodded. "And cream, please." She liked her tea to be a treat. As a child it had been either too bitter or too weak, depending on the supply of leaves, and never flavored with any kind of sweetness or milk.

Her hostess offered her a cup of tea that looked and smelled perfect. "I brought sandwiches as well."

Vivian thanked her, and hoped the older woman didn't hear her stomach rumble. She took a sip of the glorious tea, and then set the cup and saucer aside to drop three little cucumber sandwiches on a plate. There were beef and ham sandwiches as well. She took one of each, not caring if she looked greedy. She hadn't eaten since breakfast and she was famished.

Miss Cooper-Brown took several sandwiches herself. "I'm glad to find myself in the company of a woman who enjoys food as much as myself," she remarked with a smile.

"Thank you for your hospitality." It wasn't exactly a lie. She might be Temple's prisoner, but this woman allowed her to be there. This woman showed her more kindness than any of her sex had in a long, long time.

"I hope the other ladies haven't bothered you too much?"

Vivian took a bite of sandwich, chewed and swallowed. "Bothered me? Oh no, no one has said a word. But . . . they do stare at me." She raised her gaze to the other woman's. "Do you know why?"

For a second, it seemed as though Miss Cooper-Brown might choke. But then she took a sip of tea and her countenance regained its normal composure. "I'm sure no one means any offense—"

"Oh, no offense taken," Vivian interrupted. "I just find it a little . . . disconcerting."

A doll-like hand rested fleetingly on her knee. "Many of the girls who work here have never experienced the world beyond this island, or our neighbors on the mainland. They know only of their tiny spheres, and what is expected of them."

Vivian stared at her. "Are you saying they see me as exotic?" The thought was laughable. But there was a fine line between freak and wonder, wasn't there?

"Quite. They've never seen a woman in trousers. They've never witnessed an independent woman with the means to travel by herself. And they've certainly never seen a woman so strong and capable be so lovely and feminine. In short, you are something of a novelty."

Lovely? Feminine? Her? "But why don't they speak?"

Her hostess looked as though that should be obvious. "They've been taught not to speak to their betters without being spoken to first."

"I'm no one's better," Vivian replied a little more forcefully than she liked. "I was raised in a manner similar to these women and do not see myself as elevated above them in any way."

Her words were greeted by a charming, dazzling smile that left Vivian feeling a little dumbstruck. "Then I shall tell them to make free to converse with you. As well, please do not hesitate to engage them, if the mood strikes you."

She would. She would show them she wasn't some snob—or some "novelty." Perhaps she might even make some friends.

But she shouldn't make friends. Friends would make it more difficult to leave this place. More difficult to do her duty. And besides, she had no idea how to make friends. She'd never had any.

Temple was the closest thing she'd ever had to a friend, and that was simply twisted.

"Perhaps there is something I can do to help out around the school?" Vivian detested being idle. And having an occupation would keep her away from Temple long enough so that her head might remain clear. It would also provide her with the opportunity to question the staff, skulk about and find information to report back to Rupert.

But first she had to find a way to get that information to him.

Miss Cooper-Brown was obviously both surprised and delighted by the offer. "Are you at all skilled in the art of pugilism?"

Vivian laughed. Of all the things she might have speculated being asked, this was not one of them. "As a matter of fact I am." She knew Queensbury's rules and had fought in both a fair manner and a not so fair. She even knew some Oriental styles of fighting.

"Oh, excellent!" Miss Cooper-Brown clapped her hands as Vivian finished off a ham sandwich. "Would you consider teaching some of the ladies how to defend themselves?"

Vivian didn't question why. She knew full what a woman needed to defend herself against. "I would."

This time it was her hand and not her knee that her hostess seized. "Marvelous! Oh, Miss Vivian, I'm so very happy that you have come to us!"

Perhaps it was only because Vivian was unaccustomed to such exuberance, or perhaps she was merely overly suspicious, but there was something about the brightness of Miss Cooper-Brown's eyes that gave her pause. There was something this woman withheld from her.

Why did it seem as though everyone concealed their intentions from her?

"I am glad to be here, Miss Cooper-Brown." She would be even more pleased when she uncovered just what the hell was going on. Perhaps some of the other women might be able to tell her.

"Oh, please. You must call me Kimberly, or Brownie."

"All right." She would also call her a liar, although not strictly to her face. She didn't believe Kimberly bore her any ill intent, but even good intentions could have catastrophic consequences.

"Perhaps you could start your lessons tomorrow?" The other woman asked, oblivious to her companion's suspicions. "I imagine you will be much distracted when Temple's friends arrive, and I do want the ladies to learn as much as they can before you are diverted."

That brought Vivian out of her own thoughts—and damn near robbed her of breath. "Temple's friends?" The only friends she knew of were his fellow vampires.

"Yes." Kimberly appeared slightly bewildered. "He sent the telegrams out a few days ago. I expect some of them to begin arriving late next week."

Not much time, then, Vivian reflected, her heart thrumming in anticipation and a little fear. Was this why he kept her unharmed? He was waiting for the others to arrive before deciding what to do with her? Perhaps he'd let his friends have a go at her as well. Perhaps they'd send her corpse back to Rupert, bitten and defiled.

Or worse, perhaps they planned to make her one of them.

It was hard to imagine, but not so difficult that she dismissed it. Time to stop waiting and take matters firmly in hand. If Temple's brethren were coming, she had to let Rupert know. "Kimberly, would you be able to send a telegram for me?"

"Of course. I have several of my own to send. Can you have it to me within the hour?"

"Without question."

"Then I will include it with my own. Now, shall we enjoy our tea? Let us talk of frivolous things, such as how I would love to have hair like yours."

Vivian laughed, even though in her mind she was mentally composing the missive she would later send to Rupert care of his post box. She would warn him that Temple had called for reinforcements in the code only the two of them knew.

And then she would have to figure out how to protect herself against five angry vampires.

Chapter 7

"**W**hy does Rupert hate you?" Vivian asked him.

It was evening. Temple and Vivian were on the back terrace sharing a light supper. Kimberly had business to attend to and couldn't join them, but promised to bring a tray of tea and sweets later. Vivian expressed a great deal of enthusiasm about the prospect of cakes and biscuits, even as she filled her belly with bread, cheese, and an assortment of cold meats.

Temple ran the tip of a finger along the rim of his wineglass. He'd eaten a little of the supper prepared for them, surprising Vivian. She hadn't known he could eat "real" food. "I have no idea."

"None?" Her tone and expression were incredulous.

He took a piece of cold ham from the platter and popped it into his mouth, licking the salt from his fingers. He noticed Vivian watching him as he did so, her cupid's bow lips parted.

Damn but the attraction between them hadn't lessened since that first night, or the second. It seemed to grow, dig its claws in deeper and deeper until he felt it pressing upon his insides.

"None," he replied, jerking his gaze away from her mouth. "I'm surprised you don't know the answer."

Vivian frowned, and looked away. "He's never told me. In fact, he's never used the word *hate*. I just assume that he hates you because . . ."

He couldn't help but smile. "Because he took me prisoner, drugged me, and locked me in a cage?"

She smiled a little as well. "When you put it like that, it seems fairly obvious, doesn't it? But I've never been able to figure out why he seems to both admire and despise your kind."

His kind. Her kind was far more rare. Did she not wonder why Villiers took her in to begin with?

"It must be difficult giving your loyalty to a man who doesn't trust you." He couldn't resist baiting her.

Tempest-hued eyes met his. "Rupert trusts me."

He arched a brow. "Just not enough to share why he wanted to keep me prisoner. Not enough to tell you why he sent you after me."

She held his gaze, but he saw the turmoil there. Leaning forward, he rested his forearms on the table. "Why are you here, Vivian? Are you supposed to distract me? Feed me tidbits of information and make me believe you're on my side?" When she colored, he snorted, surprisingly disappointed though he'd known the truth. "How stupid do the two of you believe me to be?"

He had to give her credit for not looking away. "I don't think you're stupid. And are you not trying to use me for your own advantage as well? Trying to turn me against Rupert with all your insinuations and seductions?"

"Of course I am," he admitted. "Your mentor is my enemy, Vivian. It would be to my advantage to convince you to feel the same way. Just as it is to my advantage to keep you here rather than kill you and send your body back to him wrapped in a big red bow as I should."

Her eyes widened as she paled. "You'd never kill me." A slight tremor marred the certainty in her voice.

"No," he grumbled. He shouldn't admit to it. "But I should. I suspect it would really ruin Villiers's plans if you were dead."

She just stared at him, and it was all he could do not to shift uncomfortably under her gaze. "How old were you when Villiers told you about vampires?"

Vivian started. Shaking her head, as though to clear it of whatever horror his talk of killing her had put there, she pulled herself together. "I was sixteen. I thought him mad as a loon."

"How did he convince you?"

"He showed me one."

Temple's hand froze over the platter of meats. "What?"

She thought for a moment, plucking a piece of cheese from a platter. "We were in Germany meeting with some of Rupert's friends. They had a man there in a cage . . . only he wasn't a man. He was a vampire, but he didn't look like you."

"We don't all look alike, you know." He meant it to sound jesting, but it came out much harsher than he intended. "In a cage like an animal?" Then he couldn't resist adding, "Like a freak?"

She paled under the terrace lamps. At least his remark struck a nerve. "There was something wrong with him. Something strange about his face. His eyes were too large, his teeth like the fangs of some great beast." She looked at him helplessly, as though frustrated by her own ability to explain— to make him see that this vampire deserved to be locked up. "He did not look human as you do."

Large eyes and teeth. Inhuman. "Nosferatu." A monstrous vampire turned so by drinking diseased blood. Mad, dangerous, and more animal than anything else. "No wonder they caged it," he allowed. "What the hell was Villiers thinking bringing you there?"

Her expression changed, became almost guarded. "He thought I needed to see what a true monster looked like."

"Is that how you saw yourself?" he asked, easily picking up on her meaning. How could she think such nonsense? He could flay her father for putting such thoughts in her head. Flay him and toss him into a vat of boiling salt water.

"I used to," she replied. And he knew from her tone that sometimes she did still.

Reaching across the space between them, he took her hand in his. He wasn't playing this time, he was sincere in his attempt to connect to her. "There is nothing monstrous or wrong about you, my delicious Amazon."

She frowned once more, but didn't pull away from his touch. "Why do you do that?"

"Do what?" As if he didn't suspect where this was going.

"Talk to me like you care for me. Treat me like your lover. We both know you despise me for my loyalty to Rupert."

"Do I?" He smiled, but not with any real joy. "You're mistaken. If anything I pity you. Distrust you. But despise you?" He shook his head. "I told you before I don't hate you. Do you think I could want you like I do if I hated you?"

Now she snatched her hand away. "You should hate me. I should hate you!"

"But you don't, do you?" Poor thing. What disappointment waited for her when she learned that nothing Villiers did was out of love for her? At least Temple respected her. Desired her for the woman she was, not what she represented.

Her blood, her heritage was only part of it. An undeniable part of it.

"No," she replied defeatedly as she glanced away. "I don't. But I won't betray Rupert for you."

That was as good as he was going to get from her, he knew that. He also knew that he wasn't being fair to her, using every charm he possessed, every seductive trait to keep her with him. He wanted her on his side, and not just because it would piss off Villiers.

"Of course you won't." Oddly enough he respected her even more for it. "But don't fool yourself into thinking I'm going to make that easy for you, sweetness."

Their gazes locked, understanding passing between them with an intensity that gave his heart a jolt. In all his long life, he'd never been locked in a battle like this one. Defeating her would allow him such sensual pleasure, yet the idea of destroying her ideals and hopes left a sour taste in his mouth.

There was so much more at risk than just lives here. He had to win, because keeping her out of Villiers's hands was more important than his own safety. That was why he didn't—couldn't—let her go. He had to protect her, even as she fought against him.

Villiers had known exactly what he was doing sending her after him. He had to know that Temple would see what she was, that he would never dare harm her. Bastard.

Had Villiers known what a temptation she would be? That Temple would react to her not only as an adversary and a vampire, but as a man? That his dusty heart would feel a flicker of something he thought he'd stopped being capable of years ago?

He could not fall in love—or rather he could, but he could never allow it to go beyond the limits of human mortality. Once, a long time ago, he had made that mistake and the consequences of it—and there were always consequences—weighed heavily on his soul still.

He had already killed one woman he cared for. He would rather not do it again. He had to keep Vivian alive—and he had to keep his emotions out of it.

"Would you like to take a walk?" he asked, wanting a distraction from his thoughts.

She looked surprised—and wary. She hesitated, then nodded, obviously sensing that he meant her no harm. Could she ascertain his emotions as easily as he could sometimes sense hers? He chuckled when she began piling pieces of meat and cheese in a napkin, and she smiled self-consciously.

"You must think me an ox," she murmured as they walked along a gravel path, but that didn't stop her from biting into a piece of chicken.

Temple lifted his face to the night, enjoying his mistress's cool caress on his brow and cheeks. "I find you interesting."

"Rup . . . I'm told that a lady should never be 'interesting'—it is synonymous with gauche."

Laughter, sharp and true tore from his throat. He tossed a broad grin at her and snatched a morsel from her store. "Do you aspire to be such a boring creature as a lady, Miss Vivian?" How easy things were between them now. For a second, he wondered what could have been were circumstances different.

She shrugged, trying to appear nonchalant, but he could see the blush in her cheeks—a benefit of his keen vision. "I was given lessons in how to be one."

"Clearly you saw reason."

She chewed and swallowed. "You think it a foolish pursuit?"

"Certainly not, if that is the desired outcome, but I've always had a partiality to women rather than ladies."

"There is a difference, you are right. Ladies are fine creatures."

"But women are much more enjoyable."

"Oh?" There was little coyness in her voice. "How so?"

Temple knew a challenge when he heard one. He stopped walking and seized her by the waist, hauling her close. She moved her hand to avoid smearing his shirt with food—though she probably did it more for her own stomach than concern for his clothing.

"Women have much more exquisite *tastes*," he informed her, dropping his voice. "Much heartier . . . *appetites*."

Vivian's response was to shiver delightfully in his arms. "How can you talk of killing me and then say such a thing?"

He leaned close, brushed his lips against the soft curve of her ear. "Because I take pleasure in your reaction when I say it."

Another shiver. "You have a rather strange sense of pleasure."

He laughed at the seductive huskiness of her tone. He laughed often in her company.

"This way," he whispered, drawing her toward a copse of trees where two sturdy specimens held a hammock between them. Once there, he took the napkin—now empty—from her hand and stuffed it in his pocket.

"I take pleasure in your appetites, sweet Vivian." As he spoke he pulled her to him once more and grinned against her lips. "And now I want to taste you."

"I know," she murmured, heavy gaze meeting his. Was that regret he saw in her eyes?

"Say no and I'll stop." She might see him as a monster, but he wasn't going to prove himself one.

"And if I say yes?"

A low groan tore from Temple's throat. Vivian put up no fight as he swept her up into his arms and placed her in the hammock. Easily, he lay down beside her, sliding his hand up her hip, tugging her shirt from the waist of her trousers to slip beneath. Her skin was warm silk beneath his palm. Her stomach quivered at his touch, the soft flesh there supple and heated.

"You have a fascination with doing this outside," she said, tone dry.

"Only with you." It was true. He might use her, but he'd never lie to her. "You were made to be worshiped by moonlight."

She made a face that would have crumbled a lesser man's self-worth, but there was humor there as well. "You don't have to say such things. I have no will where you're concerned."

That raw honesty tugged at his heart—and scoured his conscience. "I never say anything I don't mean." He kissed her throat, felt the fluttering of the pulse there against his lips. "That reminds me; I made a promise to you when you first arrived."

He could almost taste the flush that swept up her throat and cheeks as she remembered that night in the tub. He felt most wicked—and proud of himself at the same time for eliciting such a response.

"I always keep my promises."

She gasped. It was a soft, breathy sound that seemed so strange coming from her lush lips. Uncertainty was not an emotion Vivian wore well.

Chuckling yet again, Temple took those lips with his own, sucking on the full lower one as his fingers made short work of the falls of her trousers. Lifting her hips, Vivian wriggled to help him remove the offending garment.

She was so innocent in her desire, so unabashed in her eagerness for him. How could he not take her? How could he not worship her as she so deserved? Any man, mortal or immortal, would have to be an unfeeling monster to refuse her.

With her boots and trousers removed, Vivian's thighs were long, shapely pillars of pliable alabaster in the night. Temple slid down, pushing her shirt up so that he could kiss her from the hem of her demi-corset, down to her navel, and along the soft curve of her stomach. He could smell her arousal, and when he nudged those delectable thighs apart to bury his face between, the scent of her intoxicated him. He managed to hold back with the first stroke of his tongue against her slick flesh, but when Vivian moaned appreciatively, his hold on his control snapped.

He was ruthless with his mouth and tongue. He licked her, sucked on her until she writhed beneath him, making the sweetest noises he'd ever heard. He made love to her with his tongue, filling her and withdrawing. Then, he licked upward, finding

that sensitive tuck of flesh that had her hips buck-
ing in response. He slipped two fingers inside her,
her juices soaking his hand as he reached for and
found a place deep inside that had her gasping in
response. Her thighs tightened, clenching at him
as he used his mouth and hand to carry her closer
to climax. And then she came in a sweet rush of
wet heat that had her shouting her release to the
canopy of leaves and clouds above them.

Temple didn't give her time to recover. He was
hard and eager to be inside her—desperate to be
inside her. Rearing up, he braced his hands on
either side of her. The hammock swayed gently
as he positioned the head of his cock against the
soaked door to her sex, and slowly slid inside. She
was so hot, so snug, and she drenched the aching
length of him as she stretched to take it all deep
inside.

"You're heaven," he rasped against her throat,
kissing the hammering pulse there. "The closest
I'll ever know."

Strong arms wrapped around him, held him
tenderly, so much so that his heart ached with the
simple action. He bit her then, unable to stop himself. Vivian cried out, arching her hips upward
and wrapping her legs around his hips so that he
was completely buried within her.

Easing his fangs from her neck, Temple suckled gently at the wound, taking just a little of the
sweet bouquet of her blood before closing the

holes with his tongue. His hips continued to rock against hers, the sway of the hammock adding to the glorious friction between them.

He couldn't remember the last time he felt so complete, so whole and . . . happy.

Vivian quickened beneath him and Temple felt the answering tightness in his own body, the heavy pressure that signaled that the end was almost upon him.

"Come for me," he growled. "Sweet Vivian, come for me now."

And she did. It was as though her body responded to the demand instinctively, and when she practically sobbed her release a second time, Temple's body reacted to that in turn. A ragged cry ripped from his throat as he stiffened, pumping himself into her, emptying himself inside her.

He collapsed on top of her, savoring the sweat-sweet heat of her body beneath his. Savoring the taste of her that lingered in his mouth. Savoring that for now she was his.

Because someday he knew she was going to have to make a choice, and he couldn't let himself want her to choose him.

Vivian did not appreciate having her judgment clouded. This realization came into clarity as she took a quiet luncheon with Kimberly in the small pink parlor on the south side of the school.

Even more frustrating was how much of the

responsibility for it came to lay at her own feet. She had no one but herself to charge for the conflict between her head and heart this afternoon. As much as she might want to, she couldn't even blame the man sleeping below ground.

Her head told her not to trust Temple. Her heart said otherwise. What did her heart know? Why would she want to put her faith in a man who claimed to have no idea why Rupert hated him, but sent out word to his vampire friends to join him. If that wasn't a man building an army, she didn't know what was.

And what part was she to play in all of it?

"Vivian?"

Glancing up, she caught Kimberly watching her questioningly. She really should be paying better attention to her hostess. After all, this woman had known Temple for a long time. She could provide valuable information.

Information that she would then turn and send to Rupert, which was her duty. So why then did it feel as though she was planning a betrayal? "I'm sorry, Kimberly. Did you say something?"

"I asked if you would like more soup."

Her bowl was empty, and as distracted as she was, there was little that ever robbed Vivian of her appetite. "Yes, thank you."

Her hostess smiled as she ladled the rich, fragrant broth into Vivian's bowl. "I apologize for interrupting your reverie."

"Oh, please don't. It was rude of me to drift off when I could be conversing with you. Tell me about how you came to run this school."

"I began this academy years ago." Gimlet eyes sparkled. "But you don't care about that."

"No?" Honestly Vivian was a little surprised by the statement. She did want to know about the school and why Temple had a hiding spot there.

"No. You want to know if Temple and I were ever lovers."

Heat rushed into her cheeks. "That is none of my business." But she did want to know—and she didn't as well.

"That does not stop us from wondering these things." The older woman took a sip of wine. "Do you honestly want to know about my past with Temple?"

What was that pain in her heart? Was that jealousy? "Yes."

"Temple and I met because of my involvement with the Sisterhood of Lilith. We revere the goddess whose blood made Temple and his friends vampires. Temple purchased this place years ago to use as a safe house for himself and others. He thought I might be able to make use of it as well—for the sisterhood. That's when I started the academy."

Vivian popped an olive into her mouth. "It seems a rather inconvenient spot for a school."

Kimberly merely smiled. "Perhaps. This school

was started so that young women could have an education similar to that afforded to men. Our students learn Greek as well as French and German, Classics and Mathematics. I also offer classes in History and Art as well as the usual in feminine deportment."

Vivian's own education had included very little of those, save for deportment. She learned what a lady was supposed to be and she learned how to fight. Oddly enough, the opposing lessons never seemed to battle for dominance inside her. Being a lady seemed so unimportant next to being able to protect herself. She'd learned the fancy lessons for Rupert and the rest for herself.

"Your students must come from very liberal-minded families." She may not know much about the world, but she knew that many men—many women for that matter—wouldn't allow their daughters to have such an education.

"They do. Those who share my beliefs don't mind the location. In fact, our seclusion gives us an air of exclusiveness our patrons appreciate."

Vivian wondered just what kind of patrons the school served. Were these girls special to their families, or discarded to this island like garbage?

An awkward silence fell between them and Vivian didn't know what to do about it. She liked Kimberly and didn't want the woman's past with Temple to interfere with that. She'd never had a female friend before.

They stared at each other for a moment. Damn it all, she could end this.

"Are you in love with him?" she asked.

The expression on the other woman's face was worth the embarrassment of asking such an intimate question.

"Not in the way you suspect." Kimberly laughed. It was a delicate sound like chimes or tiny bells. "My dear, you don't mince words do you?"

Vivian laughed as well—although nowhere near as delicately. The tension between them had eased and she was glad for it. "My apologies. Tact has never been a virtue I possess."

"Never apologize for being open and honest, my dear girl. I much prefer plain speaking." Kimberly poured herself another glass of wine. "And to answer your question, Temple is one of my dearest friends. Nothing more. What is he to you?" The gaze she shot Vivian was curious at best.

Vivian hesitated. Nemesis. Lover. Conscience and thorn in her side. "Honestly I don't know."

Kimberly didn't look convinced. "Fair enough." She paused. "Will you begin your lessons with the girls today?"

Grateful for the change of subject, Vivian nodded. "Yes. In fact I should go prepare." Not that she had much to do, but she was nervous about becoming a teacher rather than a student and wanted to do all she could to make sure things went well.

After finishing her soup, Vivian took her leave of Kimberly and made her way to the ballroom where the lessons were to take place. She did some stretches and thought about what she wanted to teach and before she knew it, she had several young women standing before her eager to begin.

She began with simple jabs and blocks—the basics of pugilism. Better to start with how to throw a punch and how to block one. Most of the women made up in eagerness what they lacked in experience. They apologized every time they managed to land a blow on Vivian and apologized when they didn't, but there was much laughter, and it was the most pleasant afternoon she'd passed in quite some time.

And they didn't treat her like some kind of mythical creature—at least not that much. Most gave her more deference than she preferred, but there weren't any secretive looks and whispers. Perhaps Kimberly spoke to them.

Her good mood did not last long unfortunately. It began to disintegrate right around the time the housekeeper came in and told Kimberly that a telegram had arrived for Temple.

From one of his vampire friends, no doubt. The suspicion put a frisson of fear at the top of her spine and then shoved it all the way down. Fear was not an emotion she had much experience with or was remotely comfortable with, but she was smart enough to face it when she felt it.

She had no reason to trust Temple, except that he had yet to hurt her. She had no reason to distrust him either, save that he was Rupert's enemy and in some regard that made him her enemy as well. No, she didn't know what she felt for Temple, but she knew what she felt about four more vampires arriving at the school—vampires who might not take so kindly to her having been part of a plan to hold their friend prisoner.

She promised Temple she wouldn't try to escape, and not just because he'd given her more pleasure than she'd ever given herself. She'd given her word because she subscribed to the old adage of keeping enemies close, and because Rupert wanted her to get as close to the vampire as she could.

And she stayed because she liked it. She liked him. As twisted as that was, there was a part of her that liked Temple. She was drawn to him, true, but she wanted to know more about him. She liked his smile. Liked his laughter. Liked that he made her feel sensual and wanted.

She liked that she knew exactly where she stood with him. He spoke easily of killing her, yet she knew she was of more use to him alive at this point.

She didn't plan on running just yet, not before she had reason. When she knew for certain that the vampires were coming, then she would have to make a decision. Would she run to Rupert, or would she stay and face the consequences?

Regardless of what choice she made, be it stupid or wise, she had best be prepared for any eventuality. That meant working on her own fighting skills when she was alone and finding an escape route if she needed it.

"Beg your pardon, miss."

She was walking through the front hall when the little housekeeper caught up with her. The poor woman was puffing to catch her breath as she hurried after Vivian's much longer stride.

"I'm sorry." Vivian crossed the floor to meet her. "Did you need me for something?"

The petite woman's breath came in labored gasps. "I have a message for you." She offered Vivian a folded piece of paper, warm from her grip.

"From who?" Vivian asked as she accepted the missive.

"I don't know, miss. A young lad brought it round the kitchen just before I delivered Mr. Temple's telegram."

Vivian froze, note tucked in her tightened fist. "Did you mention this to him?"

The woman looked affronted. "Of course not, miss."

Relief made her almost giddy. "I appreciate that, thank you. And thank you for bringing it to me so quickly."

That seemed to soothe the housekeeper's wounded pride. She smiled and bobbed a quick curtsey before rushing off to her duties. Vivian waited until she was gone to open the letter.

Meet me on the cliffs near the forest. I have news for you.

It wasn't signed and the handwriting wasn't familiar, but that didn't matter. She knew who the news was from. Her mysterious contact had word from Rupert.

She didn't say anything to anyone. She simply walked out the door without anyone raising so much as an eyebrow. Of course, they wouldn't. The island was so isolated, and the tide had yet to turn so there really wasn't any way she could escape. Even Temple, who was no doubt awake now and reading his telegram, wouldn't worry about her roaming around. There was nowhere she could go on this island that he wouldn't find her.

Oddly enough, that realization was as comforting as it was unsettling.

It was a warm day, the sun high in the sky with a warm breeze blowing off the sea, sending the grass and flowers swaying as though dancing to a melody only they could hear.

Vivian walked, feeling that same breeze ease through the thin fabric of her shirt and brush her skin. The sun was warm on her cheeks and head, filling her with a sense of well-being despite the uncertainty in her heart.

She walked toward the cliffs, pausing just for a second to gaze out over the waves crashing against the shore. She was careful not to get too close to the edge, and then because she didn't want to keep her contact waiting, she continued to walk toward the forest that was a few hundred yards farther on.

There was a young man standing at the edge of the trees, just inside the thickening foliage where he wouldn't be easily spotted from the school. In fact, she wouldn't have seen him yet had she not terribly acute vision to go along with her other abnormal traits.

He lifted his head as she drew closer. He wasn't familiar, but that was no surprise. When they were within speaking distance he held up his hand for her to be silent, then gestured for her to follow him deeper into the forest. Vivian did so without hesitation. He was young and not very big. Unless he had friends or a weapon she would be able to take him down in combat should he prove a threat.

The air was cooler there, where the trees grew thick and high, their trunks slightly bowed by years of being pressed upon by the wind. Here, the ground was spongy with moss and the air was rich with the smell of dirt and leaves. Here it was as though the ocean disappeared and there was nothing more to this world than sun-dappled darkness and the sounds of little forest creatures.

She followed him for a few yards before he

stopped and turned to face her. Even then, he didn't speak, he simply held out a telegram for her to take. She did. Glancing down she saw that it was indeed from Rupert—the code was unmistakable.

"Leave your reply and any future correspondence underneath the statue of Lilith in the garden," the young man instructed in a thick Irish brogue. "There's a loose stone. That's where you will find replies from now on as well."

"Thank you." That was all Vivian had time to say before he turned and began walking away, deeper into the forest. Good thing she didn't have any questions for him then.

She sat down on a fallen tree just a little distance away and read the telegram. It wasn't very long. Rupert told her how proud he was of her for learning that Temple had already sent for his friends. He told her to find out when they could be expected to arrive, and had Temple given her any other useful information? Also, for her to be careful and to have an escape route planned—just in case things turned ugly.

That was certainly not what her confidence needed to hear. But he was right. She needed to be prepared.

He told her where to go if she needed to get off the island in a hurry. Apparently he had a contact with a boat. How convenient. With all these contacts, Vivian wondered what the devil he needed her for. Of course, she knew that she was the only one who could get as close to Temple as she. Did Rupert wonder if she shared the vampire's bed? Did he think less of her for it? How could he when it was his idea to begin with? Maybe he hadn't come right out and suggested it, but Vivian wasn't that thick that she hadn't understood what "everything necessary" meant in terms of distracting Temple.

What bothered her, was how had Rupert known that Temple would be attracted to her? How had he known that Vivian would be attracted to Temple? Perhaps he hadn't. Perhaps he expected her to play false if necessary. Or maybe he knew about the strange connection she and Temple seemed to share. If so, why had he never explained it to her?

He kept so much from her. Yes, she knew it was so she wouldn't be able to reveal too much if tortured or pressed. He claimed it was for her own good, but didn't she deserve to know information about herself? What else had he kept from her for "her own good?"

She stood up. She couldn't doubt Rupert now, not after all they had been through. Not after all he had done for her. It was going to take more than a few nights in a vampire's arms and isolation to make her doubt the man who had been like a father to her. She had no reason to distrust Rupert, and every reason not to trust Temple—even if she didn't know what they were.

Since she was out, it only made sense to look around. It would be wise to get a lay of the land now that she was out in the daylight. Perhaps she'd map out the route to Rupert's associate with a boat. She reread the directions he gave, looked around to orientate herself, and then began walking away from the cliffs. As she neared thinner cover, she turned left as Rupert instructed. Here, the ground looked patted down, not as overgrown, as though this had been a well-traveled route once upon a time.

A twig snapped under her boot, then another, so she adjusted her path hoping for more quiet ground. There wasn't much of a path, but there was definitely enough for her to follow. It seemed to run parallel to the main road, so hopefully it would lead her to a clearing. Temple would be able to track her, so the best she could hope for was a fast escape—and if she was really lucky she would be able to get away during the day just like she was now.

Suddenly the ground seemed to open up beneath her, sucking her down. Vivian fell into darkness.

Chapter 8

Running across Europe with four vampires and a priest was not the way Marcus Grey originally planned to spend the summer. He had set out to uncover what he hoped would be the Blood Grail in Cornwall, and learn the truth about the legends of his long-dead ancestor Dreux Beauvrai.

Instead, he found himself embroiled in a plot by a sinister group called the Order of the Silver Palm, and face-to-face with a man who could give him personal details about Dreux—firsthand.

In June he had been nothing more than a simple scholar—an archeologist. Now he carried a pistol at all times. He hadn't shaved in two days, and not only had he been introduced to a world the likes of which horrifying novels were based upon, but he was damn sick of vampires.

So was it any wonder that when they stopped in at the safe house in Vienna whilst en route to Italy, that he rose at daybreak and went for a walk about the neighborhood? So much of his life was lived at night now, and darkness grew tedious for an outdoorsy sort as he.

So it was he who offered to go to an establishment run by a friend of Chapel's to check for messages. The vampires couldn't go, and Molyneux wasn't feeling well, which was good because Marcus would have fought the old man for a chance to get out in the sun. Everyone hoped that there would be news of Temple. Marcus didn't say anything, but he had an awful suspicion that whoever took the vampire might have already disposed of him.

The door to the bookseller's shop stuck a little as he tried to open it. He gave it a shove and set it crashing against the bell. So much for trying to be inconspicuous.

"Gun moang, mein herr," the man behind the cluttered counter greeted him brightly. "May I help you?"

"Good morning," Marcus replied with a smile. "Would you by chance have anything by Severian?" It was the exact phrase Chapel had instructed him to use. Severian was Chapel's real name—or rather, the name he used for the first one hundred or so years of his life. Once the Church got a hold of him and the others, everything changed. Even their names.

Some of the brightness left the little white-haired man's face to be replaced by wariness and suspicion. "That is very rare, *mein herr.*"

Again, Chapel had prepared him for that response. "Indeed. I'm interested in first edition only."

The old man nodded, his expression now grave. "Come with me. I have what you are looking for."

Marcus followed him, his hand within easy reach of his pistol. Chapel might trust this old coot, but Chapel wasn't as easily killed as Marcus could be.

The shopkeeper led him to the back of the store and through a heavy, narrow door into a small office. There, he unlocked the top drawer of the desk, but instead of reaching into the drawer, he turned his hand and removed something adhered to the underside of the desktop. Marcus mentally shook his head. All this intrigue and secret behavior. One would think the old man guarded state secrets and not notes to a man believed to have died six centuries earlier.

He held out his hand for the single letter his companion palmed, but the old man surprised him further by slipping the note into an old book first. He then offered book and all to Marcus.

"I hope you enjoy it, *mein herr.*"

Marcus stood there, caught between amusement and dread. Whatever he might think, this man took his position as keeper of Chapel's mail as very important. The Order wouldn't hesitate to use or even kill this man, so if he wanted to play at being a spy or something equally as dangerous, then Marcus would not mock him for it.

"Thank you." He slipped the book inside the leather satchel slung over his shoulder. "I hope I shall. *Gun moang.*"

Marcus left the shop with the foolish urge to cast a glance around to see if he was being followed. Instead, he kept his gaze focused straight ahead. If he wanted to look suspicious—which of course he did not—all he had to do was act like it.

It would be hours before the vampires rose from their slumber. No doubt they were snuggled in their beds—he hoped all they were doing was snuggling—whispering little love poems to each other in their sleep. It was disgusting, really, how they mooned over one another.

He shuddered and gave himself a little shake. For now Vienna was his and he planned to make the most of it before returning to the safe house.

He went to a café where he sat outside and drank strong coffee. He indulged sugary pastries that thrilled his tongue and delighted his soul. He walked the cobblestone streets and narrow lanes, marveling at the beauty of the mellow hued buildings. He spoke to people that he met, stopped to study details of architecture, art and flora that caught his eye. Twice he stopped to pet a dog and once he scratched a sleek black cat behind its ears.

When his stomach rumbled again he stopped for lunch and stuffed himself with bread fresh from the oven and meats that practically melted in his mouth. And once that appetite was sated, he found a pretty girl and fell in love with her for an hour.

And then, because it was time to return to the safe house, he decided the time had come to deal with the man following him. He'd noticed his second shadow right around the time he first entered the bookshop. Obviously the man had been watching the building.

Keeping his pace even and natural, Marcus began to walk. He didn't take the route to the safe house, but rather one he'd found the night before, that led to an area with a small, loud tavern and lots of dark places.

It was into one of those dark places he slipped after rounding a corner. His back pressed against the cool brick, he pulled a knife from the sheath he wore inside the waist of his trousers.

His pursuer paused, then moved forward, each step slow and careful. This was no novice. The realization had Marcus's heart thumping in anticipation. Six months ago he eschewed violence for books. Now he found himself almost as bloodthirsty as his vampire companions—and he hadn't their excuse.

He waited until the man had taken a step passed his hiding spot before grabbing him from behind.

His arm went around the big man's neck, squeezing hard enough to cut off the flow of oxygen. He pressed the blade beneath a heavy arm, the sharp point ready to slip between ribs.

"Easy, mate," he growled as the man struggled. A meaty fist caught him on the thigh like a bag of bricks, but Marcus kept his ground. He squeezed the man's neck harder.

"What do you want?" he demanded.

The man took another swing—clumsily this time, as he slowly drifted into darkness.

Marcus gave him a shake, pressing the blade tighter. The man jerked as the cold steel pricked his flesh. "I asked you a question."

"Fuck you, vampire lover," the man rasped in heavily accented English.

That was answer enough.

Sausage-sized fingers pulled at Marcus's arm. Marcus tightened his hold, sweat beading on his brow as he fought to remain in control.

He could kill this man who smelled of cigars, wine, and garlic, but someone would find the body and that would lead to questions. Marcus couldn't risk being one of the possible answers. Plus, he wasn't a killer. He could take him back to the safe house, but his companions weren't killers either. And no doubt the vampires were who this man was after. Better to leave him to crawl back to the Silver Palm with his tail between his legs.

Sweat trickled down his temple as the man's

struggle slowed. Finally, the large hands fell limp, as did the even larger body they were attached to. Marcus stumbled as the full brunt of the man's weight crumpled.

Panting, he dropped his would-be assailant to the dirty alley floor. He swiped his arm across his forehead before dropping to one knee to search the pockets of his unconscious foe. He found a bit of money, lint, and a flask filled with merlot.

The man's big hands were scarred across the knuckles and two fingers on his right hand looked as though they'd been broken in the past, as did his nose. He had scars on his chin and above his eyebrow as well.

A professional fighter. Marcus was lucky he'd surprised him, else there was little doubt this man would have beaten him senseless. No doubt that had been the plan—to capture him, and recover whatever information he had.

A close call indeed.

Marcus started to rise when a glimmer of silver caught his attention. On his left hand, the man wore the signet of the Order of the Silver Palm. With a glance around to make sure he had yet to be seen, Marcus lifted that hand, grasped the jewelry and pulled. It caught on the large knuckle, requiring a not-so gentle tug, and then slid off the rest of the way. He slipped the ring into the inside breast pocket of his coat. It might just come in handy some day.

Then, he rose quickly and made his way out of the shadows, straightening his clothes as he did so, and slipping his knife back into its sheath. He reentered the sunshine looking every inch the young English tourist. He wasted no time returning to the safe house. If the Order was following them, then something big was about to happen—something bigger than what the lot of them had already been through.

No, this wasn't how he planned to spend his summer. Hopefully he'd survive the rest of it.

At least nothing was broken.

This was something to be grateful for, Vivian tried to reassure herself as she slowly, gingerly rose to her feet at the bottom of the dirty pit.

Looking up, she winced at the sky darkening above. She had been down there for hours. The throbbing on the side of her head explained why so much time had passed without her knowing. Obviously the fall had rendered her unconscious. She carefully touched her scalp and felt the unmistakable grit of dried blood. Her left ankle was tender and swollen, but only sprained. It could have been much worse.

As though it wasn't bad enough. No one knew that she had even gone for a walk let alone the direction she had taken. In fact, it was highly unlikely anyone even realized she was missing.

Panic rose briefly in her breast, but she pushed it away. She was not going to die in this hole. Eventually she would be missed and Temple would look for her.

She would not think of this as the same as being in a cage. She could get out of this, unlike the cage the traveling show had kept her in those first few weeks, until certain that her will was broken and she would stop trying to run away.

That was why she had been so surprised that Temple hadn't locked her up when he caught her that night. Keeping her naked and in his bed was not the same kind of torture as putting her in a box. He could have caged her as she had caged him. Surely he might have taken some kind of pleasure from that? Some measure of satisfaction. But he hadn't, and that was worse, because that made him better and a part of her hated him for it. It was so much easier when people acted in the manner she expected, which was usually one of deceit or cruelty. Those motivations never surprised her.

There was nothing more hurtful than having kindness plucked away. Perhaps that was why she had always been so afraid of disappointing Rupert. At any moment she expected the kindness he'd shown her to be yanked away.

Sometimes, she even wished for it.

But she did not wish to languish in this prison.

"Temple will find me," she told herself aloud, calming the clamor of her heart. "The man has a sense of smell that could rival a wolf. He will find me tonight." No doubt this trap was of his making. The earth had a fresh smell to it, and the net that had covered the hole was hardly aged.

She had been so foolish. She knew better than to be so trusting of her surroundings. She should have known that a vampire refuge would have safety precautions. She had lowered her guard because it was a school. Because it was run by women, and she was thoroughly ashamed of herself for it.

Meanwhile, she wasn't about to simply sit there and wait to be found. The smooth planks lining the pit were there to make climbing impossible, but she was not so easily discouraged.

She punched at the planks with her fists, dug at them with her fingers. Then she kicked with her boots, trying to break the wood so that she could get a toe or finger hold. Splinters pierced her knuckles, stabbed beneath her fingernails until her hands were bloody and sore. Her toes throbbed in the leather of her boots, tender from being jabbed repeatedly against the planks.

She managed to climb halfway up before her foot slipped, driving easily a dozen spears of wood into the fleshy pads of her palm. The pain made her cry out, and with the blood, loosened her grip. She fell to the ground with a heavy thud, and landed on her feet. Pain screamed up her leg from the impact on her already injured ankle and she crumpled, sprawling across the dirt on her side.

She lay there a minute and let the tears come. Frustration, anger, and pain built to an overwhelming level within her and she had to let them out or risk screaming like a madwoman.

Then again, perhaps screaming wasn't such a bad idea. "Hello?" she cried. "Is anyone up there?" She continued until her throat began to hurt and her mouth was uncomfortably dry.

Exhausted, she pulled herself into a sitting position and began yanking splinters from her right hand—at least the ones she could find. She would be lucky if infection didn't set in. Her palm was a mess from what she could see in the dim light, prickly and sticky with blood.

Her ankle throbbed all the way up to her knee. Her hands stung and burned, and her head felt as though it had been kicked repeatedly. Her ribs ached mildly from the last fall, but she could still take solace in knowing that none of her bones were broken. The discomfort at least kept her from panicking over her tight surroundings.

She picked at splinters until her fingers began to cramp from the work and the light became too dim for her to see anymore. Almost sunset. Almost night. How much longer would she have to stay there? She was exhausted. Thank God the night was warm, so there was no danger of her taking a chill. She was soon going to need to relieve her bladder, a task made all the more distasteful by the small space. She would put that off as long as she could.

Finally, just when darkness had closed in and she thought she was going to have to urinate regardless, she heard something above her.

"Hello?" she called, struggling to her feet. Then silently she prayed that it was not something looking for a snack and willing to jump in for it. She balanced her weight on her good leg, propping her shoulder against the wall for extra support.

"Vivian."

Elation swept through her at the sound of Temple's voice. She could have wept. "I'm here." It was foolish of her to say it, for of course he could see her with those sharp eyes of his.

Silence followed, and for a second she feared he might have left her.

"Stand back."

He didn't have to tell her twice. She hobbled back as far as she could, pressing her back against the cool planks behind her. There was a whoosh of air against her face, the sound of something heavy hitting the ground, and then a dark, crouching shadow rose to its full height and she saw the outline of Temple before her.

She could have wept in relief. "Thank God you found me."

"He had nothing to do with it." His voice was a low growl, menacing and rough. "Put your arms around my neck."

Vivian did so gladly, clinging to him with all the enthusiasm in her heart. He seemed to hesitate before wrapping his own magnificent arms around her waist.

"Hold on," he instructed. "Bend your knees."

She did as he told, barely having time to think before he vaulted upward, sweeping both of them up into the night and out of the pit.

He carried her through the air, and as the breeze slipped over her, Vivian was able for a moment to forget about the pain in her hands, head, and leg. This feeling of freedom was unlike anything she had ever experienced, and were she not struck dumb by it, she might have laughed in sheer exhilaration.

Temple landed on the front steps of the school. Holding Vivian in his arms, he carried her in through the great hall, where several of the women stopped to stare, and then he continued up the large, sturdy staircase.

"Where are we going?" Vivian asked, confused by the new direction.

"Your room," he replied harshly.

"My room?" She blinked. "I thought your room was my room."

He didn't even look at her. "Not anymore."

She didn't ask—didn't dare say a word that might turn that cold countenance upon her.

He took her to a large room on the third floor in the west wing. It was decorated in shades of peach and cream with a delicate Oriental pattern on the wall and soft, gauzy curtains in the windows.

He set her on the bed and crouched down to silently inspect her hands and ankle, then her head. Vivian tried not to wince, but even though his touch was gentle, it wasn't gentle enough.

"Nothing's broken," she murmured. "The gash on my head no doubt looks worse than it is. My hands got the brunt of it." They were a mess to look at as well.

He pressed a handkerchief into the palm that had been ripped open. "I'll have two of the women bring you a bath and tend to your wounds." He stood.

"Temple?"

He looked down at her. He was hunched, his hands clenched into fists at his sides. She could feel the tension in him like a shove—pushing against her. "What?"

She tried to smile, but it felt forced and unnatural. How could she express any kind of joy when he looked at her like that? "Thank you for rescuing me."

If anything his expression grew more grim, his gaze even colder. "You're welcome. I hope whatever your assignation wrought was worth it."

Vivian's heart stopped cold in her chest. He knew. Of course he knew. He could probably smell the other man on her, even though their meeting had been brief.

"I—"

He held up his hand. It was just as well. What did she possibly hope to say to him? She had gone to meet someone. She would go again, and if it weren't for falling, she wouldn't have let on to him at all.

"Don't." Was all he said, the word ground out between clenched teeth. "Just don't, or so help me God . . ."

It was then that she saw how tightly clenched his hands were. His knuckles white beneath the skin. The beast inside him wanted to kill her, she knew that. It was only the man in him that stopped it.

And she knew then that despite being enemies, he had a softness for her. Rupert would call that an advantage. Vivian didn't know what it was— but it made her stomach turn even as her traitorous heart thrilled at the thought.

She didn't say anything. She just sat there mute as he slowly turned away and moved toward the exit with all the tension and grace of a lion stalking its prey.

When the door closed behind him, she heard the soft click of a key turning. The bastard had locked her in!

Vivian jumped to her feet, stifling a cry as her weight came down on her injured leg. She hobbled to the door, her sore and sticky fingers clenching at the knob. It was indeed locked.

She shook it—as though that would do any good. Panic rose within her, followed by anger. The only thing that kept her from kicking the heavy oak down was pain, and the remembrance that the door belonged to Kimberley, not Temple.

Whirling on her good leg, she hobbled toward the window and threw open the drapes. This time she couldn't hold back the bellow of rage that tore the soft flesh of her throat. The window had bars on it.

Temple had put her in a cage after all.

Chapter 9

He was such a stupid ass.

As he left Vivian's new "room," Temple berated himself for ever daring to trust in her or believe anything she said. Christ, he had told the woman she was the closest thing to heaven he'd ever seen and then she sneaks off to meet another man.

Not just any other man. He had to be an associate of Villiers.

Temple clomped down the stairs, and when he saw one of the maids, he instructed her to take another girl and attend to Vivian. Regardless of her deceit, he couldn't bear to think of her suffering—and her wounds had to be painful.

It wasn't really deceit. He knew she was going to help Villiers, just as she knew he'd use her against the same man. So why was he so . . . pissed that she had kept her word to her mentor? Why did he take it so personally that she was doing what duty demanded of her? Had he really thought he could win her to his side so easily? The thought hadn't even occurred to him until now.

When he awoke to find her gone, dread had filled his heart. When no one knew where she was that dread was replaced by cold, stark fear. And when he found her in that hole . . . well, the first thing he'd felt had been relief. The second was betrayal.

He hated that feeling.

What if he hadn't found Vivian? What if the fall had killed her?

"You look as though someone kicked your dog," a soft voice remarked as he entered Brownie's private drawing room.

He cast a brief glance at his friend. She sat on a tiny blue sofa in a demure pale yellow gown with lots of lace and ribbon. She looked like a little doll, not even real.

"I take it you found Vivian?" she asked when he said nothing.

Temple nodded as he pulled a decanter of whiskey from the liquor cabinet. "I did. She was in one of the pits in the woods."

"I told you those things were dangerous."

"That's why I dug them." He had dug three of them before Vivian's arrival on the island. With his strength and speed it hadn't taken long to set the traps meant for Rupert Villiers and his men—just in case they tracked him.

"I do hope you apologized to her for any injury."

He snorted as he poured a liberal amount of whiskey for each of them. Then he joined his friend, seating himself across from her and handed her a glass. "I did not."

"Temple!" She looked positively aghast. "How could you? The poor thing could have been killed!"

"That poor thing can hold her own, Brownie. You needn't worry that a hole in the ground will do her in." Oh, but it could have, had she landed the wrong way. Had one of those boards she smashed ripped through her stomach and not just her hand.

Brownie smiled in sympathy. "You're angry that she was hurt. You feel responsible."

"I am angry, damn it!" He tossed back the contents of his glass. The whiskey burned. It felt good. "As for responsibility, that falls upon her own head."

She favored him with a small smile. "You haven't told her what she is, have you?"

Temple scowled at her. "And let her use that against me? No. The more ignorant she is the better."

"Perhaps if she knew what she was she'd know why she's so important to you."

He snorted. He didn't even know why she was so damned important to him. Oh, there was the obvious, but there was much more to it than the pull of her blood.

Earlier a telegram arrived from Payen Carr. He offered whatever help he could give, and Temple was tempted to take it. If Carr could give him anything to make Vivian see how dangerous Villliers was—anything that could lead to the downfall of the Order of the Silver Palm—he would be grateful.

Shrewd eyes narrowed. "I probably shouldn't tell you this, but I would be remiss as your friend if I did not. Vivian gave me a telegram to send for her the other day."

Temple's head jerked up. All melancholy was gone, all guilt and uncertainty evaporated. "To whom?"

"A man named Vincent?" Brownie frowned. "No, that's not it. Valance?"

It was as though his heart turned to stone in his chest. Softly, he set his glass on the polished cabinet. "Villiers."

"Yes! That's it. Villiers. Wait, Temple. Where are you going?"

He was going after the man who Vivian met in the woods, something he should have done before this. If the man carried a message from Vivian to Villiers, he might already be too late to prevent it from being delivered. Damn her eyes, he'd been too distracted with fear and anger to think straight.

He ran out the front door and bolted straight into the sky, flying over the spot where he had found Vivian. He didn't need to pick up on the scent; it was burned into his memory thanks to anger and jealousy. Yes, he had been jealous as hell over Vivian meeting another man, until he realized why, then jealousy turned to rage.

Soaring through the cool summer night, Temple followed the scent to a small cottage half a mile from the school. It was a little ramshackle, but cared for, sitting at the bottom of a low hill that was its only protection from the wind that blew across the cliffs from the sea below.

He landed on the dirt path leading to the door, and was on the steps, his hand clutching the latch before he realized what else he smelled. Blood. It was fresh—and human.

"Christ." He pushed the door open and stepped inside.

The man whose scent clung to Vivian was on the floor, blood pooling beneath him from the single bullet hole in his head. He had obviously outlived his usefulness to Villiers. And whatever information he might have obtained from Vivian was now long gone.

He could follow the scents that filled the cottage, but there was no knowing which one belonged to the killer. Whoever he was, it wasn't Villiers. Temple would know if that bastard had been here, and there wasn't a trace.

His only option now was to return to the Garden Academy and confront Vivian.

The return flight to the school did nothing to cool his temper or lighten his mood. He stormed into the foyer, stomped through the hall, and bounded up the stairs three at a time. And when he reached Vivian's room, he did well to remember to use the doorknob rather than kicking it off the hinges as he wanted.

The maids attending Vivian's wounds gasped as he stormed in. Vivian didn't look the least bit surprised to see him—or impressed—as she sat on the bed in a simple nightgown.

"Leave," he ordered the women. They were obviously done with their task, judging from the fresh bandages Vivian sported. He tried not to look at the pile of bloody splinters in the small glass dish one carried on her tray. And he tried to ignore the smell of blood—Vivian's sweet, intoxicating blood—mixed with the sweetly scented soaps the women had used to bathe her as well.

The maids left in a hurry. Good servants that they were, they remembered to close the door behind them. Temple waited until the latch clicked before turning on the woman sitting on the bed.

"What did it say?" he demanded

"What did what say?"

"The telegram you sent Villiers. Or perhaps he sent one to you. 'Dearest Darling, my maniacal plans are empty without you by my side.'"

Her jaw lifted defiantly. "What did you say in the telegrams you sent your friends? 'Come for dinner boys, I've got dessert'?"

He took a step toward her and she immediately came to her feet and lifted her fists, even though both hands were bandaged and no doubt sore as hell. She wasn't too steady on her feet either, one ankle obviously swollen beneath layers of white gauze.

"Good God, do you think I'm going to hit you?"

"If I were a man you would. You've talked of killing me, why wouldn't you stoop to violence?"

He ignored the last part. "If you were a man I wouldn't have fucked you."

She didn't flinch at his crude tone, she just watched him with those damn storm-hued eyes. He'd never seen those eyes so cold. "Why did you?"

He met her gaze with an icy one of his own. "For the same reason you let me."

Vivian didn't say anything to that. She looked away, her jaw tight.

"What does Rupert have planned?" Temple demanded a few seconds later, before the silence between them could linger.

Her chin lifted as her fists lowered. "I don't know."

He moved toward her. "What does he have planned?" Barely an inch separated them.

"I. Don't. Know."

Did he kiss her or kill her? "Did you tell him I sent for the others?"

She had the balls to lock her gaze with his. "Yes."

He turned away. "Fuck!"

"What did you expect me to do, Temple?" Vivian demanded as she lowered herself to the bed once more. "Sit here like your good little whore and wait for your friends to show up so you could kill me together?"

"Kill you?" She had to be insane, and he looked at her as such. "Have I even so much as harmed a hair on your head?"

"You punched me."

He dismissed that with a wave of his hand. "Only to make you calm down."

She laughed at that, but without humor. "I'm sure it wasn't the first time you've used such tactics on a woman."

Temple was sure the blood drained from his face. "You bitch."

Now it was she who went white, but she did not back down. She did not look away. In fact, she smiled in a way that was nothing short of mocking. It was a mean and bitter smile and he hated to see it on her beautiful face.

"Don't play noble with me, vampire. You've played games with me since the first time we met. And as soon as you got the chance you took my virginity and got me into your bed."

"As I recall it was easy."

"Yes, and I'm ashamed for it."

Ashamed? That word struck Temple deep inside, twisting like a dull and rusty blade. She was ashamed of what they had shared.

"Rest assured I will not trouble you with my attentions again. In fact, when you have recovered from your wounds, I want you to leave this place. Go find the man who pretends to be your father but wants to be your lover. Ask him if he's responsible for the murder of the man you met earlier." To hell with using her for leverage. She deserved whatever plans Villiers had in store for her.

She went pale. "He's dead?"

"Undeniably so."

She tossed her head, sending that glorious hair rippling down her back. "You could have killed him." But he could see in her gaze that she was more hopeful than convinced.

"You think that if it soothes your conscience," he replied. "How many people does Villiers have to harm or kill before you see the truth?"

A sneer distorted her lovely features. "You'd say anything to make me believe the worst of him."

God, if she showed him a quarter of the loyalty she gave Villiers he'd be a fortunate man. "I don't have to say anything. If you took your blinders off, you'd see it for yourself."

"You are impossible," she responded. "You know nothing about him."

"I know enough."

"This isn't going to end until one of you gets hurt."

He stared at her, too tired and too incredulous to do anything else. Had she truly not thought this through to the logical conclusion? "Sweet, one of us isn't going to be just hurt. Villiers or I will die. I hope you don't regret whichever one it is."

White as a sheet she went. For a second he thought she might faint. He didn't dare hope the reaction was for his benefit. "Go to hell," she rasped.

Temple shot her a smile over his shoulder as he walked toward the door, to leave her once more.

"I'll see you there."

If only she could walk, Vivian would have left the Garden Academy the very next morning. Unfortunately for her, she had an ankle that refused to accept her weight for more than a step or two, hands that were stiff, sore, and bandaged to the point of uselessness, and a lump on her head the size of a small egg.

She wasn't going anywhere for a few days, she realized darkly as she lay on top of the light quilt that covered her new bed. All she could do is hope that she would be recovered by the time the vampires arrived. That seemed more realistic than hoping they wouldn't kill her and send her corpse back to Rupert.

Why did Temple remain here? Wasn't the simplest course to leave now that he knew that Rupert knew his location? He could go someplace Rupert would never find him.

Or perhaps he was tired of doing just that, and wanted to put an end to whatever strife lie between them. Would one of them truly have to die for that to happen?

She didn't want Rupert to die. And though it might make her a betrayer, she didn't want Temple to die either. She didn't want anyone to die—particularly herself. She knew Temple was capable of murder by simple virtue of his vampire nature. But Rupert? She couldn't believe he had the messenger killed. She just couldn't.

But Temple believed it, there was no denying that. She might have taunted him with the suspicion that he had been the killer, but she knew in her heart that he had told the truth. No matter what he might be capable of, this was one death that didn't fall upon his shoulders.

She didn't blame him for being angry at her, but he should have known that she would do all she could to help Rupert. Did he expect her to blindly follow him—give up everything she'd been taught and believed—because of a few nights in his bed? She didn't expect him to give in to her so easily.

Although it would be nice. He didn't have to be so cruel about it, though. He didn't have to make it sound like she had betrayed him.

Oh! These thoughts were beginning to take their toll. Vivian wasn't accustomed to being idle, and this just lying around was beginning to wear on her despite her physical discomfort. She needed to do something to take her mind off the pain, to take her mind off of Temple and Rupert.

She picked the lock on the door. It took her almost a full quarter hour, but she did it.

No doubt Temple would chain her to the bed or something equally as nefarious if he discovered what she had done. There was no way she could escape in the shape she was in, and she only wanted to get something to eat—not aggravate him. Not really.

One of the maids had brought her a set of crutches earlier that morning, so she used those to maneuver her way down the broad staircase to the main floor. There wasn't anyone about, and breakfast had long been cleared from the dining room.

Slowly and clumsily she made her way down the back stairs to the kitchen. She ached from the effort by the time she reached her destination, but the smell of fresh scones and tea made it worthwhile.

"Oh, come on now, girl!" she heard an exasperated female voice cry. "Just climb down!"

Several other women voiced their agreement, save for one querulous one who replied, "I can't!"

Vivian hobbled into the kitchen to find several of the maids gathered around another who was up on a ladder, clinging to a cast-iron pan on the wall as though it was all that kept her alive.

"What's the matter?" she asked.

All the maids turned with a collective gasp. "Miss Vivian!" one named Shannon cried. She was tall and buxom with hair the color of cinnamon and eyes the color of moss. "You shouldn't be here."

Vivian smiled at them. "I'd rather be here than alone in my room." She nodded at the girl on the ladder. "What's wrong?"

Another of the girls snorted. "Agnes climbed up to get a pot and now she won't come down again."

Agnes was a young girl of perhaps eighteen years of age who might weigh seven-and-a-half stone soaking wet. She fixed Vivian with a teary gaze. "I'm sorry to be such a coward, miss."

Smiling, Vivian shook her head. "We all have fears, Agnes. Would you feel better if I came up there with you?"

There was that look of amazement again—the one she had hoped the maids would stop giving her. "Oh, miss, there's no need . . ."

Vivian stopped listening. The other maids jabbered as she limped toward them. Some chastised poor Agnes, bringing a fresh outpouring of tears from the girl's eyes. Others tried to talk

Vivian out of helping in her wounded state. They simply didn't understand that she wasn't a normal woman. Then again, from the way they looked at her, maybe they did understand after all.

She put her weight on her crutch, then propped her good foot on the first rung of the ladder. She stepped up and repeated the process. When her crutch couldn't reach the floor anymore, she handed it to one of the maids and used the ladder itself for support. Agnes wasn't far up, maybe five or six rungs, but it was high enough. Fortunately, the ladder was one that folded, so it had an extra set of legs beneath it, giving it the strength to support Vivian's added weight.

She lifted her leg to brace her lame foot on a higher rung. Her thigh was positioned directly beneath the girl's bottom. "Can you sit down, Agnes?"

The girl nodded with a sniff, gingerly lowering herself downward. She was so afraid it broke Vivian's heart. She didn't mind the little bit of weight coming down on her leg, and onto her sprained ankle. It hurt, but she ignored it as she reached up and hooked her left arm about Agnes's waist. "Wonderful. Now, put your arm around my neck."

The girl did, clutching Vivian like she was a buoy in a raging sea. "A little looser, dear. I've got you."

Lowering her lame leg, Vivian took the full—
and almost inconsequential—brunt of Agnes's
weight against her, lifting the girl with her arm as
she slowly inched down the ladder.

By the time she reached the ground, her leg
was throbbing from ankle to thigh. Agnes, now
safe and secure, threw her arms around Vivian's
waist and hugged her. The girl's head could have
rested on her chest. It was odd, being hugged by
another woman with such feeling. She hadn't
been embraced so since before her mother died.
The realization brought a hot prickle to the back
of her eyes.

"Thank you, miss!" Agnes cried, still squeezing. "I was ever so afraid of falling."

Vivian patted her back. "You're safe now." She
cast a glance at one of the older women as the
young maid released her. "Those scones smell delicious. Might I join you for tea?"

More astonished glances exchanged and directed at her. "You want to take tea with us,
miss?" It was Agnes who spoke, her voice so full
of wonder and gratitude that Vivian squirmed.

"My name is Vivian," she told them. "And yes,
I would like to take tea with you, if you do not
object to having me."

Judging from the cacophony of pleasure that followed, the women did not mind at all. One pulled
a chair out from the table for her and she hobbled
toward it, thanking the woman as she sat.

They treated her like a queen, placing a plate of warm scones before her complete with strawberry jam and clotted cream. Tea was served in an old but unchipped china cup, and tasted strong and sweet.

Soon they all were seated around the table, eating and drinking. If they were uncomfortable in Vivian's presence they soon recovered from it, and regaled her with talk of their everyday lives, as they joked with one another in a sisterly fashion.

"I envy you," Vivian told them, helping herself to yet another scone, which she heaped with jam and cream. "Your friendship. I don't have any women friends."

They looked at her with a mixture of shock and sorrow. "You have us miss, er, Vivian." It was Shannon who spoke, and one of the older women patted her on the shoulder in praise for it.

Vivian's eyes filled, and a tear spilled over before she could stop it. Hastily, she wiped it away with the back of her hand. "Thank you, so very much."

They talked some more. A few made ribald comments about Temple and how fine he was, and Vivian tried to ignore how they watched for her reaction whenever they made these comments. She refused to add her own opinion, because right now she was torn between wanting the man in her bed and wanting to string him up by his testicles.

"Do all of you revere Lilith?" she asked as Agnes topped up her cup with fresh hot tea.

"We do now," Mary, one of the older women replied for the group. "Mrs. Cooper-Brown introduced us to the goddess and put us on the path. She saved us from bitter lives, Miss Vivian. My husband cast me out after our third stillborn. I'd be dead if not for the missus and this place."

Another of the women hugged her and Vivian's heart pinched a little at the sorority between them, and the circumstances that brought them together as they each revealed the tragedy in their past that had led them to the school. By the end, she was convinced that Kimberly Cooper-Brown was nothing short of a saint.

"My father sold me to a freak show," she admitted when all the rest had spoken.

Little Agnes reached across the table and seized her hand. Despite the difference in size, the young woman had a grip that could crack walnuts. Vivian had to fight a wince as pain shot up her fingers. "You're one of us, Vivian. Lilith will look after you as well. She has to."

Mary gave the girl a sharp nudge, the reason for which Vivian had no idea, and the girl let go of Vivian's hand, glancing away.

"How does Temple fit into your worship?" she asked, not sure she wanted to know. "He has Lilith's blood, does he not?"

"He's something special, he is," a girl whose name Vivian didn't know replied. "I suppose he's like a priest or a prophet."

The idea of Temple as a prophet was almost laughable, but these women held him in high esteem, so Vivian didn't make her derision known.

"I should like to know more about Lilith," she said. "Will you ladies teach me?" The more she knew about where Temple and his abilities came from, the more she might be able to figure out why Rupert despised him so.

And maybe along the way she'd find out not only why these women treated her so royally, but also maybe she'd find a measure of peace herself. Maybe Lilith could give her that.

The women exchanged glances, as though they weren't certain, but it was Agnes who spoke, Agnes who looked at her with a determination far beyond her years. "I'll tell you all I know." Then she looked around at the others. "We all will, won't we? Because Miss Vivian is one of us."

Murmurs of agreement came forward and, one by one, every woman turned her gaze to Vivian and smiled. Vivian, for the first time since her mother fell ill, felt like she was accepted for who and what she was, with no agendas and no expectations. Neither Temple nor Rupert offered her that, despite the connection she felt to Temple and Rupert's kindness.

It was as though she finally had a family.

And she knew that the longer she remained in this place, the harder it was going to be for her to escape and leave it, and all the people in it, behind.

Chapter 10

It was Vivian's blood he craved, not her.

This was what Temple told himself as he sat in the library that evening, hunger gnawing at him. It made perfect sense, of course. Vivian's blood made him stronger, sharper. When he bit her, tasted her, he felt as though he were more than invincible. He felt as though he were a god.

It had to be her blood that made him feel like this, because he would accept no other explanation.

It didn't help, of course, that her scent was everywhere he went. Did she think he wouldn't discover that she had gotten out of her prison? He didn't know whether to be insulted that she believed him that dumb, or impressed by her cunning. She was a never-ending source of amazement, his Vivian.

But she wasn't his. She belonged to Villiers—in every way that mattered. The coded telegram and her refusal to suspect her mentor in the death of the courier was proof enough of that.

Logically he knew better than to feel as betrayed as he did. He would have done exactly the same thing as she, were the situation reversed. But that didn't ease the disappointment churning in his gut, souring there.

She had given him her blood and her virginity. And though he hadn't asked for her trust—done nothing to warrant the giving of it—it pissed him off knowing that she reserved that part of herself for Villiers, a man who didn't deserve to even know her name. A man who only sought to use her.

But then, was he much better? In the beginning he wanted to use Vivian against Villiers. He still did, so how could he think himself any better? Villiers was a white knight to Vivian and he . . . well, he was a black-hearted villain for the most part.

And why should he care? He didn't want her. He couldn't completely have her while Villiers stood between them. And once the problem of Villiers was eliminated, Vivian would hate him too much to ever give herself to him again.

"You look decidedly brooding," Brownie remarked pertly as she entered the room.

Temple frowned. "What are you doing here?"

She shot him an amused glance. "I run the place, remember?"

He didn't bother to remind her that he had paid for it—long before she'd ever been born. He couldn't remember the exact date, but it was no doubt written down somewhere. He'd put her in charge of it because the sisterhood had been good to him.

"That doesn't answer my question," he replied.

"I'm looking for a book." Her gaze traveled quickly over a large selection of leather-bound spines. "Apparently Vivian has decided she'd like to learn more about Lilith."

If Temple's heart could beat like a human's it would have pounded in his chest. Instead, it gave one mighty thump and then went back to its usual slower-than-molasses rhythm. "Does she?"

His former lover turned her head toward him. "Would you have me try to stop her?"

"No, that would only encourage her all the more. Let her read. The worst that could happen is she could learn the truth."

"About you, or about herself?"

He shrugged. "I don't imagine she much cares to learn about me."

"You don't think? I suspect it's because of you that she's interested in the Mother to begin with." Like all disciples of the sisterhood, Kimberly believed that Lilith was the mother of humanity rather than Eve—at least in Ireland. Legend had Lilith giving Adam children who were as "otherworldly" as their vampire step-siblings, only looked upon much more kindly by the Creator. There were those who believed that Danae, the mother-goddess of Celtic lore to have been one of these children, and that she and her issue peppered this blood throughout Ireland. Red hair was a sign of Lilith's lineage. There were other traits as well, more rare than hair or eye color.

"Suspect all you want. I know better than to attempt changing your mind."

She made a face. "You are ill-tempered. Could your falling out with Vivian have anything to do with this sour mood?"

"Bugger off."

She laughed and turned her attention back to her books. "Ah, here it is." She plucked a large and tattered volume off the shelf. "This should keep her occupied for a while."

"Don't underestimate her," Temple advised. "You'll regret it."

"I would never underestimate Vivian!" Indignation colored her smooth cheeks. "She's a lovely young woman."

Temple sneered. "Of course you would take up her defense."

Brownie watched him for a long time. Long enough that he shifted uncomfortably in his chair.

"You are pale, my friend," she said softly. "Can I get you something?"

"I'm hungry." Christ, he sounded like a whiny child.

"I have a bottle—"

"I want a person, Brownie."

Her gimlet eyes narrowed. Setting the book aside, she turned and tilted her head. "Will I suffice?"

His gums began to itch a little, then stretch as his fangs distended from his gums. It always made him feel vaguely serpentine when that happened and he wondered if there was a biblical connection there as well. There were those who thought Lilith to have been the snake in Eden.

He rose to his feet and took her in his arms. She trembled a little, sending a wave of shame through his veins. It wasn't fair that he do this to her, even though it was part of the arrangement of running a safe house. The people in charge had to provide blood, whether bottled or fresh. He'd taken from her before, and enjoyed it. They both had, so why now did it feel so low, so dirty?

He imagined his fangs breaking her fragile flesh, the taste of her on his tongue. It would be good for her—much better for her even than him. He had been bitten by only one vampire, and that had been many, many years ago, but when he thought of her teeth in his flesh, he still shivered just a little bit.

And he had killed her, so the bite had to be good for him to have such a reaction to it now.

But it wasn't Brownie's blood he wanted. It wasn't she that he wanted moaning softly in his arms, silently pleading for more than just his fangs. He wanted Vivian. No one else would satisfy. And, damn it, anyone else would be wrong.

His hold on her relaxed. Brownie gazed up at him, her pale brow knit with concern. But there was a hint of rejection—and was that relief in her eyes? "Would you prefer a different vintage?" The humor in her voice was appreciated, no matter how forced it was.

Temple gave her a gentle smile as his fangs slid back into his gums. No, he didn't want a bottle. He wanted Vivian, and if he went after her, he would take her, whether she welcomed him or not. And she most assuredly would not welcome him.

"Actually," he said, letting her go, "I've decided I'm not hungry after all." And then, before she could see what a lie that was, he turned his back and left the room. He needed to get as far away from this place, and from temptation, as he could.

Two hours later, Temple returned from the mainland, his hunger sated and with several paper-wrapped packages in his arms. In them were clothes for himself and some for Vivian. She didn't have much and he wasn't spiteful enough to keep her in rags. He bought her trousers and a couple of shirts, stockings, undergarments too. The underthings were fine and delicate—a bribe as well as a peace offering. Plus, he wanted to see her in them. He knew he would—neither of them could deny what was between them for long.

She was a weakness he couldn't afford to have, and yet could not seem to bring himself to get rid of. The excuse that she was useful against Villiers just wasn't as convincing as it had been a few days ago.

He also brought back chocolates for the ladies of the house. His reasons for this were not entirely made up of heartfelt generosity. He knew the sisterhood would gravitate toward Vivian, that they would instantly accept and adore her. He needed to keep some of that adoration for himself. The last thing he wanted or needed when going up against Villiers and the Silver Palm was a school full of disgruntled women aligning against him.

He put the box of chocolates on the table in the kitchen where it would be certain to be found the next morning. And then stealthily climbed the stairs to the upper floors and left the packages for Vivian outside her door.

He stood there for a moment, listening. He could hear her in there, the softness of her breath, the *woomp-woomp* of her heart that was like music to him. And he could hear the occasional flipping of pages. She was reading—the old book Brownie found for her no doubt.

Would she uncover the truth? Would she believe it if she did? And if she did believe, would she see Villiers for the villain he was? Or would his armor remain untarnished?

He spent far too much time thinking about her. That was no doubt why Villiers sent her after him.

He knew she would be a distraction. Did Vivian know she was supposed to be a distraction as well? Had giving herself been part of the plan?

Of course it had, but the passion she showed him was no act. She had wanted him almost from the very beginning, he knew that. It was the one thing he could be certain of. Whatever lies there were between them, her body hadn't told one of them.

He turned away from her door before he could do something stupid, such as let himself in and throw himself at her feet. He went to the library instead, where he hoped to find distraction. He would resist the urge to go to her and beg her forgiveness for locking her up. She must hate him for that.

In the library he poured himself a glass of bourbon and plucked a copy of *Tom Jones* off the shelf. Obviously, Brownie didn't believe in censuring her students' reading material. The story was entertaining enough that it helped take his mind off Vivian. In fact, he was jerked out of the world of young Mr. Jones when he heard a knock on the front door. It echoed throughout the school. Who the hell would be calling at such an hour?

Suddenly alert, he listened. The housekeeper answered the door, speaking loudly to the guests. A man replied in a familiar voice and asked for Temple. He stopped listening then, knowing what would happen next.

A few minutes later he was not disappointed. The housekeeper, in her cap and wrapper, came into the library with a knock and a smile despite having been pulled from her bed.

"Beg pardon, Mr. Temple, but you have guests awaiting you in the big parlor."

"Thank you. Are they vampires?"

It often amused him that this question was never considered strange to the people who knew him. "I believe so, sir."

It didn't matter that he was ancient, or so familiar with the ways of the world. A little burst of happiness blossomed in his chest at her words. He'd been right. The visitors were his kind.

His friends.

He sent her off to bed, assuring her he could take care of rooms et cetera, and then made a mad dash to the room where his guests were waiting. He burst into the room with his excitement and smile scarcely contained.

Standing in the parlor were two lovely women and two mangy curs of vampires, if he ever saw any.

"Hello, boys," he said. They grinned and descended upon him like wolves returning to the pack.

Reign and Saint had arrived.

Chapter 11

Vivian had not forsaken him.

Ensconced in his new lodgings on the shore near Louisburgh in County Mayo, Rupert Villiers's dislike of Ireland and all things Irish was overshadowed by the pleasure of knowing that at least something was going as he planned.

Chapel had surprised them in England, but then those men had been idiots led by an even bigger one. In Rupert's estimation they had deserved to die. At least Cecil Maxwell had managed to escape Bishop in Romania. Maxwell should arrive tomorrow. Unfortunately, his fabulous monster—an exceptional nosferatu—had been destroyed by the vampire Bishop, along with it most of his research.

Constantin Khorza was lost to them now that he had reconciled with his dhampyr daughter, and that was all right. He wasn't all that useful anymore—and not even enough of a threat to kill.

Baron Hess was on his way as well, the last of Rupert's lieutenants. He was also the one responsible for the fantastic debacle involving Justin Fontaine. Fontaine had thought he found the perfect woman for their final ritual, and while the boy had done a bang-up job of collecting the necessary organs, he had called far too much attention to himself, and earned Saint's ire. Hess had reclaimed much of Rupert's trust by taking care of the Fontaine "problem."

That was all who was left whom he truly trusted. Even Dashwood was dead, killed by his own son in Scotland while trying to apprehend Reign. Thankfully the vampires retained enough predictability that they jumped whenever Temple called. Really, their nobility would be their downfall—running off to rescue their former leader would lead to their deaths.

And give Rupert more power than any human could possibly imagine.

It was enough to give him an erection.

As if by divine providence, a maid knocked on his study door to bring him a fresh bottle of port. She kept her face averted, head down, but her figure was lush and round and entirely adequate to ease the ache between his thighs.

"Come here, girl," he said in his silkiest tone.

Of course she did as he instructed, good servant that she was. She'd even closed the door behind her, making sure the guards outside would hear little of their encounter. Maybe the Irish had more to offer than he originally thought.

The guards were a precaution he sometimes took in precarious situations, and given his proximity to Temple, and recent sighting of Payen—which may or may not have been his own imagination—it was only smart to have extra protection.

"Is there something you wish of me, sir?" the maid asked, setting the tray on the smooth surface of his desk. She could not have been in service long, given the fine state of her hands. He liked the soft huskiness of her voice. It reminded him of a time long ago.

"Indeed," he replied, raising his hand to a glossy sable ringlet that bobbed beneath her cap. He'd always been partial to dark brown hair, ever since Violet. Too bad Vivian's hair was so unapologetically red. "I have something very special to ask of you. Something that would make me very happy."

Her face was still downcast. "Of course I desire your complete happiness, sir."

A little thrill of victory raced through Rupert. He wasn't one of those men who liked to force himself on unwilling women—he much preferred when they gave into him on their own.

"Up on the desk, lass," he instructed softly. "Lift your skirts."

She was a reasonably tall girl, so her delectable derriere scooted easily onto the desktop. Rupert lazily unfastened his trousers as the girl's pretty hands clutched and slowly—teasingly—lifted her drab skirts. First he saw her lovely ankles, then shapely calves, both of which were encased in pale pink stockings.

"Those are very pretty," he commented, reaching inside his clothing to free his throbbing erection. "Did a man give those to you?" Certainly they were too expensive for her to have purchased on her own.

"Aye," she replied. "My husband."

Ah, good. She wasn't a virgin. God, she had delicious thighs. She stopped there, playing demure. Rupert stepped between her knees. "Spread your legs for me."

She did, still not raising her face. This downcast gaze was beginning to grow tiresome. He wanted her to look at him as he ploughed into her. He wanted to see lust and pleasure in her eyes, wanted that power.

Wanted to pretend she was Violet. Twenty years and the memory of her was enough to make his cock twitch.

"Spread them further," he commanded, stepping deeper into the valley of her thighs. "Look at me."

She did, meeting his gaze with one that was far from coy and nowhere near submissive. Her eyes were the most clear and bright shade of hazel—layers of green, blue, and gold rather than a muddy mixture. For a second he thought it was his mind fooling him again.

He knew those eyes.

"Hello, Rupert."

Violet.

He heard the port bottle smash, felt the potent wine splash on his hand and face, knew it stained his sleeve. The bottle arced upward and, somehow, he managed to flinch just in time. The movement saved him from losing an eye and half his face. Instead all he got was a jagged slice across his cheekbone.

He screamed and reeled toward the wall. Hand pressed against the wound on his cheek, Rupert's hand was clumsy with fear as it searched blindly along for the bellpull.

Violet hopped off the desk and came toward him, holding the broken bottle by the neck. His blood ran down the tinted glass, over her slender fingers.

She was going to kill him.

"This is going to end," she informed him coolly. "Here and now."

"You're not a killer," he muttered, breathing a silent sigh of relief as his fingers closed around the silken cord.

"Maybe not," she replied, pretty face grim as she advanced. "But I can and will kill you to protect my husband."

Husband. Payen. Bastard. Once his plan came

to fruition, he was going to hunt down and kill that son of a bitch.

But for now he would have to be content with calling for help. He pulled the cord, ringing a bell out in the main hall. He didn't just pull it once, but kept yanking at it, creating a clanging panic that echoed throughout the house.

The door burst open and as the guards rushed in, Violet gave Rupert an exasperated glare. "I should have killed you the minute I walked in."

"Yes," he agreed. "But you didn't. You never were all that bright, my dear." Then to his guards. "Shoot her."

Pistols cocked and in that second before anyone could fire, Violet grinned coldly at him. "I'll see you again, Rupert. And for God's sake, pull your trousers up."

And then she was up on the desk as shots rang out, running for the windows with the speed of a panther. He couldn't tell if she was hit, but bits of plaster sprayed from the walls from bullets that missed. Arms extended high over her head, she dove through an open window—no doubt quickly taking to the air, or dropping gracefully to the ground below. His men rushed to the window, but Rupert knew she was long gone before they ever got there.

Legs trembling, he expelled a shaky breath. He was going to have to be more careful now. Much more careful. Still, there was some satisfaction in knowing the vampires realized he was a force to be reckoned with.

That thought alone put a smile on his face and restored much of his earlier calm and sense of accomplishment.

Then, because his erection hadn't failed during the exchange, but rather hardened all the more, and because he didn't want his men to see, Rupert took Violet's advice.

And pulled up his trousers.

Chapel and Bishop arrived at four o'clock that morning. With them were their wives, the lovely Prudence and exotic Marika. They also had Chapel's old friend Father Francis Molyneux and a young man named Marcus Grey with them. The group of them were assembled in Temple's rooms.

There was something oddly familiar about Marcus Grey. Temple recognized the sound of his voice from his brief time in Cornwall, as Mr. Grey tried to dig his way into his lair, but it wasn't the man's voice that perplexed him. There was something in his scent, something in his person that made him seem an old friend.

"He's descended from Dreux," Chapel explained, when he caught Temple staring at the young man. "He was in Cornwall looking for answers about certain legends surrounding his ancestor and his 'friends.' "

Dreux. Half a millennium had passed since his death, but Temple felt the loss all the same. Everything changed the morning Dreux walked out into the dawn, unable to live with what he had become.

Temple nodded. "That explains it." But before he could speak to the young man, the door to his apartments opened. Saint, Reign, and their wives, Ivy and Olivia, entered. Olivia looked a little pale, and Temple wondered if Reign's suspicions might be true. He asked Temple not to say anything to the others, but Reign feared his wife might be pregnant. Temple didn't even know if such a thing were possible let alone what the eventual outcome might be.

A vampire baby. Born, not bitten. Would it be born human? Vampire? Would it age? How awful would it be for it to remain ever an infant? Or would it grow as a normal child? There was no way of knowing, and according to Reign, Olivia was terrified. Temple didn't blame her. With so much on their minds, the last thing the two of them needed was to face a showdown with the Order of the Silver Palm.

But Olivia didn't hold his attention for long once he noticed the expectant silence that fell over the room. He turned his head and saw Saint and Marika staring at one another, wonder clearly written on their faces.

Saint took a step toward her, and his wife, Ivy, let him go with a happy smile. Bishop didn't seem quite so eager to release his spouse, but he let her go all the same, a hopeful expression on his austere face.

Like everyone else, Temple simply watched as the two met for the first time.

They walked toward each other, stopping just within reach. Saint reached out first, tilting his head thoughtfully, his dark eyes glistening with moisture. His fingers touched Marika's cheek, then her hair, then her cheek again as a smile curved his lips.

"You look so much like your mother," he said. Temple, not prone to displays of emotion, felt a lump in his throat. He could not imagine what his friend felt at that moment.

A tear trickled down Marika's smooth cheek as she took Saint's hand in her own, holding it against her face. She closed her eyes and wept. And then Saint took her into his arms and held her as tears ran from his eyes.

Everyone   discreetly   looked   away—even Bishop—giving them a little time alone. There was no harm in delaying talk of the Silver Palm for a few moments.

Temple took the time to instead study his companions. How happy his old friends were. Chapel, usually so brooding, was positively grinning at his bride, who obviously returned his adoration.

Bishop was like a wolf protecting his mate. Saint—
who treated romance like a game, always leaving
before he had to lose another loved one, had finally met his one true love. And Reign was reunited with his wife after thirty years apart. Each
of them had someone to share eternity with.

Except for him.

For a second, his mind jumped to the woman
who slept several floors above. How would his
friends react to her?

"Temple?"

He raised his head to find Saint and the others
watching him. "You're done?" he asked stupidly.

Saint smiled that little roguish smile of his.
"Marika and I will have plenty of time to acquaint
ourselves. Right now, I think what we all want to
hear is what the hell happened to you—and just
what the devil is the Order of the Silver Palm up
to?"

There were murmurs of agreement and Temple
ran a hand over his face. "I wish I knew. I have
someone here who might be able to answer some
of our questions, but I suspect she'll resist."

"She?" Saint's grin widened. "I've never known
you to have trouble with women."

"Except for Lucinda," Bishop remarked drily.
Chapel, Saint, and Reign shot him looks that
ranged from shock to downright anger. Perhaps
Temple should have been offended on his own
behalf, but he wasn't. He understood Bishop. His

old friend was worried about losing his wife to Saint, even though he knew it was a foolish fear. And because he felt so helpless, he was going to lash out at the person he blamed for all of this. Temple.

"Yes," he replied with a forced smile. "But then I killed her and she wasn't any trouble at all."

The women, the priest, and Mr. Grey gaped at him, but Temple ignored them. Let the others explain. It had been two centuries, and he was not going to talk about it. Not now that he was thinking he may end up with yet another woman's blood on his hands if he didn't protect Vivian from his friends.

And his friends from Vivian. He couldn't forget that.

"As for what happened to me, it's a strange but short story." He proceeded to enlighten them as to his abduction: He told them how the Order drugged him and how they knew about his plans to meet the others in Italy. He told them about Rupert Villiers and he told them about Vivian.

But he didn't tell them what he suspected about her, not yet. He wanted to see their unbiased reaction to her. They had enough against her knowing her association with Villiers, anything else might make them far too wary of her.

Why he should want his friends to have a good opinion of her was beyond his own comprehension. Obviously while he had been trying to seduce her into loyalty for him she had been doing the same to him. The only difference was, she seemed to have succeeded where he failed.

To think he had once thought of himself as a great warrior. His reputation had been the stuff of legends. Now, to be brought so low by a woman. Lucinda must be laughing in hell.

"Rupert Villiers," Marcus mused after Temple fell silent. "I've heard that name before."

The boy was already proving himself useful. No wonder Chapel kept him around. "Where?" Temple asked.

Marcus thought for a moment, blue eyes narrowed. "I think I stumbled upon his name in my research. Twenty years ago he was going to marry a woman named Violet Wynston-Jones. The nuptials were interrupted by a vampire named Payen Carr."

"I've been contacted by Carr," Temple informed him. "He was once a Knight Templar."

"And a protector of the Blood Grail," Marcus added. "Perhaps he can help us determine exactly what the Order wants."

"They want the Grail." Temple looked around at his friends. "That's why I sent a piece of it to each of you—to keep it safe."

"Why the Grail?" Reign somehow managed to look both fierce and bewildered at the same time. "All they need to become vampires is our blood. If that was all they wanted, they could have gotten that from Olivia when they kidnapped her nephew."

Temple arched a brow. "Obviously the four of you need to share your experiences as well. I think that is the best place to start."

Reign glanced at Olivia, whose eyelids were decidedly heavy. "Can we perhaps do this later? We've been traveling nonstop. Olivia needs to rest."

"So does Frank," Chapel interjected, referring to Father Molyneux.

The old priest shot him a dark look. "I am very much able to make that decision for myself, *mon amie*."

Marcus interrupted the power struggle with a wide and obviously false yawn. "Perhaps you aren't tired, Father, but I certainly could use some sleep. Besides, it's almost dawn."

He was right. Yes, very useful this descendent of Dreux. Much more rational than his ancestor.

"There are rooms on the north wall that have shutters and heavy drapes," Temple revealed. "Father Molyneux and Marcus can sleep in the west wing. Many of the students are gone for the summer, so we don't have to bother ourselves with trying to maintain secrecy."

"Secrecy is rather tedious," Ivy agreed, speaking for the first time as she linked her arm through Saint's. "Let's go to bed."

The expression on Saint's face was as hot and predatory as it was loving. Temple was uncomfortable seeing it—like he was intruding upon a private moment. None of the others seemed bothered, except for Marcus Grey, who actually rolled his eyes.

The couple said their good-nights and Saint stopped briefly to give Marika another hug, which was enthusiastically returned. Bishop's jaw tightened.

Desire. Protection. Jealousy. How Temple envied his friends these emotions. When he saw how Saint wanted to love Marika and how Bishop wanted to protect her, it warmed his heart—and made him want to cuff both of them upside the head. There was room for both of them in her life, and Bishop needn't worry that Saint would ever overshadow him or somehow harm his bride.

But, he knew how hardheaded Bishop could be, and there would be no telling him these things. He would have to work it out on his own.

It worried him, though. It worried him because it was going to be a distraction for both vampires. And he worried because it was obvious that Francis Molyneux was not long for this world, no matter how much Chapel might wish it otherwise. Worried because Reign's mind was obviously on his wife and not on the danger they faced.

And he was worried because all he wanted

to do was climb into bed with Vivian and feel her strong, supple limbs wrapped around him, breathe in the scent of her hair, and feel a measure of peace. She could probably rip out his heart and he wouldn't care, so drugged he would be on her scent and her touch.

The others made their good-nights as well. Bishop came to him before leaving. "Forgive me," he said.

Temple smiled and clasped the slightly smaller man's hand his in his own. "You know better than to ask."

When everyone else left, there was only Temple and Marcus left in the room. The human eyed him without a drop of fear, but with a great deal of speculation and, oddly enough, respect. What had he done to deserve that?

"Aren't you for bed, Mr. Grey?" Temple smiled slightly. "I thought you were exhausted."

"Marcus," came the instant reply. "And I am, of course. Did you really kill her?"

Temple didn't need clarification. He understood the young man perfectly. He wasn't offended, nor was he particularly persuaded to be gregarious on the subject, but he could at least be honest. "I did."

"Why?"

"Because she was a monster, and because it was my fault."

Marcus nodded, as though he understood,

which was of course impossible. But at least he seemed satisfied because he didn't ask any more questions.

"I might not be a vampire," he said, "but I'm not sick and I'm not in love and I will endeavor to do whatever you require of me."

As far as pledges of allegiance went it wasn't much, but Temple hadn't had anyone swear fealty to him in centuries, and even then there hadn't been half the integrity behind those flowery speeches as there was in Marcus Grey's voice.

"Thank you." It wasn't much in way of gratitude either, but it was just as sincere.

Marcus gave a curt nod. "Good night, then."

"Good morning, Marcus."

The young man departed, leaving Temple standing there alone, silence weighting down upon him. Oh, he could hear the muffled footsteps of his companions as they went their separate ways, hear their soft whispers, but he was not part of that. Those words were not meant for him.

Was it weakness that made him feel so terribly alone? He'd spent so many decades by himself, with no other thought than protecting the Blood Grail. But now, he thought perhaps the only thing he'd been protecting was himself. He stayed away from people because it only reminded him of how alone he was.

Relationships had consequences. If the last two hours in the company of his friends had screamed anything at him, it was that. Relationships made a man vulnerable. Better to be empty and alone than vulnerable and distracted.

He glanced toward the bed. The sheets still smelled of Vivian, and he knew he would sleep with his face buried in her pillow just as he had since he'd put her in a different room. He should have the bed made up clean, but he couldn't bring himself to do it, not yet.

He extinguished the lamps and stripped off his clothes in the darkness. Marcus Grey's words came back to him as he crawled into bed, letting Vivian's scent ease the hollow ache inside him.

It was a good thing Grey had a clear head because Temple didn't. The second he closed his eyes, he could see Vivian on the back of his lids. He could almost feel her breath on his cheek. Like Molyneux and Olivia there had to be an ailment behind this obsession. Perhaps he suffered from a sickness of the mind, of which he had yet to discover a cure. One thing was for certain.

It sure as hell wasn't love.

Chapter 12

Vivian woke that morning to find the little maid Shannon standing over her, smiling as bright as a sudden burst of sun on an overcast day.

"Mr. Temple left these outside the door for you." She held up several packages in her arms. "And he says that I'm to give you the key to your room."

Blinking, Vivian sat up and rubbed the sleep from her eyes. After her earlier escape, Temple had kept the lock blocked up so she couldn't pick it. She didn't think it was so much because he could keep her locked up, but rather to prove that his will was greater than hers.

"The key? Really?" She sounded like an idiot, but she hadn't slept well, and her mind wasn't quite functioning as it should.

Shannon handed her the slender brass key. Vivian stared at it as it gleamed in her palm. He hadn't only let her out—but he'd given her the ability to lock him out as well. She could read so much into that if she wanted, but she would rather not.

And he'd brought her things. Why? To soften her up? To distract her? Or was this some kind of apology? It might not be much of one, but damn if it wasn't effective.

"I brought you water to wash with," Shannon informed her, setting a porcelain pitcher on the washstand. "I thought you might like to join us for breakfast."

The hopeful expression on her face destroyed any thought Vivian might have had of refusing. She didn't need to worry about running into Temple just yet, and she did miss her new friends.

"I'd love to," she replied. "I'll be down as soon as I've dressed."

When Shannon had left, shutting the door behind her, Vivian opened the packages from Temple. He'd bought her clothes—nice, new clothes—some of which were very delicate and pretty. The thought of him picking out such intimate items brought a rush of heat to her cheeks— but it wasn't embarrassment that warmed her. It was the idea that he might have imagined what she would look like in fine lace and satin.

She climbed out of bed and quickly washed. She was able to stand now without much pain. Even walking didn't hurt much at all. Her ability to heal quickly was a godsend, especially in this instance. Even her ruined palm looked much

better. She put some salve on it and a clean ban-
dage before slipping into some of the undergarments Temple left for her. Pride demanded she
send them back, but feminine vanity won out.

Oh! They felt lovely. A clean shirt and new
trousers followed. He'd chosen her size well. Why
wasn't she surprised?

She didn't need the crutches to go downstairs,
though it was still a bit of an ordeal. Her foot was
stiff, and achy and kept her from moving quickly.
Normal movements were awkward and tedious.
But, she managed to make it to the ground floor
without falling and without breaking a sweat, so
she counted herself lucky. Then she continued on
in the direction of the kitchen.

The sound of footsteps made her halt, and lift
her head. She saw the strange man before he saw
her.

She watched him from around the corner as he
walked lazily toward the back stairs to the kitchen.
Who was he? He was reasonably young—probably
close in age to herself. His shoulders were broad,
his hair dark and wavy. A very pretty face too. But
pretty did not mean safe. Lions were pretty.

And this lion was headed toward the place
where all of her new friends worked, ignorant of
his approach. Temple was asleep, and even if he
wasn't, the sun was too bright through the windows in this part of the house for him to appear.
That left Vivian alone to protect the house.

She might not be able to run, or even walk for a great distance just yet, but she could sneak up on this man with relative ease. She could take him down and find out exactly who he was.

She crouched, whipped herself around the wall, and ran for him. He turned at the last second as she launched herself through the air at him.

"What the—?" That was all he managed to blurt out before she knocked him to the floor, piling the full of her weight on top of him.

He put up more of a struggle than she thought he would. He was strong and muscular—the kind of strength that came from hard manual labor. And yet he had the face of a gentleman. He fought, however, like a street brawler, and Vivian thrilled a little at the physical exertion.

He tried to pin her, tangling his legs with her own to prevent her from kicking. She managed to plant a fist hard in his belly as he tried to seize her wrists.

"For God's sake, I'm not trying to hurt you!" He was scowling at her, panting with the effort to subdue her. "Calm the hell down!"

"Who are you?" she demanded, flipping him onto his back. "What are you doing here?" She straddled him, pinning his wrists to the smooth floor.

As he smiled, she realized that he had stopped fighting her, and was perfectly content to lay there with her on top of him. "My name is Marcus Grey.

And you must be that resistant person Temple spoke of."

Resistant? Temple called her resistant? She wasn't certain how she felt about that. How exactly did he mean it?

"What are you doing here?"

"I'm here with Chapel and Bishop." His eyes narrowed thoughtfully. "Do you know who they are?"

Vampires. Oh God, the vampires were here. Stunned, she rolled off of Mr. Grey, and landed hard on her backside. "They're going to kill me," she lamented.

Mr. Grey sat up so that they were practically shoulder to shoulder. "Why would anyone want to kill you?"

If he was with the vampires, then her next statement would draw some kind of reaction from him. "I work for and was raised by a man named Rupert Villiers."

The rosy hue of his cheeks faded to a pallor. In a blink he rolled to a crouch and Vivian found herself with a pistol pointed at her head—just out of arm's reach.

Suddenly, Mr. Grey didn't look so friendly anymore. "You belong to the Silver Palm?"

Vivian didn't dare move. "No."

"But you are aligned with them."

She said nothing. What could she possibly say that would convince him she wasn't his enemy?

Hell, she *was* his enemy! And he was hers, and right now she was better off letting him believe he was in control, which he unfortunately was.

His handsome face turned to a mask of cold disgust. "If you're with the Order, why are you here?"

Yes, why was she? Really, she could offer any number of excuses, both to him and to herself, but would any of them be the truth? "I'm Temple's prisoner." That at least was fact. Or rather, it had been.

A loud click echoed in the quiet hall, jerking Vivian's gaze upward. Mr. Grey had gone quite rigid, and with good reason—he had a rifle pressed against his back. Holding it was Shannon, the housemaid. Her hands held the weapon steady, and her lovely freckled face was set with fierce determination.

"You will drop that pistol, sir."

"Shannon," Vivian began, "it's all right." She didn't want the young woman to get into trouble with Kimberly for assaulting one of Temple's guests.

But it was nice to know at least someone was on her side.

"It's not all right," Shannon insisted, giving Mr. Grey a poke between the shoulders with the tip of the barrel. "If you would, sir, I asked you to drop that pistol."

Slowly, Mr. Grey leaned forward, uncocked the

pistol, and laid it upon the floor. This surprised Vivian, because the man could have easily taken Shannon's weapon from her, of that she had no doubt.

"Now, get up," Shannon ordered and the man rose to his full and rather impressive height. "Be a gentleman and help Miss Vivian to her feet."

Expression mutinous, Mr. Grey nevertheless thrust his hand in Vivian's direction. She took it and stood as well. And she thanked him for his assistance.

"You can put the rifle down, Shannon. Mr. Grey isn't going to hurt either of us. He's merely being cautious."

Shannon didn't look convinced, but she lowered the gun all the same. "Anyone who knows you knows you wouldn't hurt a mouse."

That was so far from the truth Vivian could have laughed, but so sweet that the laugh dissolved around the lump in her throat. "Don't make a saint out of me, Shannon. I would hate to disappoint you." Then she turned to the man beside her. "Mr. Grey, I'm about to go downstairs for breakfast. Would you care to join me?" She wasn't trying to fool him with false kindness, she truly wanted to speak to him. He was the first non-vampire she'd met who knew about Rupert and the Order. It was obvious he thought them as despicable as Temple did.

Vivian knew very little about the Order of the

Silver Palm. It was one of those things Rupert kept from her. Perhaps it was time she learned what she could about the organization—even if the information was biased.

There had to be a reason for this hatred. Maybe Mr. Grey could tell her why Rupert had abducted Temple in the first place.

Marcus seemed surprised by the suggestion. "Given that I am famished, I believe I would, yes."

"Follow me." She moved passed him, presenting him her back in what she hoped was not a misguided gesture of trust and proceeded down the stairs. Shannon came behind them, rifle in hand, but no longer pointed at Mr. Grey.

The kitchen bustled with energy and conversation—all of which came to a halt when the women saw Marcus.

"Jesus, Mary, and Joseph," an older woman practically sighed. "Who's this pretty lad?"

"Marcus Grey," he replied with a charming smile and a bow.

The women giggled and blushed. Perhaps he wasn't so bad after all, Vivian thought.

"Mr. Grey is going to join us for breakfast, if no one objects," she said. And of course, no one did. Not even Shannon.

Breakfast was lively as always, though the women kept their conversation much more tame than usual. They were interested in Marcus Grey and asked him numerous questions about himself. He was charming and intelligent and just open enough that all the women were half in love with him by the time the meal ended.

Only Shannon seemed unimpressed. She sat beside Vivian and frowned at the handsome man the entire time. He wisely ignored the feisty Irish woman.

As the dishes were cleared, the maids broke off to attend to their various duties. Most were loath to depart the company of their guest, but the older ones shooed them away. Shannon was the last to rise.

"I'll stay with you if you want, Miss Vivian." She glared at Mr. Grey as she spoke.

He grinned at her. "Do you honestly believe I'd be foolish enough to assault Miss Vivian with the lot of you Amazons around?"

The girl didn't blink. "I'd rather not comment on how much of a fool I believe you to be, sir."

To his credit, Marcus laughed. "Well said." Even Vivian wasn't immune to those sparkling eyes. How could Shannon remain so unmoved? "I give you my word, Miss Shannon, that I only wish to talk to your friend."

Vivian patted her friend's hand. "It's all right, really."

Only then did the young maid leave, but not before shooting another heated glance at Marcus Grey before she stomped off.

He watched her go. "What an amazing creature," he murmured before turning his attention back to Vivian. "You certainly have a devoted friend in that one."

"I'm lucky to have her."

"Indeed you are." His expression turned thoughtful. "Such devotion cannot be undeserved, so I feel I must apologize for my actions earlier. I am . . . distrustful where the Silver Palm is concerned."

"So I guessed." Vivian smiled at him. "But you didn't kill me, and for that I am grateful."

Mr. Grey leaned forward. "Miss Vivian, might I ask what happened to your hands?"

She glanced down at the few scraps of bandages wrapped around her hands. "I fell into a pit."

"Honestly?"

"Yes." She would give him honesty. "I went out to meet a messenger and I fell."

"Are you really a prisoner here?" Disbelief colored his tone as he glanced around. "You seem rather free for one."

Vivian squirmed uncomfortably, remembering the bargain she made with Temple when she first arrived. She missed that. "Let's just say I have a suspicion Temple's friends will not be as kind to me as he had been."

"No one would hurt you if he told them not to."

She met his gaze evenly. "I have no idea what he will tell them."

He regarded her warily, but with great curiosity. "What do you know about the Order of the Silver Palm, Miss Vivian?"

"Rupert and most of his acquaintances belong to it. I've always assumed it was some kind of club for gentlemen with a keen interest in the occult."

"But now you're not so certain?"

"No," she admitted. "I'm not."

"And you honestly had no knowledge of their activities?"

She shook her head. He made it sound so sinister. "No. Other than occasionally having me with him as his protector, Rupert didn't share that part of his life with me. I met many members, but I was never privy to their meetings. He didn't even tell me what he wanted from Temple."

He scratched his jaw. "No. I wager he didn't. You were Villiers's protector?"

"Surely you noticed that I am not like other women, Mr. Grey?"

"Yes, I had noticed that you are rather . . . talented." Rather than condemning, his tone was light, almost flirtatious.

Vivian smiled once more. "Rupert helped me hone those talents."

"You were his ward but he trained you to be his guard."

"Exactly."

"Miss Vivian, would you like to discover the truth about the Order?"

Her first instinct was to say no. She didn't want
to hear things about Rupert, things she might not
like. But if she was honest with herself, she would
acknowledge that she already had huge doubts
where her mentor was concerned. She needed
to hear the charges against him so that he could
defend himself later.

"Yes," she replied. "The truth would be nice.
Can you give that to me, Mr. Grey?"

"I can give you some." His expression turned
grim. "You will have to face the others for the rest.
Can you do that?"

She was going to have to face them regardless
sooner or later. "Yes."

The legs of his chair scraped across the floor as
he pushed away from the table and stood. "You
have courage, Miss Vivian, but I don't envy you."

"Because they'll despise me?"

He gazed down at her, eyes full of pity. "Because by the time you're done listening, you might
just despise yourself."

"What the hell are you doing here?" Temple
demanded as Vivian walked into the drawing
room alongside Marcus. The drapes were drawn,
shrouding the room in heavy darkness to protect
the occupants from the morning sun.

There could be no doubt that he spoke to her.
All gazes turned on her, more curious than ag-
gressive. Obviously he had yet to tell them who

she was. Vivian held her head high. "I would like
to learn more about the Order of the Silver Palm,"
she told him calmly. Could he smell her fear? She
wasn't so much afraid of him as she was of the
others. What would they do to her? What would
he allow them to do? That was why he let her
out—so she'd find her way here.

"So you can report all we know back to Villiers?" It was an honest question, but Temple's
purpose in asking was less savory. He wanted
her to face the vampires' reaction to her. She supposed she couldn't blame him. There was something satisfying in the harsh lines of his face, in
knowing she had hurt him. It meant he cared, and
as twisted as it was, she liked that.

The vampires eyed her warily, with some dis-
dain. The women made their dislike more appar-
ent than the men, but no one objected to her being
there. And no one moved to touch her.

Odd. She would have thought they'd make
breakfast out of her.

"I would like to know with what crimes the
Order is charged. Perhaps I can answer questions you might have, and maybe you can answer
mine."

He looked like he wanted to believe her, but
didn't dare. "Fine. Have a seat. Everyone, this is
Vivian Villiers."

"Barker," she corrected, feeling less guilty than
she should have for rejecting Rupert's last name.

What difference did it make what her surname was? "My name is Vivian Barker."

Temple stared at her, an odd gleam in his eyes. How could the two of them harbor such distrust and hard feelings toward each other when he obviously desired her as much as she desired him? It made no sense.

He introduced his friends to her, skipping Marcus Grey, of course. She sat next to the young human. He wouldn't offer much protection against the vampires, but they might think twice before mowing through him to get to her.

Plus, she liked the way Temple's jaw tightened when she put herself next to the handsome human.

"Does anyone object to Miss Barker's presence?" His teeth were clenched as he spoke.

No one objected. Temple gave her one last chance to prove herself a coward and run. "You are not going to like what you hear."

Vivian kept her face as expressionless as possible. "I don't suppose I will, no. Fortunately, the truth of it doesn't depend on my pleasure."

One of the male vampires, a rugged looked one with dark hair and piercing pale eyes, arched a heavy brow. "I think she can handle it, Temple. Let's get on with it, shall we?"

Jaw clenched, Temple nodded. "Fine." Maybe he was the coward, Vivian mused. Was he worried that she wouldn't be swayed, or that she would hear something that changed her opinion of Rupert? No, she couldn't believe he was that concerned for her feelings. His only concern was his agenda. He and Rupert were very much alike in that regard.

The truth didn't scare her, but finding out that she was nothing more than a pawn to either side did.

"Marcus, why don't you start?"

The man shot her a brief glance before turning his attention to the rest of the room. "I was approached by the Silver Palm because of interest in a site in Cornwall where the Holy Grail was supposedly buried. The Order encouraged me to dig, saying they would give me information about Dreux Beauvrai, my ancestor, in exchange for the Grail. What I didn't know was that it was Temple's lair they used me to uncover. When I learned the truth of what they were up to, I told Chapel. The Silver Palm attacked and would have killed us all if not for Chapel's quick thinking."

Vivian's ire immediately sparked. "How can you be so sure the Order would have killed you?"

Marcus turned to her with an unsympathetic but calm expression. "Because they shot at us."

It was like someone put an icy hand into her chest. She couldn't even speak. The Order—Rupert's friends—shot at people?

The fairest of the vampires, the one named Chapel spoke next. "When we made it into Temple's lair, it was too late. The Order had taken him." He took his wife's hand. "Pru was poisoned by a trap, and almost died."

Prudence squeezed his fingers as she gazed lovingly at him. "I remember what they did to you, how they hurt you. They tried to take you too."

On one hand, Vivian was able to tell herself that they were vampires, and therefore not human, but Prudence hadn't been a vampire then. Marcus Grey and Father Molyneux were human still. How could the Order risk harming mortals? And if she was honest, she couldn't understand why they would want to hurt vampires either. So far she'd seen nothing that made her think of these people as the monsters she always thought them to be.

The one who looked like a hawk—Bishop— went next. He kept his eyes fastened on Vivian as he spoke, and it took all of her resolve to hold that sharp gaze. He didn't look upon her with hate, but his distrust was obvious.

"I went to Marika to investigate the disappearance of a friend's brother," he told her. "I never did find him, but the Order is suspected of having abducted creatures other than vampires as well."

There was more? She didn't know anything about that. She didn't tell him that, though.

"Marika had been approached by the Order, who told her they would give her information on Saint, who she blamed for the death of her mother, in exchange for capturing me."

"How did she do that?" Vivian didn't want to interrupt and risk this vampire's ire, but she knew no human was a match for a vampire.

"I was a dhampyr," Marika explained. "Saint tried to turn my mother before I was born, and the result made me a halfling."

Vivian stared at her, eyes wide. "I didn't know such a thing was possible."

Marika gave her a rueful grin and a shrug. "I managed to trap Bishop and take him back to my camp. Eventually he convinced me that the Order was only trying to use me. When I refused to turn Bishop over, the Order not only threatened my father, but my brother as well. When that didn't work, they attacked with a nosferatu who poisoned my blood and almost made me one of them."

Vivian cast a glance at Temple. He was watching her carefully. Was that pity in his eyes? No doubt he remembered the two of them talking about the nosferatu she had seen. Rupert and the others hadn't killed it. What had they done with it? Had they set that monster free? She shuddered at the thought—then chastised herself for daring to think it. Rupert wasn't a killer.

Was he?

Next was Saint, who had a most grisly tale of a Jack the Ripper–style killer preying upon the women of Maison Rouge in London and taking their wombs. "I was abducted using silver, but thanks to Ivy I managed to escape." He put his hand on his wife's thigh. "The Order wasn't done with us, however. One of them took Ivy and tried to use her in a sick ritual involving the trophies he claimed from his victims. I managed to stop the ritual and the killer was apprehended by the police."

"And his trophies?" It was Temple who asked this.

Saint shot him a glance that said more than Vivian could ever hope to decipher. "They disappeared. Soon after his incarceration, the killer was found dead in his cell. I have no doubt that it was his own brethren that killed him," the dark vampire insisted. "I still have no idea why he killed those women to begin with, but I don't think it was a coincidence that there were five victims and there are five of us."

Vivian's head swam. Her stomach churned at the idea of five women being so brutally murdered and desecrated. There was no way Rupert could possibly be involved in such a horror. Never. Bile crept up her throat at the thought.

Reign—she remembered his name now—told his tale next, and Vivian's nausea eased somewhat.

"The Order made Olivia believe they had kidnapped her nephew and blackmailed her into giving me to them in exchange for the boy. When Olivia reneged on the agreement, they not only tried to kill her, but her nephew as well."

Vivian pressed a hand to her mouth. She couldn't hear anymore. She just couldn't. She had expected it would be difficult to hear what they had to say, but she hadn't thought it would be so horrific. Rupert couldn't know. He just couldn't.

"It appears they don't just want the grail," Chapel mused. "They want us."

Temple had to agree. "They've tried to abduct us all in one way or another."

Reign glanced around the room. "So whatever they're up to, they need wombs, the grail, and us."

"That can't be good," Bishop commented drily, cracking his neck. "And you say this Villiers is behind all of it?"

Temple nodded. "According to Payen Carr, the Order of the Silver Palm's resurgence began twenty years ago. Right around the same time Villiers was supposed to marry Violet Wynston-Jones." He turned his attention to Vivian. "Do you know anything about that?"

All this time Temple had been too intent upon the discussion to notice Vivian's reaction. Now that he looked at her, his blood ran cold. She looked like a child, afraid and alone and on the verge of tears. When she met his gaze, however, that expression instantly vanished, to be replaced by one of indignation.

"Except for Temple, have any of you met Rupert Villiers?" she asked, rather than answer his question. She couldn't know anything about Villiers, his past or his exploits, or she wouldn't look so surprised. Or so hurt.

Of course none of them had encountered Villiers that they knew of, and they said so.

Her tempestuous gaze pinned him to the spot. "I know you think him the worst kind of villain, and maybe he is. But Rupert Villiers saved my life."

"Did you ever stop to ask yourself why?"

She swallowed. "Of course."

"You know he wants something from you, Vivian. You cannot tell me you don't."

A complexion such as hers could not hide a flush. "He has never been anything but kind to me."

Damn her for the blinders she wore. How could she give her loyalty to that man, who only wanted to use her, and not to him when all he wanted was to have her in his arms again? "Because you're of use to him. Why won't you see that? He's only using you."

The flush in her cheeks turned into a fire. "And you're not?"

Silence followed as she walked out the door, slamming it behind her. Everyone stared at him—he could feel their gazes—but Temple's attention never left the door. Her words left him cold, even though he knew them to be true, he wanted to explain that he was different from

Villiers, but he had to admit that he wasn't. He'd planned to use her to his advantage even before realizing what she was.

Come back, he pleaded silently. *Come back to me.*

She didn't. Instead, one by one, the women in the room rose to their feet.

"We'll talk to her," Prudence promised as they walked to the door.

"Thank you," Temple said, unable to hide his surprise. Obviously they had seen that Vivian was ignorant of the Order's true nature as well. That pleased him on so many levels, but he hated to see her hurt at the same time. She wasn't a villain. She was a pawn. An innocent pawn who had no idea the man she revered only wanted to use her.

"Don't worry," Saint told him. "The girls will make everything right."

Bishop shot him a glare. "You don't know any of them well enough to know what they'll do."

The other vampire remained unruffled, but Temple knew from experience that Saint was like a snake. He might look perfectly still, but that didn't mean he couldn't strike at any second. "If thinking that makes you happy, then by all means, think it."

"I don't mind thrashing the shite out of both of you if necessary," Temple warned them. "I'm in the mood to do it."

"Fighting amongst ourselves won't solve any-thing," Chapel reasoned. "We have to fight beside each other if we're going to destroy the Order of the Silver Palm and have any semblance of normal lives.

"Chapel's right," Reign agreed. "So if the two of you need to knock heads, do it and get it over with so we can move on to more important things, like protecting our women from these sick bastards."

Saint and Bishop watched each other for a moment and then shared a stiff nod. There would be a truce for now, it seemed.

"Speaking of women," Reign began. "What of Vivian? Is she the Order's puppet or another of its victims?"

Temple ran a hand over his face as he began to pace. "She's so god-damned blind where Villiers is concerned, I want to believe her innocent, but she'd do anything for him, and that makes her dangerous."

For the first time since the group came together that evening, Father Molyneux spoke. Temple had almost forgotten the old priest was there, he'd been so quiet.

"Is it safe for me to assume that you harbor some affection for the girl?"

He couldn't meet the priest's gaze. He couldn't meet anyone's gaze—and they were all watching him, the bastards. "I don't know that either. She's been getting messages from Villiers—and reporting to him as well. Christ only knows what she told him."

"I think she's a puppet," Reign remarked, returning to his earlier comment. "The Order tried to use Prudence's quest for the Holy Grail against Chapel. They set Marika after Bishop, and Olivia after me. And they tried to involve Ivy in their plans as well. It stands to reason that they're using Vivian."

Saint's lips curved into a crooked smile. "Well, if that's the case, you might as well marry her now, Temple. You're going to end up with her anyway."

Temple shook his head. "That's not going to happen. Even if she is as innocent as I would like her to be, there's no future for Vivian and me."

"Why not?" Chapel demanded.

"Because she's mortal."

"You can change that." Reign shrugged. "It might not be easy, but we've all done it."

Temple sighed. "The last time I did it, the woman I loved turned into a bloodthirsty monster and I had to kill her. I won't risk that with Vivian."

Saint scowled at him. "Vivian is not Lucinda."

"No," Temple agreed. "She's not. But neither is Vivian completely human."

Chapter 13

"Are you in love with Villiers?" It was Prudence who asked the question.

"No," Vivian replied quickly, looking up from where she sat in the parlor. "He's been like a father to me."

The pretty, slender redhead sat down next to her. "What of Temple? Do you love him?"

Vivian practically choked on the breath she'd drawn. "God no! I'm attracted to him, but I'd never be foolish enough to fall for a man who only wants to use me." She couldn't be that foolish. Could she?

It looked as though she was foolish enough to believe in Rupert why not Temple as well? God help her, but the vampire's words had cut her to the bone. He'd made her doubt the one man to ever be good to her. How could she trust a man who'd locked her in a cage over one who had set her free from one?

Olivia, a striking brunette who looked very

tired, but could no doubt tear Vivian apart, came to crouch in front of the sofa where Vivian sat. "I want to believe you are innocent," she said softly. "But if you're part of the Silver Palm, I will kill you."

"I know," Vivian replied evenly, even as her heart beat quickened. "I'm not a threat to you."

"Not to me, or to us." Olivia encompassed the other women with a wave of her hand. "But you are a threat to Temple. That's why you were sent after him."

"I was sent after him because I'm stronger and faster than most men."

Olivia smiled. "You're not stronger and faster than a vampire."

"No, but Temple and I have fought and I have held my own." She was proud of that fact.

"Whoever sent you knew you'd be a distraction. You're just to keep him busy until the Order can collect itself and launch an attack."

The idea of Villiers . . . er, Rupert, using her in such a manner went against everything she wanted to believe, and yet it made sense, knowing how crafty her mentor could be. He knew Temple wouldn't hurt her, just as he knew there was no way she could subdue a vampire on her own.

Had she been sent after Temple to distract him, or to distract herself? If she wasn't there, Rupert wouldn't have to worry about her asking questions, would he?

She raised her gaze to meet Olivia's first, then swept it around to meet those of the others as well before coming back to Olivia once more. "I don't want anyone to get hurt, but I don't want to be anyone's puppet." She'd been used for the gain of others too much, and the only person who could stop that, was her.

Olivia smiled once more and gave her a little pat on the knee. "We will help you with that."

And then they gathered around her and told her everything that hadn't been told in the room with the men.

Her head spun.

After the women left her, Vivian sat for a long time trying to collect her thoughts, and make sense of everything she had heard that night.

There was no way she could believe it all and not think the worst of Rupert. But how could she call the vampires liars? They had suffered horribly, and with the exception of Olivia, the women had all been human at the time. She could almost excuse—although not condone—hatred of vampires, but she could not excuse what they endured.

Had the last decade of her life been a lie?

Slowly, she shuffled through the dark halls of the school. She didn't know where the vampires were, but if they were in this building they were being very quiet. There was only one vampire she was concerned with, however. And despite the fact that he might not even be there, Vivian found herself standing outside his door, afraid to knock, but unable to turn away.

The door opened, taking the choice away from her. Temple stood before her, backlit by a wash of golden light from the lamps within, naked from the waist up.

Her hungry gaze roamed over the heavy muscles of his arms and upper body, the dark hair that covered his chest, the salty bronze of his skin. Perhaps the women of this place were right to treat him as a god—he certainly looked like one.

"You're still here," he murmured softly.

She looked up. "Where else would I be?"

He shrugged, looking a little unsettled. "I thought you would have swum to the mainland to get away from me."

"Is that why you gave me the key to my room, so I'd run?"

He shrugged his wide shoulders. "I wasn't sure I could protect you if the others wanted blood. I thought you deserved the chance to escape."

Her heart pinched. That was more than she or Rupert had given him. Or maybe she had given him such a chance when she forgot to tell Rupert about the opium losing effect. Thinking about it now, she thought there had been part of herself that wanted him to get free.

All these years she hung so much on the kindness Rupert had shown her, but Temple had shown her what it was to be considered an equal. He'd treated her like he'd treat any other threat, not like she was something to mold and shape for his own pleasure. "I could run all the way to Italy and I wouldn't get away from you."

Pale green eyes darkened. "If you did run, I think I would have to chase you."

She shivered. What more invitation did she need? Whatever it was that tormented her and drove her to him, also seemed to drive him to her. Palms flat on his chest, she pushed him into the room and followed immediately after him. "I want you."

"Vivian . . ."

"Right now, it's all I have that is honest and real. Nothing else makes sense to me anymore." To say anything more would be to slice open her chest and lay her heart bare before him.

He gazed down at her, taking in every feature, every hair, and pore it seemed. "I'm sorry for what I said earlier."

"I know." Vivian pressed her hands to his cheeks. "You are more than you should be to me," she whispered, finally admitting aloud what was in her heart.

He kissed her then, inhaling any words that might have lingered on her tongue. Thank God he stopped her from saying anything else. Wrapping her arms around his lean waist, Vivian kissed him back, tasting him with her tongue as his nudged open her lips.

Their caresses were inelegant, almost frantic. Temple yanked her shirt over her head and then fell to his knees to relieve her of her boots and trousers. When she was naked except for her corset, he pressed the rough stubble of his jaw against the soft flesh of her stomach and rubbed his face against her.

"I love your scent," he confessed hoarsely. "I love your taste." And then that stubble abraded her thighs as he forced her legs apart and shoved his face between. Vivian cried out, gripping the hands that held her hips tightly in her own as he licked her, ate her—drove her into a frenzy with his tongue until she jerked against his mouth, coming in a violent torrent of hot, wet, spiraling pleasure.

When he rose and kissed her again, Vivian could taste herself on his lips, feel the wetness of his chin against her own, and it stoked the fire within her once more. She pushed him onto the bed, and he fell willingly. He sprawled atop of the sheets, with heavy-lidded eyes and trousers that strained from the erection contained within them.

Vivian crawled onto the bed. Her fingers went to the fastenings on those tight trousers and began working them free. As she did, Temple's hands came up to cup her breasts, freeing them from the cups of her corset to pinch her nipples. She hissed in response, feeling the pressure of his fingers deep inside.

She wanted him again—so badly she ached with it. When his trousers were unfastened, she pulled away from his hands to peel the light wool down his strong thighs and long calves. Dropping them onto the floor, she turned her attention to the length of hard flesh standing tall and thick between his legs.

She took him in her mouth—all the way to the back of her throat and out again. Temple shuddered, arched his hips. He swore softly when she did it again, this time applying the firm pressure of her tongue against the underside.

What power this simple act gave her. She gave him pleasure because she wanted to, and because she wanted to know that she could bring him to his knees, make him want her as much as she wanted him. She sucked, licked, and nibbled with her teeth, bringing his breathing to a rough and shallow tempo. Strong hands pushed against the back of her head, urging her to take him deeper. He moaned, and Vivian smiled.

And when she lifted her head, his cock trembled before her. Temple looked up at her, his lips parted, eyes heavy and glazed. "I'm yours," he rasped, coming up on his elbows. "I want to feel your hot quim wrapped around me. I want you screaming my name when you come."

Shuddering, her skin a mass of sensitive goose-flesh, Vivian climbed on top of him, straddling his hips so that the smooth tip of him pressed against the cove of her body. Slowly, she widened her thighs, lowering herself onto the satiny length. He stretched her, filled her until the back of her thighs rested on the top of his and there was no more of him to take. He was completely engulfed within her and the sensation of it had her almost delirious.

Yes, this was honest, even if it wasn't right. It was true and pure and there were no lies or mistrust between their bodies. She rocked against him, savoring every thrill and tingle, every shift of him against the walls of her sex.

"Lean down," he commanded. She did, bringing the tight, aching peaks of her breasts within reach of his mouth. He took one between his lips and sucked hard, drawing a little cry of pleasure from her. She rocked her body a little faster against his.

Then he bit. His fangs pierced the puckered flesh of her areola and lights flashed behind Vivian's eyes. She lifted her hips and came down hard upon him, taking his entire length deep inside with one powerful thrust that had her screaming his name as climax tore through her. His hips pumped fiercely, his mouth clamped around her nipple. His groan vibrated through her flesh as she felt a wash of heat inside her.

She collapsed on top of him.

A few moments later he ceased the delicious tugging of his mouth around her nipple and swept his tongue over it before releasing her breast all together.

Vivian lay beside him as her breathing returned to normal, trying to contain the maelstrom of emotions swirling inside her. If anything she was even more confused than she had been before coming to him. And yet, some things seemed so perfectly clear in her mind.

Either she was falling in love with this man, or she was losing her mind. Perhaps both.

Gentle fingers brushed her cheek and she squeezed her eyes shut to keep tears from falling. They scorched her eyes, pooled around her lashes.

"You're perfect," he whispered, his breath warm against her ear. "Perfect to me."

Oh, God.

Pushing him away, Vivian jumped off the bed and grabbed her discarded clothes. She didn't know if she got all the items—she didn't care. Temple didn't speak, didn't try to stop her, but she could feel his confused gaze on her. She ran out of the room, naked with the bundle in her arms, and she didn't look back. She couldn't.

If she looked back, she'd see Temple, and if he looked at her with even the barest hint of caring, she'd run to his arms and beg him to keep her with him always.

Right now she needed to run away rather than toward. She needed to be by herself, stand on her own and follow her own council rather than Rupert's or Temple's. Because she was going to have to choose between them. It was a choice that might end up costing them all very dearly. A choice, she feared she had already made.

Forget kindness. Forget equality. Temple treated her like something no one else ever had.

A woman.

Having spent the rest of the evening in the library researching what Temple had told them about Vivian, Marcus stumbled to his bedchamber a few hours before dawn. He was exhausted.

And he had to be delusional, because as he reached the top of the stairs, he thought he caught a glimpse of a woman ducking into a room down the opposite hall, and she was naked.

He shook his head. That couldn't have been Vivian, was it? Surely his eyes were playing tricks on him.

All thoughts of Vivian and what she might or might not be, clothed or unclothed, fled his mind as he entered his room and discovered that he had company. He was even more surprised by just who that company was.

Shannon, the feisty maid, stood beside his bed in nothing but a plain linen nightgown that grazed the tips of her breasts and the round curve of her hips in a most tantalizing manner.

He didn't speak and neither did she. They simply came together in a fierce embrace and fell together onto the mattress, tearing at each other's clothing in a fever to press skin to skin.

And Marcus discovered that he wasn't that exhausted after all.

"We cannot meet again," Rupert told the woman in bed beside him. "It's too dangerous. You will have to bathe before returning to the island, or Temple will smell me on you."

His lover stretched languidly, not at all concerned by the potential danger. Hubris was an awful thing. He had seen it happen to better people—with ruinous results. He would not allow her pride to destroy all he had worked for.

"Do not worry yourself," she cajoled. "I have fresh clothes at the inn and I will bathe before I return. Temple will suspect nothing."

"You underestimate him. Don't."

She didn't like his tone, judging from the mulish set of her jaw; the gleam of maliciousness in her pretty eyes. "And you overestimated your precious Vivian. She was in his bed that first night, did you know that?"

Rupert looked away. It didn't matter that Vivian

had given herself to the vampire. Her maiden-
head was not why he had taken her in and kept
her close all these years. Thanks to Temple, Vivian
would enjoy her first time in his bed more now
than she would have as a virgin. And that was
a good thing for both of them. Given her importance in his plan, he only wanted her happy.

"Is she in love with him, do you think?" He
made his voice drip with disinterest. "It would be
most inconvenient." He liked to think his little pet
smarter than that, but he had made the mistake of
sheltering her for the last few years.

"I think he has deeper feelings for her than she
for him, though he won't admit it."

"Good." His sweet protégé was every bit the
distraction he knew she would be. Temple would
be captivated by her looks and form, he would
sense what she was. He would be drawn to
that. No doubt the vampire was driving himself
mad trying to suss out just what the Order had
planned.

"Are you certain of Vivian's loyalty to you?" his
lover asked.

Rupert smiled bitterly. Jealousy was so unbe-
coming in a woman. "I am more certain of hers
than I am of yours."

Twin blossoms of crimson stood out on her fair
cheeks. Delicate nostrils flared. Ah, anger. That
was much more flattering to her. "Then you are
a fool," she snarled. "She's already encountered

Marcus Grey and agreed to meet with the vampires. How long will it take for them to turn her mind against you?"

"Vivian adores me." He said it as much for himself as for her. "She will not be so easily swayed."

"Not even when she discovers that you plan to kill them all? What will she think of what you have planned for her?"

He knew it had been a mistake to share his plan with her. Normally he knew better. No one but his most trusted allies knew the extent of what was going to happen in the warehouse he'd secured for the ritual. By the time it was over he would be a god, with the power of Lilith at his fingertips.

"No woman would turn down what I offer Vivian." That wasn't hubris on his own part, it was certainty. "Would you?"

She glanced away and everything became crystal clear. "Ah, that is your complaint." He chuckled. "You are jealous of my Vivian."

She turned on him with the ferocity of a jungle cat. "I am not jealous! I am enraged! How can you choose that thing over me?"

He slapped her—hard. Her head snapped back against the pillow, and he positioned his body over hers before she could retaliate. "She is a creature of a higher plane than you or I and she deserves your respect."

She glared at him, her cheek burnished and hot where his palm had struck. Her lovely breasts quivered as she shook with rage, their tight little ginger-hued nipples brushing against his chest. Her thighs were tight beneath him, trying to keep him out.

Rupert smiled. He liked making her realize how much she wanted him. It made him think of Violet, and what he'd do to her if only he had the chance. He'd make her want him, make her scream it.

He pushed between those rigid thighs, shoving his hard cock into her waiting wetness even as she fought beneath him. "Go ahead and fight," he told her. "Your soaked twat tells me how much you want me."

She cried out as he thrust deep, rolling her head against the pillow in pleasure. His sweet little Kimberly Cooper-Brown liked it as rough as he did. Nails scored his back as he moved inside her. Parted lips begged for him to bite her, and he did. Not hard enough to draw blood, but enough to make her shove herself into his thrusts like the most seasoned whore. He'd never had a lover as enthusiastic and as tuned to his needs as she.

It really would be a shame if he had to kill her.

Chapter 14

The night was empty without Vivian in it. That was the last thought that came to Temple when he fell asleep just after dawn, and the first thought when he woke as sunset approached later that day.

He had wanted to chase her when she ran from him the night before. Wanted to bring her back to his bed and hold her until sleep claimed them both. He wanted to wake up beside her and see her smile with slumber still clouding her eyes.

Why? What was it about her that drew him? It wasn't her blood, as he first thought. It wasn't what she was, it was who she was. He respected her determination and strength. There was a vulnerability about her that made him want to protect her from the world. And when she gave her heart, she would be as fierce as any lioness. He wanted her fierceness. He wanted her tenderness. He wanted everything she cared to give him, any little scrap of feeling.

She terrified him, and even though his head knew he should stay away, his heart refused to believe that she was any danger to him.

He had planned to use her to lure Villiers in, use her as a bargaining tool—threaten her if he had to. But he couldn't do that now. Vivian had been used enough for one lifetime.

He would face Villiers without using her as a shield. And now that the others had joined him, there was no need to put it off any longer.

It was that realization that drove him to action. He rose from bed, washed, and dressed in a simple pair of trousers and a fresh white shirt that he left open at the throat. There was no need to be a fashion plate here.

His hair was still damp when he went in search of Vivian. He had an idea of where to find her. She'd begun researching Lilith on her own after spending time with the women of the school. Out of curiosity about the sisterhood, or because she wanted to know more about him? It shouldn't matter, but it did.

Maybe, a dark voice in his head suggested, she was digging up what she could to assist Villiers.

Temple decided not to listen to his head anymore.

He found her in the library, sitting at one of the large tables usually filled with young ladies doing their schoolwork. She actually looked small sitting there all by herself. She wore clothing similar to his, although he thought she looked far better in it. Her hair, tied back in its usual braid, glowed pure red under the mellow lamplight.

"You should have more light," he admonished. "You'll strain your eyes reading like that."

Her head jerked up and a blush suffused her cheeks at the sight of him. She hadn't heard him enter the room. No doubt she would chastise herself for that, even though he could sneak up on a cat.

Was the memory of their coupling as fresh in her mind as his? Her scent called to him, made him want to bury his face in the hollow of her neck and breath her deep inside.

Drink her deep inside.

When she said nothing, he nodded toward the large tome open before her. "Good book?"

"It's the Bible," she replied as though that were answer enough.

He chuckled as he moved closer. "I'm going to take that as a no."

"There's hardly any mention of Lilith at all." Her scowl would have intimidated most men. Temple found it charming.

"That's because you're reading the wrong one. The English versions rarely ever discuss her. You need something older."

She glanced at the shelves where holy texts in different languages and from different religions were housed. "I can't read those."

"I can. Some of them at any rate."

She met his gaze, surprise widening her eyes. "Are you offering to help me?"

He nodded. "I am."

"Why?" Her eyes narrowed now, suspiciously so. "What are you about, vampire?"

He loved it when she called him that. It was like a special name she had for him, and even though she meant it to be impersonal, it wasn't. He knew it even if she didn't.

Temple sat on the table and swung himself over so that he sat facing her, his legs hanging over the side. "There's something I want to talk to you about."

She glanced away. "If it's about me leaving you last night—"

He cut her off. "That's not it."

Her head tilted at the serious note in his voice. Then she closed the large, dusty Bible and pushed it aside so that she could climb up beside him, sitting so that they were thigh to thigh, hip to hip. Shoulder to shoulder.

"Talk," she commanded.

It took all of his strength not to reach over and wrap his fingers around hers, hold her hand as they talked. He wanted so much to be at ease with her—to offer up his trust without wondering if he had hers.

What the hell had he gotten himself into?

"You know the story of how I became a vampire?"

She nodded, her gaze lifting to his. "You found the Blood Grail and drank from it."

"That's part of it. The Grail was made from silver—silver imbued with the essence of Lilith."

"Her lover Sammael cursed her into the silver for revealing his plan to destroy humanity to God."

Temple smiled. "That's the Sunday sermon version, yes. Sammael cursed her to be passed from man to man as he thought she deserved. Eventually that silver found its way into the hands of Judas Iscariot."

Her dark brows arched. "Are you saying that Judas was a vampire?"

He shrugged. "I have no idea what he was. I've never met him, so I cannot say."

Now she looked downright astounded. "He's still alive?"

"I've heard rumors," he replied with a smile.

He let her mind move past that before continuing, "Somewhere along the line the silver was forged into a chalice. The Knights Templar appointed themselves the protector of this cup, wanting to prevent it from falling into hands that might abuse the power it contained. Some of them even drank from it to ensure their ability to protect it."

"They weren't afraid of becoming vampires?"

He flashed an indulgent smile. "Not all vampires are evil, Vivian."

She scowled, indignation coloring her cheeks. "I know that. I thought perhaps men of God, however, might see it differently."

"Without Lilith no one would have known what the angels had planned. There might not have been a Fall. There are those who credit her with Lucifer's expulsion from the Kingdom."

"No wonder no one writes about her." She rolled her eyes. "Heaven forbid a strong woman appear in the Bible who didn't lead to the downfall of man."

He smiled at the sardonic lilt of her voice. "I expect she's been written out because her story makes it much more difficult to call all angels good and demons evil. Regardless, she's been imprisoned in that cup for centuries."

"But you melted the cup down into amulets?" She looked aghast. "That wouldn't hurt her, would it?"

"I doubt it. It's her soul in there, not her physical being." From his pocket he withdrew one of the amulets and held it by its cord, extending it toward her. "Take it."

She was hesitant, but she reached across and took the silver from him.

Wonder lit her face. "It feels warm." She laughed shakily. "Alive."

His suspicions were right. It came as no surprise. He took her hand. "Come with me."

Holding the amulet—and his hand, she hopped

off the table with him and let him lead her from the room, into the main body of the house.

"Where are we going?" she asked as he led her upstairs.

"Brownie's room," he replied. He hoped his friend didn't mind the intrusion, but she had been so scarce of late he'd be surprised if she was there. Odd behavior for a woman who normally would have been waiting on vampires hand and foot, but perhaps she wanted to give them time alone to make their plans and reunite. "There's something there I want you to see."

He kept his grip on her fingers as he opened the bedroom door and pulled her inside. Vivian's hand in his own felt natural, as though their fingers were meant to entwine. He fought the urge to tighten his grip, he was so afraid she might try to pull free once she saw what he wanted to show her.

"You wanted to know why the women here treated you so oddly at first." He put her in front of the ancient painting of Lilith. "This is why."

Perplexed, Vivian turned from him to study the art. Her eyes narrowed, then widened as her lips parted in a silent gasp. "She . . . she looks like me."

"Something else that isn't in the books you've been reading." He angled his body to face her, and her gaze flickered between him and the painting in a manner that damn near broke his heart. She was so confused, poor thing. "Some claim God banished the children Lilith had with both Sammael and Adam to punish them, but I think it was a way of protecting them—of replacing the angels he could no longer trust on earth.

"The children of Sammael went on to become vampires. The children of Adam were sent to their own world, but like the angels, they were enamored of humans, and some consorted with the people of a land that would become known as Ireland. They dipped into England, Scotland, and Wales as well, but that's not the point. Where is your mother's family from, Vivian?"

She blinked at him. "Ireland. Around Kilkenny I believe." Then a bark of laughter burst forth from her. "Are you saying I'm part . . . faerie?"

Temple didn't laugh. "I'm saying that you're a descendent of Lilith."

All of Vivian's humor faded as she stared at him. Her cheeks were pale, her eyes large in the starkness of her face. "My God, you're serious."

She tried to pull away, but he wouldn't let her. He reached down and grabbed her other hand as well, forcing her to face him. He could only imagine how difficult this was for her—how fantastic—but she needed to hear. She needed to know the truth.

"Some of Lilith's descendents, especially women, exhibit certain traits."

Her attention engaged, Vivian relaxed, stopped pulling at her hands. "Like what?" she asked warily.

Temple smiled at her. "Hair an impossible shade of red. Eyes that shift color like the raging sea, and strength, speed, and agility beyond normal human ability." He shook her hands when she dropped her head. "You're not a freak, Vivian. You're the child of a goddess."

"Oh, my God." She pulled at him again, but this time it was because her knees were buckling. "This can't be happening."

"It is." Temple released her hands to slide his arms around her, pulling her close and taking her full weight against him. "I know it's hard to accept, but it's true."

Dazed eyes lifted to his. "Why are you telling me this? Why didn't you tell me sooner?"

"I'm telling you now because you deserve to know. I didn't say anything before because I wasn't certain how much you knew."

"How much I knew?" She pushed at him but he didn't let her go. "How could I know . . . oh, hell. Rupert. He knows, doesn't he?"

He wanted to make Villiers as much of a villain as possible, but he wouldn't lie to do it. "I think it's why he 'rescued' you in the first place."

It cut to see pain wash over her face. All these years she believed Villiers loved her like a daughter and now she was faced with the possibility that she had been little more than a part of his plans and schemes all along.

"How did you know?" she asked weakly.

"I suspected something was different about you when I bit you. Your blood is different from human blood. The painting and Brownie's reaction to you solidified my suspicions."

"How is my blood different?"

He smiled. "I feel connected to you. After I taste you I feel as though I could do anything."

Her lovely lips curved slightly, and some of the color had returned to her cheeks. "You can do anything."

"But you make me want to."

He saw the surprise and pleasure on her face and he kissed her then, before she could turn away to try to hide it from him. She relaxed in his arms, opening her mouth and letting his tongue inside to rub against her own. Kissing her was like kissing heaven—or the sun. So incredibly wonderful that it was almost awful in its sweetness.

Temple pulled away. He didn't want to, but he had to. There was more to say. He ran his hands along her back, tugged gently on the fat braid that lay in the slight dip of her spine.

"I've told you all of this so you know how important you are, Vivian." As much as he wanted to continue to hold her, he let her go instead. Her attraction to him could not cloud her judgment right now. He had to allow her to do this on her own. "I'm convinced that Rupert wants you for whatever nastiness he has planned, and I'll do anything I have to in order to stop that from happening."

"Even kill me?" She folded her arms across her chest and regarded him openly. She wasn't judging him, she simply wanted to know where she stood.

It felt like a knife in the heart, but he nodded. He'd killed before, but the idea of spilling Vivian's blood, of having to destroy her . . . "If I had to, I'd kill you. I'd kill myself to keep Villiers from using you."

Her expression softened and he knew his mistake then. He might as well have come out and tell her he'd die to protect her.

He would.

"You need to decide what side you're on," he told her gruffly, backing up a step. "That's not a threat, it's just advice. You need to take a side and go to it, because when the time comes that Villiers and I meet, one of us is not going to survive it."

She shook her head. "I don't want either of you to die."

"You can't stop it." He gave her a rueful smile before turning to go. "You simply have to decide who you want to fight for when the time comes."

Then he left the room, because he didn't want know if she wasn't going to fight for him.

* * *

"How long have you known?" Vivian set down her glass of whiskey long enough to ask the question to the table of women.

Guilty looks passed around those seated at the scarred but sturdy structure.

"Since ye came here," Shannon admitted. "We all knew just from the look of you that you were touched by the goddess."

Vivian might have rolled her eyes if she wasn't certain to offend with the action. "But none of you said anything. Why?"

Shannon looked away, but Agnes finally said, "The missus told us not to."

One of the older women gave the young maid a swat for tattling, but Vivian was grateful for the honesty. "What would be the harm in me knowing?"

"Beg your pardon, Miss Vivian," Shannon said, finding her voice once more, "But there's not many who'd believe they were descended from the first wife of Adam. I suppose the missus thought you'd think us daft."

Daft. Most likely she would have. "And that's why you all treated me strangely."

"Strangely?" Agnes echoed. "Why, I didn't know if I'd be able to speak to you!"

The women all laughed and looked upon Vivian kindly when she didn't join in the revelry.

Shannon reached over and took Vivian's hand in her own, strong, slightly calloused one. "You're somethin' special to us, Miss Vivian. Don't mistake our reverence for anything else."

"I don't want your reverence." She softened the announcement by squeezing her friend's fingers. "I thought you were my friends."

"We are!" Colleen, one of the older women, insisted. "Don't you think for a minute we're not, young miss."

And that's when Vivian knew that she had been accepted for who she was—because an old woman scolded her rather than treat her like her superior. It brought tears to her eyes—and the whiskey she'd consumed allowed them to fall.

"You've all made me feel so accepted." She sniffed. "Thank you."

They crowded around her, taking turns giving her hugs and kisses on the brow and cheeks. Never mind that Rupert had taken her in. These women felt more like family than anything or anyone else.

Well, except for Temple. It was odd how much she'd come to expect him in her life—how much she wanted him there.

"What's going on?" came a voice from the stairs. It was Kimberly, and she was watching them with an expression that didn't seem to know if it should be amused or concerned.

The maids pulled away from her, letting Vivian face her hostess. She wiped her eyes with the backs of her hands. "Temple told me about Lilith, about what he thinks I am. The ladies here were lending their collective shoulders."

The older woman's jaw dropped, but only for a second, before she totally regained her composure. She stood on the stairs, gripping the banister, and though her knuckles were a little white, everything else about her was perfectly poised. "I see. I confess I am a little surprised that he took that chance before you had the opportunity to learn more on your own, but Temple knows what is best."

Vivian frowned. There was nothing wrong with what Kimberly said, but it struck her as wrong in some way. Insincere, perhaps? That had to be the whiskey making her overly suspicious.

Before she could ask the other woman any questions, however, the doorbell echoed above them.

Kimberly's fair brow furrowed. "Who the devil could that be at such an hour?" Clutching her skirts, she made to return up the stairs.

Vivian rose to her feet. "I'll go." All of Temple's companions were there, so there was a strong chance that whoever it was might not be friendly. If that were the case, then Vivian was the only one who could defend herself.

Kimberly nodded. "All right, but I'm coming with you."

There was no arguing with the woman who ran the place, so Vivian took the stairs two at a time and put herself as far ahead of Kimberly as she could. She ran across the great hall, her boot heels clacking loudly and pulled open the door before Kimberly made it to the top of the stairs.

Standing on the step were a man and a woman, both of whom were handsome and pleasant of face. He was tall with sandy hair and eyes that shone like bronze in the light. She was tall as well, though not as tall as Vivian, with dark brown hair that was perfectly styled beneath a fashionable little hat, and almond-shaped hazel eyes.

"Can I help you?" Vivian asked, feeling too large, and too extraordinary at that moment with her 'impossible' hair and trousers.

Neither the man nor woman seemed the least bit startled by her appearance. "I'm looking for Mr. Temple," the man said in an accent that for some reason made her think of knights on horseback and ladies in towers.

"Mr. Temple?" Vivian folded her arms across her chest and rose to her full height—which made her just a little shorter than this man. "And who might you be?"

He grinned, making his handsome face even handsomer. He was a pretty one, this. Charming too. "I am Payen Carr, and this is my wife, Violet."

The room spun for a moment as Vivian collected herself. Violet?

"You wouldn't happen to have been Miss Wynston-Jones before your marriage, would you?" she asked hoarsely.

The smaller woman regarded her as one might any new acquaintance. "Oh dear, does my reputation precede me?" She laughed, but there was an edge to it. She was prepared to think of Vivian as a threat if necessary.

"Come in," Vivian said, stepping aside, her legs numb. "Temple and the others are in the parlor, I imagine."

Kimberly stood a few feet away watching them with a peculiar expression. "Is everything all right?" she asked.

Vivian nodded. "Temple is expecting Mr. and Mrs. Carr I believe." Was it her imagination or did Kimberly turn a little white at the mention of their names?

"This way," she said to them, and led them through the house to the room Temple had set up as a gathering place for himself and his fellow vampires. Her legs weren't steady, but they kept her upright. If this was the same Violet who Rupert had wanted to marry, then she had to be a vampire, because she didn't look a day over five and twenty. That meant her husband was undoubtedly vampire as well.

All these vampires were starting to make Vivian uneasy, especially now that she knew her blood was special. She wanted to trust them, but she'd be an idiot not to at least consider what a delicacy she'd be for them.

They reached the door of the parlor. Vivian

knocked and Temple called for her to enter. When she did, she found him sitting with the priest, Marcus, and the others. They all looked up at her entrance.

"Payen and Violet Carr," she announced, feeling like a housekeeper.

Temple came forward, and shook hands with both of them. "Thank you for coming." Then he made introductions. When he got to her, he said, "I see you've already met Vivian."

That's when Violet turned on her with narrowed eyes. "Vivien? Vivien Barker?"

Vivian nodded. "Yes."

And then she was on her back with a frenzied vampire on top of her. A vampire whose fangs were about to rip out her throat.

Chapter 15

It took both Temple and Payen to tear Violet off of Vivian. As it was, Vivian had a bite wound on her neck and Violet's nose was bleeding from where Vivian had punched her in defense. She'd been lucky to land that against a vampire intent on ripping out her throat.

"Let me kill her!" Violet struggled against her husband's hold. "If I kill her Villiers has nothing."

Vivian allowed Temple to lick the bite so it would close. Normally she wouldn't, but she still had a bruise on her forehead, a slight limp, and little welts on her fingers from falling in the pit. She'd be damned if she'd walk around with a gouge taken out of her throat as well. But why did he have to make it seem like such a tender, possessive gesture when all he did was close a wound? It felt as though he was branding her in front of the other vampires, claiming her as his own.

"No one is going to kill Vivian," Temple announced in a tone that brooked no refusal.

"Unless it's you, right?" Vivian whispered with a brittle chuckle. Their gazes locked and she shook her head at him. She didn't need him to defend her, and she certainly didn't want to be a reason for discontent between him and his friends.

Payen was a tad more restrained than his wife. "I take that Miss Barker is here because she's on our side?"

Vivian met his gaze. "I'm here because I want to be." It might not be a direct yes or no, but it was all he was going to get.

Payen smiled at her. "Please excuse Violet. She's had twenty years to work up a hatred for Rupert Villiers." He let go of his wife's shoulders.

The two women watched each other warily, but Vivian relaxed a little when the vampire made no move to attack. She was surprised when she turned, however, to find Temple's friends gathered behind her. They were showing their support. No wonder Violet had backed down. The sight of them brought a hard lump to her throat.

Perhaps Temple had claimed her after all.

Bolstered by this, and a little disconcerted, Vivian looked at the new arrivals. "I know nothing of your history with Rupert, but I would like to hear it."

"We all would," Temple added. He made no

move to touch her, yet she felt his presence behind her as surely as if he'd put his hands on her shoulders. "Why don't we sit and try to do this in a civilized manner?"

They did sit—Vivian on one side of the room and Violet on the other with her husband. And this time, Vivian was careful to sit closer to Temple than Marcus, although not too close. If Temple had announced ownership of her, she didn't want him to think she was necessarily all right with that.

Temple and the others told the newcomers everything they could about their own experiences with the Order of the Silver Palm. Vivian even told about Villiers taking her in, although she left out the part about the freak show. They didn't need to know that humiliating aspect of her life. And if Violet Carr mocked her, Vivian would find a way to make the female vampire eat silver.

When they were done catching the new arrivals up on old news, it was time for Payen to add his own story. He did so without much prompting.

"I was in hiding when the six of you found the Blood Grail," he told them. "Not hiding from the king or his men, but from the sunlight." He shook his head. "It should have been better secured."

Saint actually smiled at him. "It was very well secured, but I was always very good with locks."

Even Bishop smiled at that. It seemed the stress between the two of them had eased somewhat.

Payen smiled as well, before continuing. "In my

day, we protected the Blood Grail from a small splinter group of the Templars called the Order of the Silver Palm. They were thus named for the silver that crossed the palm of Judas. They had the Grail for a brief time, using it to cause all sorts of havoc."

Vivian could only imagine what they did—no doubt they turned themselves into vampires. It was a wonder that none of them had ever turned up on Rupert's doorstep.

"Twenty years ago I discovered that Violet was engaged to marry a man who belonged to this Order." He turned his attention to Vivian. "It was Rupert Villiers. He claimed to know nothing about the Order at the time."

Vivian arched a brow. "But?"

There was no humor in that pretty face now. "But Villiers discovered what I was, what I am. He did some research, spoke to the right people, and suddenly he was important to the Order."

"He tried to kill Payen," Violet spat out angrily.

Payen took her hand in his. "He almost did kill you."

No wonder Violet hated Rupert so much. No wonder she wanted to kill Vivian for being associated with him. And she didn't doubt for a moment that the story they told was true. No one could falsify the kind of anger that radiated from Violet Carr's entire being. It was sweet, in a way.

She hated Rupert more for what he had tried to do to her husband than for what he had done to her.

Would Vivian feel that way someday? Would she despise the man who had been like a father to her for all he'd done to Temple? What he had supposedly done to all of these vampires?

A part of her already did. The revelation surprised her. It hurt as well. It seemed as though she had begun to turn on Rupert with surprising ease, but she realized it had been coming for some time—ever since she realized that he didn't trust her enough to tell her everything.

If she'd been smart she would have left when she began to have misgivings, but he was all she had, and so she stayed, giving him her loyalty. The idea of him plotting to use her all these years sickened her. The thought of him never thinking of her as anything more than a means to an end broke her heart.

"Any idea what Villiers is up to now?" Reign asked, breaking the silence. He had his arm around Olivia, who looked stronger than she had since her arrival.

Payen gave a brusque nod. "I'm ashamed to admit that we haven't been able to find Villiers for years, not until recently, but in that time I did some research of my own, and kept my ears open for any talk of Order activity. I've heard about the recent brushes the lot of you have had with the Order. I'm sorry for them."

Temple nodded and the others voiced their thanks. "What did you uncover?"

Payen continued, "I've since learned that there might have been an ancient link between the Order and followers of Sammael, but there's no one who can verify that now. However, the Order did have many legends as to how to break the curse to harness the power of Lilith herself."

Silence fell over the room.

"You think Villiers wants to resurrect Lilith?" Incredulity rang in Bishop's voice. "Is that possible?"

"Theoretically, yes," Payen replied. "Realistically, I'm not certain. The ritual I've heard of calls for the heart of a nosferatu."

Bishop and Marika exchanged a glance. "The Order set a nosferatu on us in Romania," Bishop said. "They were making them on purpose."

"It also calls for the wombs of prostitutes, which I believe they obtained recently in London?" The question was directed at Saint, who nodded grimly as he put a supportive arm around his wife's shoulders. Vivian's heart pinched; she had been friends with several of the girls killed by the Order.

Payen continued, "They need the Grail itself, which is why I suspect they went after you in the first place, Temple."

Temple nodded. "I melted the cup down and sent it to the others in the form of amulets. I'd heard rumors that people were asking after the Grail—and me. I figured it was just a matter of time."

Vivian's eyes widened in surprise that he'd had the forethought to do that. And Rupert always said that vampires weren't very intelligent.

"But if they only wanted the Grail, why take such efforts to capture each of us?" Chapel asked. "Do they know what Temple did with the chalice?"

If possible, Payen's expression turned even more grim. "One of the final ingredients in the ritual is the blood of first generation vampires. You drank from the Grail the same as I did. You are but one step away from Lilith herself."

A chill lanced Vivian's heart. Temple's blood. That's what Villiers wanted?

There were a few murmurs amongst the others, but Temple held up his hand. "You said our blood was *one* of the final ingredients. Is there another?"

"Yes." This time Payen's topaz gaze fell on Vivian herself. "It requires one of Lilith's natural bloodline. I'm sorry Miss Barker, but we've been looking for you for some time as well—that was why Violet tried to kill you."

The chill in Vivian's chest worsened as the handsome vampire continued, "You're the key to everything the Order has planned."

* * *

"Are you all right?" It felt trite to ask, but Temple didn't like the strain around Vivian's eyes and mouth. They were finally alone, the others having retired or gone in search of blood. Payen and Violet had gone to the mainland to search for signs of Villiers, after Vivian revealed he'd planned to set up base there. She hadn't been able to tell much else, but Temple had been surprised she revealed that much. Could it be that she was finally seeing the truth?

She nodded, sipping at the glass of whiskey he'd poured for her. "I'll be certain not to turn my back on Violet any time soon."

He smiled, deciding not to mention that he hadn't meant physically. "Well, she did try to kill you."

"And Rupert." Payen's wife had recounted to them how close she had come to putting an end to all of this.

Temple's smile faded. "She fears for her husband. She'd do anything to protect him, even kill."

Vivian walked over to the desk, trailed her fingers over the glossy surface. "I envy them that."

So did he, but that wasn't a conversation for the two of them to have. "Would you mourn Villiers had she succeeded?"

She didn't seem the least bit surprised by the question. Her head tilted in contemplation. "I would mourn the man I knew. The man I thought he was."

"I understand." And he did. After Lucinda's death he had missed terribly the woman she had been, but he was glad the monster she had become was dead.

She turned to him, rolling the glass between her palms. She watched it rather than him. "It's very difficult for me to accept the truth. I don't want to believe that he never cared for me."

That she admitted that vulnerability to him was a huge show of trust for her, and he knew it. Temple went to her. He took the whiskey from her and set it on the desk. When he slipped his arms around her waist, her hands settled on his biceps.

God, he loved her touch.

"He cared for you," he insisted. If it was a lie, what difference did it make? Would it harm her to think that someone in her life had at least a modicum of affection for her? "I care for you. That's why I think you should leave."

She pushed out of his arms. "You want me to run?"

He nodded, didn't reach for her again though he wanted to. "You're in too much danger. If you are the key to what Villiers has planned, the farther away you are the better." But Christ, the idea of her out there on her own terrified him, almost as much as the thought of what Villiers had in store for her.

She frowned. "You're scared."

Another nod. It wasn't hard for him to admit this, not if it saved her life. "I am."

"I don't believe it. You're not afraid of anything."

"I'm afraid of you." That was something he couldn't take back now that it was out there.

Vivian stepped closer, lifting her head so that when she pressed her face to his, they were cheek to cheek, her mouth close to his ear. "You scare me too," she whispered. "You make me feel special. I want to trust you with everything and yet I'm terrified of what will happen if I do."

Temple closed his eyes as a shudder raced through him. How she killed him with her simple honesty. Thrilled him with her sincerity. He pulled her tight against him, and kissed her, licking sweet whiskey from her lips, tasting it on her tongue. They broke apart long enough for shirts to be pulled over heads and discarded, and then came together once more.

Her hands stroked his bare back, up his neck, into his hair. He wanted to arch into her touch like a house cat. Christ, he'd purr if he could.

Her hips were flush against his and he held them there so she could feel his hardness, so he could feel her softness. A little sigh escaped her lips as he rubbed against her. He was hard already, eager for the hot, moist embrace of her sex. She made him feel like he was a boy again, like

this was some grand adventure he had never em-
barked upon before.

He slid his hands up the curve of her full hips,
to the dip of her waist, and around to her front to
pop the hooks of her corset, one by one, until the
stiff garment fell off her shoulders and the heavy
weight of her breasts rested against his chest. She
lowered her arms so the corset fell to the floor,
and then arched her back, until her lips pulled
free of his. She leaned back in his arms, knowing
he would support her weight, the posture bringing her beautiful bosom upward, a slight invitation for his mouth to sample them at his leisure.

So honest in her desires and needs. She brought
him to his knees with her unabashed sexuality. It
was just for him, only him. Yes, her blood called
to him, and yes she was just as drawn to him, but
this had nothing to do with blood and everything
to do with plain and simple need.

Temple lowered his head, taking a nipple into
his mouth and sucking it gently. Vivian sighed
and squirmed in his arms. He smiled against
her silken flesh, sucking harder as he knew she
wanted. Then he turned his attention to her other
breast, giving it the same attention before literally
dropping to his knees before her.

He unfastened her trousers with trembling fingers. *Trembling*. As he pulled the worn wool down
over her hips, he pressed his lips to the soft flesh

of her belly, swirled his tongue in the shallow indent of her navel. She shivered and he rubbed his cheek against the slight jut of her hip bone as he cupped the cheeks of her sweet, plump arse. Then down his fingers slid, down the back of her round thighs, to tug her trousers over the strong curve of her calves. The fabric caught around her boots and he pulled those off as well, finally stripping her completely and leaving her naked and gorgeous before him.

He rose to his feet, put a hand on either side of her waist and lifted her onto the desk so that her bottom rested right on the edge, taking her mouth again, ruthlessly plundering with his tongue as he was lowering her onto the smooth oak. Her legs came up to wrap around his waist, pressing the damp heat of her against his abdomen. He could smell the sweet musk of her arousal and his gums tightened in response. His whole body tightened.

His mouth traveled down her body again, savoring every inch of her pale skin, every sweet lick. Delicate veins pulsed just beneath the surface, warm and flush with desire-quickened blood. Temple's mouth watered for her in more ways than one.

Down he slid, until his mouth hovered above the dark red curls that framed a slit of glistening pink flesh. She was plump and swollen with need, and when he pulled her thighs apart, lifting them so that they rested on his shoulders, she arched her hips in invitation.

"Tell me what you want," he demanded silkily, trailing the tip of his finger along the soaked cleft, feeling her shiver in response. He wasn't trembling like a boy anymore. He was as brash and confident as a god, stuffed with pride knowing that this amazing woman was his for the taking.

"Your mouth." It came out breathy, like a pant.

He planted a chaste kiss at the top of her mons. "Like that?"

Vivian groaned in frustration and he grinned as she grabbed at his hair, trying to shove his face deeper between her thighs.

"Do you want me to lick you, Vivian?" He ran his tongue over her, drawing a shuddering moan in response. "Do you want me to eat you?"

"Yes." Her hips arched again. "Please, Temple. Lick me. Eat me."

There wasn't a man immortal or otherwise who could resist a plea like that.

He filled her with his tongue, using it on her like he was going to eventually use his aching cock, and then moved upward to search between the slick folds for the little knot of flesh that he knew quivered for his attention. When he found it, Vivian's hips lifted off the desk and her heels dug into his back as she cried out in tormented pleasure.

He teased her, bringing her to the brink and backing off again and again until she was practically begging for release. Then, lifting his gaze so he could watch her, he began stroking her with his tongue once more. This time, there would be no retreat.

She was up on one elbow, her other hand cupping his head, pushing him deeper into her wetness. Her face was flushed, contorted with bliss. Her glazed gaze met his, and he knew from the surprise that passed over her features that looking at him, seeing what he was doing to her was going to send her over the edge. He licked harder and was rewarded with a flood of hot wetness as she arched and came, crying out his name.

Her release almost sent him off as well. His cock throbbed and strained against the front of his trousers, demanding for its own release. As Vivian fell back against the desk, gasping for breath as her thighs quivered and twitched, Temple straightened.

He ran a hand over his face, wiping away her juices, and when he saw her watching him, he made a great, slow show of licking the wetness from his fingers. She visibly shivered in response.

Had there ever been a woman so affected by him? A woman who affected him so deeply? He didn't think so. Not even Lucinda seemed to react to his touch as Vivian did, and he certainly didn't remember craving Lucinda like he craved blood or air. Not like he craved Vivian. Right now, his head and senses full of her, he was certain that she was as necessary to his survival as darkness itself. As necessary as the very life he drank to survive.

He unfastened his trousers and kicked them off along with his boots. He wanted to be as naked as she was, nothing between them that might prevent every inch of their flesh from touching if it so wanted.

Then he took his straining erection in hand and led the moist head to the tight, slick cove between Vivian's thighs. There was little resistance as he slowly eased himself inside her—only the natural spreading of her body to accept his.

So tight. So hot. So wet. He ground his teeth as he slid fully inside. She was a glove around him, a vice designed to rob him of reason.

Temple moved slowly, easing in and out of her with agonizing strokes. He didn't want to come too fast. He wanted to savor this. Savor her. Inside Vivian nothing else mattered. Villiers himself could barge through the door in a hail of silver bullets and Temple wouldn't stop making love to Vivian.

Making love. Christ, he thought that term was only for poets or virgins. He pushed the thought away. Thinking was something he shouldn't be doing right now. He was doing something wrong if his mind was actually able to work.

Vivian squeezed his cock with her internal muscles and all thought evaporated. Jaw tight, Temple shoved his hips against her buttocks burying himself to the hilt inside her. Then he withdrew and shoved again. Reaching down he found that little knot between her slick lips again and stroked it with his thumb. She made a little cooing noise in appreciation.

His free hand gripped her thigh, holding it tight against his shoulder as he quickened his thrusts. Pressure built inside his sack, tightening inside him. When Vivian arched and cried out in climax, the tightening let go like a snapping spring and orgasm rocked through him, almost knocking his feet out from underneath him it was so sudden and powerful. He fell onto his hands, braced on either side of her, head bent so low his nose brushed her ribs.

Being a vampire had its advantages, and one of them was having enough strength to carrying Vivian to the sofa when he should have collapsed in a boneless heap. The length of padded velvet wasn't quite long enough for them, but they made it work.

Another advantage was a quick recovery time. It wasn't long before his lower body began thinking he'd like to be inside her again. Vivian felt the stirring against her stomach and smiled at him.

"I feel shameless with you," she confessed. "I

don't think there's anything I wouldn't let you do to me."

Oh God. Was that a groan? "You're the most incredible woman I've ever known."

She blushed a little but didn't look away. "You always ask what I want. What do you want?"

From behind. Standing up. Sideways. Her mouth on him while he licked her. So many things.

"I want you to ride me," he told her. "With your hair down."

Her brows lifted. "That's all?"

He grinned. "For now."

Smiling naughtily, she rose up and reached behind her to gather the thick, braid. Releasing the tie, she untwined the ropes of hair until the mass of incredible waves hung around her pale shoulders like rivers of ruby over delicate alabaster.

Temple sat up as well, taking strands between his fingers. He'd often heard of women's hair described as silk, but Vivian's was more than that. It was as shiny and sleek as satin, so thick and long. It surely had to fall to her waist if not lower.

"Is it heavy?" he asked.

She shrugged. "Not really, but I'm used to it." She swung her leg over his. "Now I have something I want you to do for me."

He would have agreed to anything at that moment, as she took him inside with one easy stroke. "What?"

Vivian began to move. Up and down. Up and down. So slow, so wonderfully slow. "I want you to bite me. I want to feel your fangs inside me like your body is inside me. I want to know that a little of something of me is inside you."

Temple shuddered. The things she said. They were always the right things. His gums tightened and contracted, the muscles there pushing his fangs to full distension with ease.

Vivian bent her neck to the side, giving him full access to the sweet vein that pulsed there. Temple wound her hair around his fist, tangling his fingers in the thick mass as he leaned forward. He bit her gently, in the way he knew would give the most pleasure, with just the right amount of pain. She shivered as the sweet taste of her filled his mouth. As he suckled, her movements quickened, her moans deepened, and closing his eyes Temple drank from her, wishing with all his damnable heart that she was a vampire too so they could share this connection to its fullest.

But he had vowed to never turn another human into a vampire—and even if he hadn't, there was no telling what the change might do to someone of Vivian's blood. No, this was as close to her as he was ever going to get.

And then climax struck once more, and Temple was saved having to think about that awful realization any longer.

* * *

Dawn was a pale shadow across the sky as Marcus stood at the window, naked. Watching the sun come up was nothing new to him, in fact it had become as normal as seeing it set, but it was the first time he'd watched the sun come up in the company of a beautiful girl who made his heart beat all the faster and his breath catch in his throat.

Shannon stood beside him, naked as well. There was something natural and yet arousing about having her strong, lithe body lean so comfortably against his, without shame or unease.

"I'm going to pay for this," she remarked with good humor as Marcus stroked his fingers down her arm. "I'll not be good for anything today."

"I can think of something you're good for," he replied, nibbling on her shoulder.

She laughed and lifted a hand to his hair, ruffling it in such a way that he couldn't help but grin like a giddy idiot. Infatuation was surely God's gift to man for all the other shite he had to put up with.

He pulled her tighter against him, feeling her silken back against his chest, their bodies fitting together like pieces of the same puzzle. He was just about to nuzzle her once more when movement caught his attention out of the corner of his eye.

Curious, he turned his attention to the window, and the figure hurrying away from the building on the grass below.

"Is that Missus Cooper-Brown?" he asked.

Shannon glanced in the same direction. "Oh, aye."

That his lover seemed so nonplussed should have been good enough for Marcus, but it wasn't. "Does she sneak out at dawn very often?"

"No, but it's become a habit as of late. The last six months or so she's been taking trips as well. We all assume there's a man involved. A lady who works as hard as the missus deserves to take a lover."

Marcus admired her loyalty and gave her a quick squeeze for it. "What about a maid who works hard. Does she deserve a lover as well?"

She turned in his arms, rubbing herself against him. "She does," she purred. "The question is, what will the lover do to deserve her?"

He swept her up into his arms, and laughing, carried her to the bed. He joined her on the mattress, tangling his limbs with her own, but before his mind was taken over with thoughts of her lovely body and all the things he wanted to do to it, Marcus couldn't help but wonder where Kimberly Cooper-Brown was off to.

And just who she was meeting.

Chapter 16

Instead of returning to her own room after the "incident" with Temple in the parlor, Vivian went with him to his rooms instead. There were many things she wanted to ask him now that she didn't feel as though the world had been pulled out from under her.

And she didn't want to sleep alone.

She'd never been one to lean on another emotionally, but she found herself doing just that. Temple's strength was a comfort to her, and when she found herself thinking that no one had ever cared about her, that she was somehow lacking as a person, all she had to do was look at Temple and realized that wasn't true.

She felt it in the way he touched her, the way he seemed to worship her body with his own. Every time they came together it was her pleasure that seemed to matter most to him, and he always knew exactly how to please her.

And she knew him well enough to know that

when he was afraid, or when he didn't want to admit to tender feelings, they manifested themselves as anger. When he was angry at her for falling in the pit, it was because she was hurt, even though he knew she'd try to get word to Rupert. She knew this because Agnes told her how he had inquired after her when the maids tended her wounds.

Temple cared for her, and he had given her more honesty than anyone since her mother, even if it wasn't delivered in a totally direct manner.

Her mother had been a good woman, deserving of much more than the man she got. Like Temple she had kept much of her emotions to herself, but she had been loving and openly affectionate with Vivian and her siblings. Now that she thought about it, she thought perhaps her mother had treated her differently than her brothers and sisters. Perhaps her mother had known the truth about her. Perhaps that extra attention had been what finally turned her father against her. He hated anyone being more important than he.

When Vivian heard the news that her father had died, she returned home immediately. Not for her father's funeral, but so she could make certain that he wasn't buried next to her mother. That was her spot. Her father was buried in a simple grave near the back of the cemetery. Villiers had given her the money to buy her mother a new headstone, a pretty one with angels on it.

Now, knowing what she did about her lineage, she knew her mother would probably still be very much alive and healthy had she only known how to swim. Her father said she drowned, and now there was no way to know if that was really what happened or not.

"How could he have been so good to me and so awful to everyone else?" she wondered aloud as she lay awake in the almost pitch blackness of the room.

Temple's arms slid around her, hauling her against his chest. "Because he wanted to keep you with him. He wants your gratitude."

That was the honest answer, she knew that. She appreciated it even, but how she wished it wasn't true. She would have liked him to say that it was because she was the one person Villiers ever truly cared for.

When had she started to think of him as Villiers rather than Rupert?

"What do you want from me?" she asked him, glad that she couldn't see his face. "Don't tell me nothing, because we're both smarter than that."

Was that a chuckle? "More than your gratitude," came the low reply. His lips brushed her temple. How well could he see her when all she could do was feel him? It was an unsettling feeling being at such a disadvantage.

"I don't have much to give." She smiled just in case he could see it. "You already have my body and my blood. I've given you my loyalty, even. What else is there?"

His big hand slid up her ribs to rest just below her left breast. "I want your heart."

Said organ began to pound in a most traitorous fashion. Temple chuckled, his breath hot against her cheek. "See? It wants me as well."

Perhaps she should be embarrassed that he knew what effect he had on her, but she wasn't. She was reasonably certain that she had a similar effect on him. In fact, were he human, she was sure Temple's heart would pound as hard as her own.

"Why? I'm the ward of your enemy. I've held you prisoner. I've pursued you. I've fought you. You have no reason to trust me. Why in the name of all that's holy would you want me?"

His thumb caressed the side of her breast. "I don't know, but I do. I don't mind being your prisoner. I love having you pursue me. I want your trust and to give you mine. I don't think we're supposed to understand these things, Vivian. They just are."

She trailed her fingers down the warm wall of his chest, delighting in the springy hair there. "I'm not going to leave," she told him, holding her breath against the anger she knew was sure to come. "I'd rather fight beside you than run away like a coward."

She sensed his scowl more than she saw it. "I want you safe."

"And you want to prove to me that you're not going to use me. I understand that, Temple. But I'm not going to leave you to face this on your own. You need all the leverage you can get against Rupert, and I'm offering myself as that leverage."

"I can't let you do that."

She smiled gently. "You can't stop me."

He chuckled. "Stubborn wench."

"I think someone is working here at the school who is in league with the Order, or at least with Rupert." How could she have let that slip her mind?

Temple braced himself up on his forearm, suddenly very serious and alert. "How do you know that?"

"When the messenger met me in the woods that day, he told me that all I had to do was leave messages at the foot of the statue of Lilith in the garden, and that messages for me would be there as well. Someone would have to put them there. Someone with access to the grounds."

"Have you checked the statue?"

She shook her head. "No. I couldn't get there after the accident, and then I assumed there wouldn't be anything because I hadn't answered him." Odd, but looking back she had misgivings even then. She had to or she would have made sure she got into that garden and sent word.

"I'm going to check it."

She stopped him with a hand on his shoulder. "It's passed dawn now. You can't."

Temple fell back on the bed with a curse.

"I'll do it," she offered, already slipping from between the warm sheets.

Temple scowled again, but all he said was, "Don't take too long."

Vivian grinned. Would he really worry about her simply running out to the garden and back? No one ever worried about her before, not that she could remember.

She threw on her clothes, buttoning her coat so the fact that she wasn't wearing a corset wasn't noticeable, and hurried upstairs. The house was quiet save for voices drifting up from the kitchen— the maids starting their day. Perhaps she'd be able to breakfast with them later. Her stomach was already growling.

Outside, the sun was still low in the sky, but birds were chirping in the trees. Dew clung to the grass as she hurried through it, dampening her boots and trouser legs.

The statue was exactly where the messenger had told her it would be. At its base there was a loose stone. Vivian pulled it easily out of its spot to reveal a compartment behind. Inside was an envelope.

So she was right. The fact didn't bring her any joy. With the messenger dead, the only way a note could be waiting for her was if someone on the staff delivered it. Who else would know about the statue? Who else could come and go as they pleased without being noticed?

She waited until she was back in Temple's apartments, back in his bed before opening the letter. It was indeed from Rupert. Temple didn't look any more pleased by her being right than she had been.

"What does it say?" he asked.

Quickly, Vivian read the code. It was only a few lines. "He asks if everything is all right and why haven't I written."

He watched her closely—so much so that she immediately became defensive. "You don't believe me?"

Temple sat up. "I believe you. I think you should send a reply."

Vivian followed his logic. "You want to watch to see who picks it up?"

He nodded. "They may do it during the day, but they'll leave a scent behind. Provided most of the staff stays away from the garden—which I believe they do—I should be able to ascertain who our traitor is."

What if it was one of her friends? "The person might not know they're a traitor," she suggested. "They might think they're love letters."

He gave her a dubious glance, but he didn't argue. "Can you write a reply today?"

"Of course. What do you want me to say?"

"Tell him that the others are here and that you fear for your safety. Tell him you want to leave."

"You're hoping he'll arrange a meet?"

"I'm hoping that he might actually give you directions to his hideout." He spoke like he thought it a gamble.

"He won't risk me getting hurt." She was certain of that. "I'm too valuable to him. He sent me after you because he knew you'd feel a connection to my blood. He never thought for a moment that you'd hurt me."

Temple arched a brow. "You know him better than I suspected."

She shook her head. "I don't know him at all, but I do know how his mind works. I'll write the note later this morning and leave it in the statue."

"Hopefully," Temple began, "we'll have better luck than Payen and Violet."

"You don't think they discovered anything?"

He lay back on the bed, folding his arms behind his head. "We would have heard by now if they had."

Yes, she supposed they would have. And then she was struck by a horrible thought. "Did you hear them return?"

He yawned and nodded. "Just before dawn."

Vivian's relief was almost tangible. As much as she didn't like Violet, she wouldn't want to find out she was dead.

God, how her world had changed in so short a time! It was almost impossible to absorb all of it.

"You've gone awfully quiet," he remarked some time later, as he rubbed his hand along her arm. "What are you thinking?"

She decided to be honest, regardless of what it might wrought. "I'm wondering if I'll ever see you again once this is over."

"Vivian . . ."

She pressed her fingers to his lips, heart clenching in her chest. "You don't have to say anything. I know what we have is only temporary whether it lasts four weeks or forty years."

"I cannot make you promises. Not now."

Not now, or not ever? she wanted to ask.

"I haven't asked you for any." She sounded defensive and she couldn't help it. She felt defensive. "Nor have I offered any in return." But giving your heart to someone was a promise, wasn't it? It should mean something.

Temple sighed. Vivian sighed as well. She should have gone to her own bed.

"There's something I need to tell you."

Oh dear. No story begun with a phrase like that could ever be pleasant to hear.

"It's about a woman, isn't it?" Wasn't it always? "Someone who you did make promises to."

"Yes." His voice was low, distant.

"Who was she?"

"Her name was Lucinda."

It sounded like a very old, romantic name. Much more exotic than *Vivian* in her ears. She was probably beautiful too. And little. A normal woman who wore dresses and pretty hairstyles. A woman who threw pretty little tantrums instead of punches. "You loved her?"

"I did. She was the most—"

"I don't need to know anymore than that you loved her." She didn't care if she sounded petty or if she sounded jealous. She was petty. She was jealous. And she was stupid as well, apparently. Here she was comparing herself to a woman she knew nothing of, who was most likely dead or at least no longer part of Temple's life.

Whatever Temple thought of her shortness, he kept it to himself. "There's more to the story than my loving her."

"Continue then." She tried to sound honestly interested. It wasn't hard, if resentful curiosity could be considered honest interest.

"I trusted her. I thought she was the woman for me. She knew what I am and she said she wanted to be with me forever. I believed her."

Vivian swallowed. She didn't have to be a scholar to know that this story couldn't possibly have a happy ending. If it had, Temple would not be with her now. "So you made her a vampire?"

"I did. It's not an easy task, you know. First the vampire trying to convert a human must be at least a century old to be strong enough to give his blood."

"I didn't know that."

She felt him shrug. "Not many do. Secondly, the person being converted must possess a certain combination of attributes to survive the change."

"What attributes?"

"A strong mind for one. A will to survive. The conversion can cause changes beyond the physical. Some minds are drastically altered."

There was a distant note in his voice, as though his own mind was no longer with her, but back in some distant time, with that same woman she was so very jealous of. "Is that what happened to Lucinda?"

"Yes. You have to understand that before I changed her she was a good woman. The finest."

"I hate her." The words came tumbling out before she would stop them. "Sorry."

Temple chuckled softly. "It's all right. There are times I hate Villiers for the simple fact that he's known you longer than I have. He knows you better."

"No." She ran a hand over his shoulder, massaging the thick muscle there. "Not better." He growled low in his throat and she smiled. "Tell me more about Lucinda."

"After she became a vampire, she changed in other ways. She enjoyed her new strength, her quick reflexes. She enjoyed killing. She killed a family. There were five children."

Vivian squeezed his shoulder. "I'm sorry. Did you leave her?"

He laughed hoarsely, humorlessly. "No." He paused. "I killed her."

"It was stupid of you to come here." Rupert tried to keep his disapproval under control. Kimberly was still so very important to his plans. "Someone might have seen you."

She paced the small space before his desk. "No one saw me. I left before the servants were up and when all the vampires went to bed."

"And did not the ferry man find it odd, you coming to the mainland at such an hour?"

"I told him I had unexpected guests and needed extra supplies. It wasn't a lie. My coach man is fetching them now."

"And just who does your man think I am? Did you tell him you wanted time alone with your lover?"

She actually blushed a little, the fool.

"Of course I did not." She massaged her forehead with delicate fingers. "It's so tiring, this constant subterfuge."

He handed her a glass of sherry. "It will all be over soon, my dear. Don't tax yourself so."

She took the glass with a grateful smile. "I'm sorry to complain. You must be eager for the end as well, and here I am whining like an infant."

Rupert smiled. It pulled tightly at his lips, but his guest didn't seem to notice. "Obviously there was something of importance you wanted to discuss with me?"

She sipped her drink. "Yes. Vivian knows what she is."

Obviously Rupert hadn't heard her correctly. "What she is?"

Kimberly rolled her eyes at him. "A descendent of Lilith. Did you think she wouldn't find out?"

Actually, yes. "You promised you wouldn't say anything." His fingers twitched. A little squeeze around her neck and he would be rid of her and her big mouth.

"I didn't. Temple told her everything."

Temple told her? That was interesting. No matter, he could use this to his advantage, he was sure. "How did Vivian react?"

"She was shocked, of course, but then she seemed more accepting." Her wide gaze slowly drifted up to his. "You're losing her, Rupert. Her loyalty has shifted to the vampires."

A sudden thickness in Rupert's throat made it hard to swallow his brandy. "You're mistaken."

Kimberly looked at him with such pity that he truly was tempted to kill her. "She shares his bed, Rupert. They're lovers. She is almost completely recovered from injuries sustained during her fall, and he has told her she can leave whenever she wants, yet she stays."

He turned away. "She stays to gather information for me."

"Payen and Violet Carr arrived last night."

Rupert froze, seized by something that was a combination of rage, fear, and something he couldn't quite name. He was cold and hot, rigid yet his knees were weak. He did not turn around He dared not. "Violet?"

"Yes." There was such satisfaction in Kimberly's voice. She thought she had him now. "How long will it be, do you suppose, before they tell Vivian everything? That is if they haven't already."

"Vivian would never think me a villain." He had been too good to the girl. Too much like a father. He would not stand for it!

He heard his guest rise, the rustle of skirts as she moved closer. "So many things you never told her. Now the vampires have told her everything. Imagine what the Carrs might have told her. Vivian might have been able to absolve you of other activities, but there's no excusing what you did to them, is there?"

She didn't know what he had done. Knew little to nothing of his "activities." She was fishing for information in a woman's way, and she wasn't very good at it.

"You have to bring her to me," he announced, suddenly turning. She was right there, not even a foot away, watching him like a house cat after a very large mouse.

He wasn't a mouse. He was a very, very large rat who wouldn't think twice of tearing this little pussy cat apart.

"Bring her to you?" Kimberly's eyes were wide with surprise. "How do I do that?"

Rupert smiled, slowly. "You'll think of something. You always do."

Vivian did not react the way Temple expected to the news that he was a killer.

"I'm so sorry," she said, wrapping her arms around him. "That must have been awful for you. Why didn't one of the others do it for you?"

"They weren't there," he replied simply. "Plus, it was my problem."

"I would have done it for you—so you wouldn't have to."

Temple's throat tightened. It didn't matter that they were discussing murder. No one had ever expressed such sentiment to him before. It was . . . nice.

He would have shown her how nice had a knock on their door not come at exactly that moment.

He sniffed the air. "Reign. And Olivia." Immediately he was out of bed, shrugging on a dressing gown as he hurried to the door. Christ, he hoped something wasn't wrong with his friend's wife. Or her baby.

A lamp beside the bed flared to life. Vivian had found the matches he kept there, and now a large area of the room was filled with a warm glow. She tugged on another dressing gown, and he waited until she belted the sash to open the door.

Reign's face was etched with concern, and poor Olivia looked wan and weak, but Temple couldn't smell blood or anything remotely like sickness, so that was good. In fact, Olivia smelled lovely to him—fresh and sweet like ripe fruit. Was that how a pregnant vampire should smell? It made him want to smile.

"What's wrong?" he asked, resisting the urge to look as happy as Olivia's scent made him feel.

Reign glanced at his wife, then at his friend. "We'd like to see Vivian, if that's acceptable."

Temple pulled a face at his formality. "Of course it is. Come in."

Reign's hand was on the small of his wife's back as they entered the room. Temple closed the door behind them and turned to see Vivian standing by the bed, a disheveled angel with her hair tumbling all around her.

Even Reign wasn't immune to the sight, staring at her with more than a hint of awe. There was absolutely no desire in his friend's expression, however, so Temple wasn't tempted to rip him to shreds.

"Sorry for the interruption," Reign said to Vivian. Vivian smiled as most women did at the sound of Reign's incredibly low, gravelly voice. Damn the man. "Olivia couldn't sleep, and one of the maid's mentioned that your mother was a midwife."

"She was?" Temple stared at his lover. "I didn't know that."

Vivian smiled teasingly at him. "I deliberately concealed that fact from you." Then, when he felt every inch the proper idiot, she turned her attention to Olivia and Reign. "She was, and yes, she taught me some of what she knew before she died."

Temple watched as Vivian reached out a hand and let it hover directly over Olivia's abdomen. "I can feel it—your child."

Reign frowned. Olivia looked more alive than she had since her arrival. "You can?"

Vivian nodded. "I've realized that whenever I'm around a vampire, I feel this tug inside. With you it's stronger." Her gaze locked with the other woman's. "What can I do to help you?"

"Can you tell if the baby is a vampire?" Reign demanded, his voice so eager; Temple winced. "Is it healthy?"

Vivian shook her head. "I can't tell, but the feeling I get is normal for me. In fact, it's even more pleasant."

Olivia took Vivian's hand in her own. "I have a favor to ask of you."

"Anything." Temple's heart swelled at Vivian's generosity.

Olivia smiled. "Since you are a descendent of

Lilith, I thought perhaps . . . that is I think you could . . ."

"You want my blood?" Ever blunt, Vivian asked the question with a smile, and then shrugged when the other woman nodded. "Of course, if you think it will help. Let's sit." She led Olivia to a chaise near the wall.

Reign followed. "Sometimes my blood makes her feel better, but she doesn't like to drink from me too often."

"Not now," Olivia explained. "Not when he needs his strength." She didn't have to say any more. Temple could see from Vivian's expression that she understood perfectly. Olivia didn't want her husband weakened when the Silver Palm was so close and so dangerous.

"I think I can help you." Vivian straddled the chaise and patted a spot between her thighs for Olivia to sit. "While you take my blood I'll try some things I know my mother used to tell expectant mothers to do."

Olivia didn't hesitate. She adjusted her own nightclothes to sit on the chaise, and when Vivian instructed her to lean back against her, she did.

"Relax," Vivian instructed. "I can support your weight, trust me. That's better." She offered the vampire her wrist. "Go ahead."

Temple watched as Olivia delicately took Vivian's arm in her hands and pierced the pale flesh with her fangs. Vivian barely winced. Then, she drew a deep breath and placed her other hand on Olivia's stomach and closed her eyes.

It could have been such a terribly erotic scene, the two women together as they were, but it wasn't. Temple stood beside Reign and the two of them watched in silence as something beautiful and wondrous unfolded before them.

After a few moments, Olivia lifted her head. She licked the marks on Vivian's wrist and wiped her own mouth with the back of her hand.

"Now," Vivian instructed. "You just lay back and let me have a chat with your little person."

If someone had told him this as a story, Temple wouldn't have believed it, but watching it, he had no choice but to believe his own eyes. Olivia did as she was told and Vivian, holding the vampire like a child, her hand still on Olivia's stomach, began to sing softly in a language he didn't understand.

"Gaelic?" Reign asked in a whisper.

Temple shook his head. "I don't know. If it is, it's ancient."

Reign shrugged. "Makes the hair on my neck stand on end."

Temple placed his hand on his friend's shoulder. The hair on his neck rose as well. Vivian had a lovely, sweet voice, but that wasn't what seemed so unearthly to him. It was as though he could understand what she was singing, even though the words made no sense. She sang of love and comfort, warmth and sweetness. A lullaby?

A very old lullaby.

The two men stood together, watching in silent awe as the strain in Olivia's features disappeared, replaced by an expression of Madonna-like tranquillity. Vivian kept her hand on the woman's stomach, her other hand now gently massaging Olivia's forehead, stroking her hair.

Just like a mother.

A little chill ran down Temple's spine. It wasn't necessarily a bad feeling, but watching his lover now, he had the strangest feeling that she wasn't quite herself. Maybe it was fancy, or the effect of the lighting. Maybe it was just his romantic nature, but he could imagine that she had changed just a little, right before his eyes. That it wasn't just Vivian comforting his friend's wife, but that it was Lilith herself, giving love and strength to one of her children, working her magic through blood and song.

"She's amazing," Reign murmured, his voice thick with gratitude and relief.

"She is," Temple replied. And when Vivian opened her eyes to look at him, he was relieved to see nothing but her in her gaze. He saw her strength, and he was humbled by the power there.

And he also realized why the women of this place thought of her as a goddess.

She was.

Chapter 17

Later that morning, Vivian wrote a reply to Villiers and left the note in the statue as instructed. Then, she and Marcus took turns watching the statue from behind a hedge in the garden.

Keeping watch was tedious work, so Marcus kept himself entertained by using his archaeological tools to dig a small hole near the hedge, in a spot that looked promising. Much to his surprise, he uncovered some broken pottery that looked Roman in origin. He'd know better once he cleaned it up.

He was so pleased with his work that he almost missed the figure of a woman entering the garden, heading straight for the statue of Lilith.

The sound of stone grating against stone had him lifting his head, and peering through the shrubbery.

A house maid had opened the secret compartment and withdrawn the letter. It was Agnes.

Marcus remembered meeting her in the kitchen with Vivian. The woman slipped the stone back into place, and with a quick glance over her shoulder, hurried off, the letter shoved into her apron pocket.

Interesting. Stripping off his gloves, Marcus packed up his roll of tools and started back to the house. Vivian and the others were waiting for him in the darkened drawing room. His eyes took a moment to adjust to the lack of light after the bright sun.

"You're early," Temple commented. "What have you found out?"

Marcus turned in the direction of his voice, practically blind. "It's Agnes."

A sound of distress that could only have come from Vivian followed the announcement. Then she said, "I can't believe Agnes is a traitor to the sisterhood."

"I don't think she is," Marcus replied, finally able to see her. "I would imagine she was coerced into assistance with the assurance that she was helping the sisterhood."

Temple nodded in agreement. "Far easier than trying to convince her that all she believes is wrong."

Marcus cast a quick glance at Vivian, who was silent. He wondered how she felt about learning all she knew was false.

"I'm going to catch the next ferry to the mainland," he informed them. It was nigh on midday now, and other than Vivian or Molyneux, he was the only one able to leave. "I'm certain Agnes will be on it as well."

"What then?" Chapel asked. "She'll be suspicious, won't she if you suddenly show up on the boat with her?"

Marcus pulled the signet ring he had "borrowed" from his pocket. "Not if I'm wearing this."

Temple was suddenly on his feet. "Where the hell did you get that?"

"I liberated it from a man who attacked me," Marcus replied easily. "I thought it might come in handy. Seems I was right."

Saint flashed a grin. "You're certainly proving yourself useful, Mr. Grey."

Marcus returned the smile. "I try." Then, he slipped the ring onto his finger. It was a little big, but not enough to be overly noticeable. "With any luck Agnes will lead me right to the Order's main compound."

"Be careful," Temple advised him. "Don't call attention to yourself, and don't take any unnecessary risks."

"Yes," Marcus replied drily. "I am brilliant, thank you. You're quite welcome."

The big vampire's lips curved into a crooked smile. "Modest as well, Mr. Grey. Just don't get yourself taken prisoner. I'd hate to have to tell the

Order to go ahead and kill you because they tried to bargain with your life."

Marcus had no choice but to concede. "Good point." He checked his pocket watch. "I'd better get going. If I'm not back by sunset . . ."

"You're not coming back," Bishop finished with a grin.

Vampire humor. So amusing.

"We'll find you," Chapel assured him. Marcus flashed his friend a look of gratitude. Nice to know someone valued his life around here, especially since he was risking it to save their immortal arses.

Truth be told, he somewhat enjoyed the danger and the intrigue. Would he miss it when this was over? Probably not. If he survived it, he would be very happy at the end of it all to go back to his books and his quiet life digging up the past.

He left the others and quickly walked to the stables. He saddled a horse and urged the gelding into a fast but easy pace. He made it to the dock with time to spare. The ferry—a ramshackle device if ever he saw one—waited. There was only one other customer waiting to go over, and that was Agnes. The ferryman told him he could take his horse across but it would be extra. Marcus paid the fare and walked the gelding onto the boat.

The maid stood near the railing, shifting her weight from one foot to the other, obviously nervous. Marcus headed straight for her.

"Hello, Agnes," he said, as he stroked the gelding's neck. "May I join you?"

The sunlight caught the silver on his finger, which in turn caught the woman's attention. She looked at the ring, and recognition lit her eyes. She flashed him a bright smile. "Of course, Mr. Grey."

Marcus returned the smile. Hopefully the rest would be as easy.

When Marcus returned later that day, he gave the vampires directions to the house where Agnes had delivered the note. It was a small cottage in the village. Neat and clean, it was obvious that people lived there, but Villiers was nowhere to be seen, and it certainly wasn't big enough to house an army. Nor did it seem equipped to keep prisoners.

Once darkness fell, Payen and Violet, along with Bishop and Marika, flew over the location to investigate with their acute vampire senses. They returned before the second hour passed.

"It's obvious Villiers had been there," Payen informed the group. "His scent was all over the place."

"But he wasn't there now," Bishop added. "And Marcus was right, there's no way he could house his men there, let alone any equipment."

"He's got another location," Temple concluded, stating what they all assumed. "One that he doesn't share with others, that he only visits during the day. He wouldn't risk us finding it."

"We encountered a similar situation in Scotland," Reign remarked. "We need someone to watch the house for Villiers' return, and then follow him when he leaves."

"I could go," Vivian suggested. "If he happened to see me, he'd never suspect me."

"No!" Everyone jumped at the loudness of Temple's refusal. He forced himself to speak calmly. "But he would suspect if you tried returning to us, or attempted to make contact." What he wouldn't say is that he couldn't—wouldn't—let her out of his sight. Couldn't risk Villiers getting his hands on her.

Selfish and stupid, that's what she had made him, and he wasn't about to apologize for it.

"I'll go," Marcus announced. "Some of the staff has seen me, so they'll think I belong. Plus I have the signet if anyone asks. I can leave before dawn and be back here by sunset."

"You'll need to get across to the mainland," Temple reminded him. "The ferry comes just before dawn."

"I'm not going to take the ferry. Someone from here might see me and ask questions. I've found a man willing to lend me his boat for a small sum. I'll take that instead."

Temple's brows drew together. "When did you happen to make those arrangements?"

Marcus grinned. "When a certain young woman asked me if I'd like to cross to the mainland and spend an afternoon with her."

Bishop and Chapel made noises of approval and Pru simply shook her head. "Well done, Marcus. You've found love in a hazardous situation. Are you certain you're not a vampire?"

Chuckles met her remark and Marcus grinned at her. "I'm certain, if for no other reason than I do not claim to be in love. We humans like to take things at a more moderate pace."

Out of the corner of his eye, Temple saw Vivian glance at him, but when he turned his attention to her, she was staring out the window at the darkness beyond, her expression unreadable.

Love. Such an odd little emotion. He thought he'd loved Lucinda, but several centuries had a way of clarifying a man's vision. He had been obsessed with her, adored her even. But love? No. Because when he'd killed her, he hadn't wanted to join her, and that was what he always thought love should be. When one mate left the world, the other would want to follow because all reason for living was gone.

There were those strong enough to go on after the death of a loved one, but he feared he wasn't one of them.

He would not dare to try to entertain Vivian's thoughts on the subject. She did not love him, nor did he believe he loved her. Even if he loved her, changing her would be too much of a risk. What if it altered her personality? Or worse, what if it affected her physically? Her blood might be wonderful for him, but there was no telling what his might do to her.

"Fine," he said, tearing his gaze away from the tall redhead at the window. "Marcus will go. Once we know the location of the Order's operation, we'll go in and destroy it."

"With what?" Saint asked. "We haven't any weapons other than ourselves."

"Fire," Temple replied. "We set it ablaze."

Bishop spoke next, "Many will escape. What if Villiers is among them? We cannot risk him attempting this again." His gaze flickered to Vivian. "My apologies."

She smiled faintly. "Thank you." Then she went back to staring out the window.

Temple frowned, but concentrated on the task at hand. "We'll be there, watching for Villiers. He won't escape us." Because of Vivian, he didn't go into the gory details of what would follow once he got his hands on the man responsible for all of this. He was going to kill him, of course. Temple's duty to the Blood Grail and to his brethren demanded that he ensure Villiers did not live to hurt anyone again.

"With any luck this will be over tomorrow night." This was uttered by Saint, who took his wife's hand in his as he looked around the room, meeting each and every gaze. "It will be done."

"And we can get on with our lives," Bishop added. "Maybe Marika and I could come visit you and Ivy."

Marika flung her arms around her husband's neck and squeezed, squealing with delight. Saint's face lit up, as did Ivy's. It seemed Saint and Bishop had put aside their differences. Good. It wouldn't do to go into this battle with discontent between them.

And yet, the idea of all of them going their separate ways once more saddened him.

Especially if Vivian's "way" differed from his own.

It was because of that, because he might lose her so soon that he announced that the meeting was over. "I've got accelerant and the necessary items for burning the place," he added. "All we need is for Marcus to get the location and we're set."

Violet spoke for the first time that evening. "We must be very careful," she warned. "Villiers always has another plan. It's how he's managed to keep ahead of us all these years."

Reign nodded in agreement. "I think we've all seen that for ourselves. The Order as a collective is far from stupid."

Temple's jaw tightened, but he flashed a toothy grin at his friend. "I've yet to meet anyone who can outsmart dead."

That brought a few chuckles and soon after the group of them broke apart. Some of them were going to feed. Marcus was going to see the man with the boat to ensure its availability the next morning, and Father Molyneux said he was ready for bed. Temple didn't say anything, but he suspected the old priest wouldn't survive much past defeating the Order.

And they had to defeat it, or die trying.

He crossed the room to where Vivian stood, still by the window, and offered her his hand. "Come," he said.

She tucked her fingers into his and followed him silently from the parlor, through the house, and down the stairs to the rooms below. There, he undressed her slowly, and then himself, and placed her upon the bed, covering her with his own body.

What words would not convey, his touch would.

Bracing his knees astride her thighs, his hands on either side of her shoulders, Temple kissed her neck, running his tongue along the shallow, warm hollow of her throat where her pulse fluttered like a butterfly's wings. He tasted her there, savored the salt-sweetness of her skin, and down farther to the tender softness between her breasts where he grazed the delicate flesh with his teeth enough to draw a flush to the surface. Vivian gasped, arching against him.

He lifted his head, pinned her with his gaze. Her eyes were bright in the lamplight, a tempest of desire, and he a drowning man. "No mercy," he murmured. "Not for you. Not tonight." He was going to love her as though this was their last night together.

For all he knew it just might be.

He cupped the weight of one breast in his hand, lightly dragging his thumb across the tight, puckered nipple. Vivian sighed in encouragement. She was so receptive to his touch, her body instinctively reacting to his.

Smiling, Temple lowered his mouth to that taut, pink flesh. Sucking it between his lips, he bit gently. She writhed beneath him, lifting her hips. He bit harder, fangs sliding down until they pierced the aureole. Vivian cried out, but not in pain. Never in pain. Temple sucked softly, drawing her into himself like the most exquisite wine. Her thighs parted beneath him, wrapping around his hips so that the eager length of his cock was pressed against the equally anticipatory dampness between her legs.

Christ Almighty, he loved the way she tasted, the way she moved beneath him, opened herself to him, as though shame and fear were not words she'd ever learned the meaning of. So beautifully honest, his precious Amazon, so beautifully his.

He closed the punctures and turned his attentions to the other breast, inflicting a similar torment upon it. Vivian's fingers cupped the back of his head, holding him close as her hips rocked against him. Her breathing became harsh, and he knew that if he didn't stop her, she was going to make herself come just by rubbing against him.

Not that he minded witnessing such an act, but he wanted to make her wait just a little while longer—prolong the pleasure.

Downward he inched, kissing and nibbling the soft flesh over her ribs, dipping his tongue into her navel. He sucked on the gentle curve of her belly, drawing blood to just below the skin. She'd have a mark later. It wouldn't last long given her ability to heal quickly, but for now, he had marked her as his.

Finally, he lay between her legs, rubbing his jaw against her hips, and then down to where her flesh became baby-fine, bordered by a thatch of amazingly red curls that glistened with moisture.

She smelled of aroused woman—warm, wet, and inviting. The scent of her went straight to his head, his heart, and his cock. Gently, he parted the lips of her sex, revealing the tender pinkness there. She was shiny with her own briny juices, her body quivering in anticipation as he made her wait for the first flick of his tongue.

Holding her open he found the hard little knot hidden beneath its slick hood. The first pass of his tongue was quick—tormenting. Vivian groaned, arching quickly, trying to shove herself against his mouth as he lifted his head. When he moved in again, it was with more purpose, a more deliberate stroke that had her moaning, digging her heels into the mattress. He licked again, savoring her taste and the little sounds she made.

He became more ruthless, licking at her with determined—almost cruel—calculation. Every stroke of his tongue was measured—long and firm enough to take her to the edge, but not enough to send her over. Then, when she was practically begging for release, writhing wantonly beneath him, Temple opened his mouth, positioning his fangs higher, so that he could continue to lick her even as he bit.

She came the second his fangs pierced her. Her entire body arched as her fingers clutched at his hair, shoving his face deeper into her as she gave herself over to the pleasure of his mouth.

He sucked for but a few seconds on her before closing the little holes with his tongue. Her body jerked at the contact.

"Sensitive?" he asked in the tone of a proud male.

"Mnn," was her reply. Temple grinned. Nothing made him happier, nothing made him harder than knowing he had pleased her.

"Roll over," he told her, his voice low and rough in his own ears.

Vivian didn't hesitate, and his heart swelled with the degree of trust she afforded him. Lying on her stomach, she revealed the long length of her naked back, the firm curve of her buttocks. Temple ran his fingers along the shallow valley of her spine, down to the flushed cheeks of her bottom.

"Spread your legs," he commanded.

She did and he eased between them. "Come up on your hands and knees."

She did that as well, her spine bowing with the position. His hands were all over her, caressing her pale flesh.

"You're so beautiful," he murmured.

Vivian rose up then, onto her knees so that her back was pressed against his chest. She reached back with one arm to bring his head toward her, turning her face and tilting so that he could kiss her full lips. As he did, his hands came to stroke her nipples and sex as their tongues rubbed against each other.

Slowly, Temple sank down, until their kiss was broken and he knelt upon the bed. Legs straddling his, Vivian followed him, and he guided her so that the head of his cock fit snugly against the soaked entrance to her body.

"Take me, Vivian," he growled. "Take me inside."

The minx flashed a saucy smile over her shoulder as she slowly lowered her body onto his. She moved as slowly—slower even—than he had with her. By the time he was fully inside her hot, tight body, Temple had little beads of sweat on his brow.

The sweet grip of her body around his and the earthy words of encouragement slipping from her mouth was the most intense torture he'd ever experienced. Up and down she slid, easing his desperate prick in and out, until he ground his teeth and dug his fingers into her hips.

Her hair brushed his belly and chest, the ends tickling his thighs. Releasing her hips, Temple wound thick strands of the heavy waves around one hand and tugged gently. The other hand slid around to dip between her thighs. He could torment her just as well as she tortured him, and he proved it by finding that little knot once more and slowly rubbing it with his finger. Vivian shuddered.

Pushing her hair aside, Temple pressed his face against her shoulder and back as the tension within him pushed past plateau and headed toward release. His breath was ragged in his own ears—a wonder in itself given that he didn't breathe like a human.

There was nothing else but him and Vivian and this moment. Nothing else mattered, not Villiers, not the future. Nothing. He could die after this and he would meet his maker happily because for a short time, he had known what it was to be utterly at peace. Totally happy.

Because he had known Vivian.

"Come for me." It was his final command, because he knew his own climax could not be staved much longer. "Come *now*."

She came. It was long and powerful, and she cried out the entire time.

Her release sent him over the edge, as always. Temple's body tightened and then seemed to explode inside. He thrust upward, burying himself inside her, filling her as he groaned against her back.

They collapsed together on the rumpled sheets, falling like spoons in a cupboard. Curved together, he pulled her snug against him before tugging the blankets over them.

He stroked her hip, unable to stop touching her even though he was exhausted. "I don't deserve you," he admitted. And he didn't. What had he done to be given this gift? And why the hell couldn't he give her what she wanted?

"No," she said with a yawn. "I think you deserve better."

Temple's throat tightened at her sweetness, so much so that he couldn't speak. So he kissed her on the shoulder instead, and held her tight against him in case she tried to escape.

And then, in the darkness where no one else could see his face or guess his thoughts, he allowed himself to admit that winning her love just might be worth the risks.

* * *

The next morning, Vivian rose shortly after dawn, unable to sleep any longer. Temple stirred, but she told him to go back to sleep, and miraculously he did just that.

She bathed in the adjoining chamber, changed into a fresh shirt and trousers and then made her way upstairs. Marcus would have left for the mainland hours ago, but there were other things she could find to fill her day. She could read more about Lilith. She could continue her sparring training with the staff.

She could do any number of things to try and make herself ignore how much her feelings for Temple had grown.

It had to be the sex. That was the only excuse. She had been so overcome by pleasure that now her body thought itself in love.

Now, if only she could convince herself that was true. Her heart would have none of it, however. It insisted, even now in the bright light of day, that somehow, somewhere along the line, she had fallen hopelessly in love with Temple.

She could only hope that it was possible to fall out of love as quickly as it was to fall in.

She entered the kitchen and found her new friends sitting down to breakfast just as she'd hoped. They had a plate out for her, which she loaded from the pan of sausage and eggs on the stove. She grabbed three fresh rolls, warm from the oven and a cup of steaming coffee as well. It would take more than a bruised heart to diminish her appetite.

"You look tired this morning," Shannon commented coyly. "Long night?"

The other women giggled as Vivian blushed. "Yes, as a matter of fact. You look rather well rested, Shannon. Perhaps your night wasn't long enough?"

The laughter grew, and even Shannon herself joined in. Of course, the girl looked just as tired as Vivian herself, and she hadn't the benefit of a preternatural constitution.

After breakfast, Vivian intended to find an occupation to keep herself busy, but her plans were thwarted when she ran into Kimberly in the upstairs hall.

"I wonder if you might come to the mainland with me?" the older woman asked. "I need help with a few errands and I thought it might be nice for you to get off the island for a bit."

Vivian could have kissed her. This was the very sort of diversion she sought. "I'd be glad to help you. Let me go tell Temple."

Kimberly stopped her with a gentle hand upon her arm. "Don't wake him. I've told Agnes of my plans. She'll let Temple know if he should wake up, but I've no doubt I'll have you back here by midafternoon."

That gave her pause. Marcus said he believed Agnes an innocent in all of this. During his time with her the day before he'd concluded that she knew nothing of the Order's true intentions and believed herself to be helping Vivian—and in turn, the vampires and the sisterhood. Regardless of his assurances, Vivian wasn't inclined to trust the maid so easily.

She did, however, trust Kimberly.

"When do you want to leave?" she asked, hoping the answer would be soon. She wanted to be gone before Temple woke. Wanted to clear her head and gather her thoughts before she saw him again.

Kimberly smiled and consulted the grandfather clock just behind Vivian. "The boat I hired will be ready in half an hour. Let me get my coat and we'll take my curricle."

Vivian could not believe her good fortune. She collected her own coat as well, even though it was showing signs of being a warm day. The women and vampires at the Garden Academy might not mind her style of dress, but there were plenty of people on the mainland who were bound to be scandalized by the sight of a woman in trousers. Going in her shirtsleeves would only make it worse. She brushed and braided her hair as well.

They left not ten minutes after Kimberly asked her, the curricle having been made ready by a groom earlier.

Kimberly drove and Vivian was glad to let her

do it. She lifted her face to the sky and breathed the fresh air deep into her lungs. She loved summer mornings when the grass was still damp with dew and the air was sweet and untouched by the sun's oppressive heat.

Kimberly made small talk, discussing such things as how she was looking forward to the return of her students soon—how much she enjoyed running the school. Vivian listened with interest, speaking when the urge hit and being content to listen the rest of the time. She enjoyed Kimberly's company. To think she had once been somewhat jealous of the older woman.

They drove the curricle right onto the waiting boat and before long were driving it off again on the opposite shore.

"I often pay for passage," Kimberly remarked as they traveled along the slightly rutted path. "It's much more convenient than having to wait for the ferry. It only runs twice a day."

"I would imagine," Vivian agreed. "It must get so frustrating at times to be at the mercy of the tide."

Her companion smiled. "You have no idea."

Silence fell upon them for a while. Vivian took that time to study the beautiful landscape around her—so rustic and green, with gently rolling hills. Sheep dotted the hillside—like little white clouds.

"Our first stop is the house of a local draper,"

Kimberly informed her. "I need to purchase some fabric for new curtains in the east dormitory."

No wonder she'd asked Vivian to come with her. There was no way a woman of Kimberly's stature could lift let alone carry that much drapery material.

They drove for what might have been half to three quarters of an hour before stopping in the yard of a comfortable-looking home that was busy, but not to the extent one would expect for a business address. It didn't look like a business at all.

"It's still early," Kimberly reminded her when she mentioned the fact. "The owner is an acquaintance of mine and allows me to come outside of regular business hours."

"You're very lucky," Vivian allowed as they stepped down from the vehicle. There was something unsettling about this place, but she couldn't quite put her finger on what it was.

She followed Kimberly inside. This time she didn't feel like a lumbering oaf next to the other woman's petite stature. She felt strong and capable, ready for a fight.

That should have made her realize it was a trap right there, but she didn't realize it, not until she followed Kimberly into a large office and saw Rupert standing in front of the desk.

Shock froze her to the spot. At first the sight of her former mentor brought such a rush of joy to her heart, but then she remembered the stories the vampires had told, that he had almost killed Violet Carr, and that joy ran away like water down a steep hill.

He came to her with his arms outstretched. "Vivian! My darling."

Vivian stepped aside when he tried to embrace her. She spared only the briefest of glances for Kimberly, who stood nearby, wringing her hands. "What the hell is this?" she demanded.

Rupert took another step toward her, and when she stepped back once more, he lowered his arms, an expression of disappointment settling over his handsome features. "I thought you would be happy to see me."

"How could you?" she laughed in disbelief. "After all you've done?"

His expression hardened. "So it's true. They've managed to poison you against me."

Vivian turned to Kimberly. Several men had followed them into the room and flanked them. Protection for Rupert, she realized. Guards for her.

"What have you done?" she demanded. "How could you betray Temple this way?"

Kimberly gave her a beseeching look. "Vivian, try to understand. Lilith is more important than you or Temple. She's more important than my own life."

Vivian's jaw dropped. "You're part of this. You've been part of it for a long time."

"Since the beginning," Rupert replied happily when Kimberly said nothing. "My dear Kimberly has been a great help to me in my research and planning."

"I bet she has," Vivian replied tightly, her gaze still fixed on the woman she had considered a friend. "You've betrayed us all."

"Not all of us," Rupert reminded her. "She hasn't betrayed me. Not yet, at any rate."

Kimberly's gaze snapped to him. "I would never betray you, Rupert. You know that." She gestured toward Vivian. "Not like she has."

Oh no. God only knew what Kimberly had revealed to Rupert. God only knew how much of the vampires' plans she'd overheard or been blatantly told by people who trusted her.

Rupert moved toward Kimberly, smiling sweetly. "I know my dear. I know you'll never betray me." And then his hand whipped out, slashing the air in front of the other woman, whose expression became one of almost comical disbelief.

As blood ran down the front of Kimberly's dress, Vivian realized Rupert had done more than slash the air. He had slashed Kimberly's throat with a long, thin, wicked-looking blade. Blood dripped from its edge onto the carpet as Kimberly slid slowly to the floor, her life gushing out of her.

Vivian couldn't speak. Not even a squeak of alarm came from her throat, no sob of sorrow. She couldn't think and she couldn't move. Shock had her feet glued to the floor, despite the trembling in her knees. Even if she could move there was nothing she could do for Kimberly. The woman was beyond her help.

She'd wanted Kimberly to face consequences for her actions, but this? No, not bleeding to death at the feet of a man who didn't even have the decency to look the least bit sorry.

A man who was now advancing on Vivian, oblivious to the woman on the floor, reaching for him, blood gurgling from her gaping throat.

"Now, my dear," Rupert said as he approached, holding the blade with careless ease, like a painter with a brush. He gave Vivian a bright smile. "What *are* we going to do with you?"

Chapter 18

Vivian was gone.

Again.

"Does she make a habit of just disappearing?" Saint asked, admiring a bronze figurine on the mantel.

"No," Temple replied. He kept his eye on his old friend, despite his worry. Saint used to be a thief and some habits died hard.

Had Vivian given in to her own habits? Was she on her way back to Villiers, or was she out there, lying injured in another one of his traps?

Bishop arched a suspicious brow. "Is it possible she's betrayed us?"

"No," Temple replied sharply. He had discounted the thought almost as soon as it came to him. Vivian would not betray him. He refused to believe otherwise.

"I do hope she's all right." Olivia ran a hand over her still flat stomach as she spoke. She looked better than she had since her arrival; Vivian had definitely helped her.

"She's friends with the servants," he thought aloud. "We'll ask them if they know where she might be."

"I'll go," Marika offered in her lilting accent. "I dress like Vivian, so maybe they'll be more comfortable talking to me."

Temple agreed. Marika wasn't as intimidating as Prudence, who was an obvious lady, or as overwhelming as Ivy with her vibrant personality. Nor was she as fierce-looking as Olivia. No, Marika was strong and capable, but enough of an outcast with her dusky complexion and accent that the women belowstairs would see her as kindred.

"Thank you," Temple told her. "I appreciate your concern." Then he addressed the room. "Who's going to assist me in a quick sweep of the grounds?"

Everyone volunteered to come, even Molyneux.

Temple took one look at the priest and decided that wasn't a good idea. "Father, would you mind waiting here for Marcus's return? I'm anxious for his report and would like to see him as soon as he arrives."

Molyneux wasn't stupid, but he wasn't arrogant either. He gave Temple a grateful smile. "I am happy to be useful, *monsieur* Temple."

The group didn't even have a chance to assemble. Marika opened the door and Marcus was on the other side of it, flushed and grim. Temple knew from the look of him that the news was not good. And he was faced with having to put Marcus's findings ahead of searching for Vivian. It wasn't a choice his heart liked having to make.

"What is it?" he asked as the young man entered the room.

"We have a traitor in our midst," Marcus announced darkly.

Temple closed his eyes. *It is not Vivian.* "Who?" he demanded, directing his gaze at Marcus and no one else. He didn't want to see the speculation in their eyes.

"Kimberly." Marcus's voice was rough, full of disgust. "She's in league with Villiers."

Kimberly? Temple frowned, hardly believing his ears. "Are you certain?"

Marcus nodded. "I've seen her sneaking about before, but this morning she took Vivian to the mainland with her. Temple, she took her to Villiers's lair."

At one time Temple would have suspected Vivian of being the one to blame, that she convinced Kimberly to take her, but not now. It wasn't easy to think of his former lover and old friend as having betrayed him, but it made more sense.

Vivian wouldn't do this. Kimberly, on the other hand was a believer in the power of Lilith, and God only knew what Villiers had said to tempt her over to his cause.

"Did you see them go in?" he asked.

"I did. Kimberly led the way. Vivian looked suspicious, uncertain even."

That cinched it. His Vivian would not have appeared unsettled had she decided to toss him over for her former guardian. She would be convinced she was doing the right thing—and she would be the one in front.

"How long did they stay?" he demanded. More importantly, "Where are they now?"

Marcus's expression did little to relieve the anxiety building in his gut—in fact it added to Temple's concern.

"Half an hour after the women entered the house, Villiers sent for his carriage. Shortly after that he and Vivian came out of the house and got inside. She was very pale. Villiers seemed very pleased with himself."

The only thing that kept Temple from raging and ranting like a madman was the knowledge that Villiers would not hurt Vivian. Not yet. She was important to his plan, and he would keep her safe and alive until the time came to bring all his hopes to fruition. But now Villiers had complete control. He had to know that Temple would come to him, if not to save Vivian, then to put a stop to his scheme.

"At the same time I saw two men carrying a large sack from the house. There was blood on it."

Chapel was aghast. "He killed Kimberly?"

Marcus glanced at him. "I believe so, although I did not stay to see if she left the house." He turned back to Temple. "I followed them. I know where Villiers took her."

Temple could have hugged him at that moment. "We don't have much time," he lamented. It was just barely dark now, but the fact that it was summer and the days were longer was against them. They had less than twelve hours before the sun rose. Less than twelve hours to make a plan, go after Vivian, and stop Villiers.

Thank God they could fly.

"We've been up against it before," Reign commented. "We can do this."

"Villiers wants us to come," Temple reminded them all. "We have to be careful. We have to be smart. Tonight, being faster and stronger will not be enough."

"Temple's right," Payen agreed. Temple had almost forgotten about the new vampires. "Villiers has survived this long by relying on his wits and his friends, both of which have proven sharper than they first appear."

Reign nodded. "Those fuckers have stayed one step ahead of us the entire time, individually and as a group."

While it might not have been the most eloquent statement, Temple agreed with him. "We have to stay sharp as well. When this is over, the only blood I want to have shed is Silver Palm blood."

Blood lust, and knowing the battle was so close at hand sparked a sense of excitement throughout the room. Conversion grew, as did the volume of voices, so much so that Temple barely heard the knock at the door.

"Quiet," he commanded, with the voice of a man accustomed to being obeyed. Six hundred years without sword and armor hadn't changed that. Nor had it changed the fact that when he spoke, his men listened. The room fell silent, and he opened the door.

A ginger-haired maid stood at the threshold. She looked nervous, her gaze darting behind Temple until it settled on something, or rather someone, who made her relax and smile.

Temple glanced over his shoulder and saw Marcus behind him, eyeing the girl with a tenderness that was almost embarrassing. "Shannon," he said. "What is it?"

The girl offered an envelope to Temple. "This just arrived for you, sir. A special messenger from the mainland delivered it."

"Thank you." Temple took the letter. There was no return address, but that didn't matter. He knew who the sender was. "You may go now."

The girl bobbed a curtsy, flashed a heated glance at Marcus and scurried away.

"I believe Villiers has already sent his demands." He held up the manila envelope for all to see before breaking the seal. The note was written in a scrawling, arrogant script.

"My dear Mr. Temple: I will not waste my time

or yours with pleasantries or meaningless jabber. I have my lovely Vivian with me once more. If her life means anything to you, come to the following address before dawn. You know what will happen if you do not. Yours, Rupert Villiers."

Temple crumpled the paper in his fist. "Son of a bitch."

"At least Villiers doesn't know that we already suspect Kimberly's fate," Reign said. "That takes away some of his bargaining power, does it not?"

"He has Vivian," Temple replied through clenched teeth. "That gives him power enough."

All eyes were upon him when Chapel asked, "Do you love her?"

Temple scowled at him. "What the hell business is that of yours?"

"He does," Saint announced. "Why don't you just admit it, Temple?"

Still scowling, Temple said nothing and turned his back on them all.

"We'll do whatever necessary to get her back." It was Bishop who spoke. Bishop, who just a few minutes ago was prepared to call Vivian a traitor. This sudden change of heart was for Temple's sake, not Vivian's. "Just tell us what to do."

He faced them with hardened determination. "I'm going to do exactly what the bastard wants. The rest of you are getting as far away from here as possible."

* * *

It had been a mistake to attack Rupert, Vivian realized for the hundredth time since planting her fist in her former mentor's face. One man she could easily disarm—and she had. In fact, she thought she might have broken Rupert's jaw.

His guards, however, had been more of a challenge and she soon found herself the one overpowered.

And she was lucky her nose was the only thing broken. One of them had landed a very rough blow to her ribs before Rupert called them off. Then he had them chain her hands behind her back as blood ran down her face.

Now she sat in a chair in an old warehouse not far from his house. There was something that looked like an altar in the middle of the room with large glass jars on a table nearby. Whatever was in those jars was soaking in blood. And on the wall closest to the table were restraints—nine of them all together.

Just enough for Temple and his friends. Vivian had an awful feeling that she was going to be the one to end up on that altar. If she couldn't get free, that was. And she was going to try very hard to get free now that she knew where Rupert's hideaway was. The only reason she hadn't attacked him at the house was so she could determine the location for Temple.

Blood trickled from her nose, over her mouth, and down her chin. Little dots of crimson stained her shirt and trousers.

"Too bad your lover isn't here to lick that up for you," Rupert sneered, holding a stained handkerchief to his split lip as he paced the floor in front of her.

Vivian looked at him. Really looked. She didn't like what she saw. How could she have ever thought him a good man? She didn't have to wonder how he knew about her and Temple. No doubt Kimberly had told him that. She was so angry at him, so disbelieving of the cruelty within him that it numbed the pain of his betrayal. Knowing that she had meant nothing to him actually pleased her. She wouldn't want to have such a monster—a true monster—care about her.

"Too bad you killed *your* lover," she sneered back. He might have bound her hands, but she could still kick the snot out of him if the opportunity arose.

The light in his eyes intensified to a point that made her want to squirm. "I'll replace her soon enough."

Dear God. She hadn't imagined it all those times she thought his behavior toward her was more than fatherly. Rupert wanted her—sexually—and he intended to have her. That time when she'd thought he'd been about to kiss her, she'd been correct.

"Why?" she demanded, trying to ignore the blood that ran into her mouth. She spat it onto the floor. "You don't love me."

He laughed then, the bastard. "No, I don't and you don't love me. I don't care about any of that. I want you. You will serve my purpose, and you will be mine."

"Not of my free will, Rupert."

He shrugged. "I'm not terribly finicky about that either, my dear." He took the handkerchief away from his lip, looked at it and then put it in his pocket. "I suppose I should thank Temple for relieving you of your virginity. That will make things run much more smoothly."

She couldn't keep her disgust from showing, even though the expression hurt her nose. "Temple was right about you. I wish I had listened to him sooner."

"You listened to him soon enough," he admonished. "Didn't take you long to switch allegiance did it? After all I've done for you."

For a second—and only one—his words had their desired effect. They made her guilty and ashamed, and she felt like a traitor. But then she realized it wasn't betrayal when you'd been on the wrong side to begin with.

"You never told me who or what I am."

He looked at her like she was mad. "Of course I didn't."

Obviously he wasn't going to offer any more of

an explanation, and Vivian wouldn't want to hear it if he did. "You used me."

"I gave you everything you needed. Everything you wanted," he reminded her casually. "You *owe* me. You're going to prove very useful to me as soon as your dear Temple comes rushing to your rescue."

Vivian laughed. Laughed until tears sprang to her eyes, out of humor and pain.

Rupert stopped pacing to glare at her. "What the hell is so funny?"

"You." She gasped for breath and almost choked on her own blood. She coughed, but the chuckles wouldn't stop. Dear Lord, she *was* going mad. "Thinking that Temple will try to save me. He won't."

No, Temple was probably at that moment cursing her very name, thinking that she had finally succeeded in escaping. He probably thought the worst of her, and of himself for having trusted in her.

Or, if by some small chance he knew she'd been taken, he was smart enough to know better than to come after her and walk right into Rupert's trap. The easiest way to stop this was to not give in to Rupert's demands.

Her former mentor shoved a wad of cotton against her face. She had no idea where it came from, but it sopped up the blood from her nose. It also hurt like hell as he mashed against her swollen flesh. With her hands behind her back, she couldn't push him away.

She kicked him instead. Hard—between the legs—and had the satisfaction of watching him fall to the floor with a silent moan of agony.

Vivian jumped up from the chair, knocking it over, and ran toward the door. The position of her arms made her awkward, and each jarring step sent her ribs and nose screaming in pain, but she pressed on.

When she reached the door, she kicked it. Once. Twice. The third kick sent it flying open.

Unfortunately, the noise had also brought two of Rupert's guards running to investigate. She kicked at one, but he managed to dodge her boot.

"Secure her to the altar," Rupert demanded from behind her.

The guards each seized one of her arms. Vivian struggled, kicking and squirming despite the pain in her torso and face. They were big men, however, and without her arms free, she couldn't put up much of a fight. They dragged her farther into the room, and tossed her onto the hard altar, knocking the breath from her with their violence. She gasped painfully as they released her shackles, only to flip her onto her back and shove her wrists into hard, iron manacles attached to the altar. They restrained her legs as well, though it took both of them to hold down each one long enough to slip the restraints in place.

She stopped struggling. There was no escape and all she was doing was causing herself more discomfort. She would be wise to save her strength for when another chance to escape presented itself.

Rupert limped into her field of vision to hover over her like Dr. Frankenstein with his "experiment." Perhaps that was how he truly saw her—his creation. His *pet*.

"Make yourself comfortable, my dear," he said brightly. "This is where you're going to stay until the vampires come—and they will come. They can't help themselves. They actually think they can defeat me, you see." She thought he smiled then—it was hard to tell.

"They will defeat you," she insisted, all bravado despite the futility of her situation. Let them think they would come. Meanwhile, she prayed that she was right and that they wouldn't.

He laughed. "No. They won't. Not this time." He leaned toward her like a co-conspirator. "I have one hundred and fifty men with me at this compound."

Vivian swallowed and tasted the metallic burn of her own blood in the back of her throat. It didn't taste so special to her. One hundred and fifty. An army.

"Each is armed with weapons made at least partially of silver, and the restraints I have ready for your friends are made with silver as well. I've invested a lot of time and money into this plan, and I intend to see it fulfilled."

"You're insane."

A flash of teeth between bloodstained lips. "I prefer determined. Ever since I first learned about vampires and Lilith I knew my destiny was to be the man to raise the goddess and rule by her side."

Raise the goddess? Vivian would have gaped at him if her face didn't feel like a horse had stepped on it. "You're going to kill them." Realization burned through her, awful and hollow. Tears threatened, but she pushed them away. Time for those later—if she lived.

"Sacrifice," he corrected. "I'm going to make them a sacrifice to their mother. Along with these offerings." He gestured to the table with the jars. "The scripture says, 'The noble organs of five fallen women mixed with the blood of five first-generation vampires will give the Mother life, freeing her from her prison.' That is what's needed to give her human form."

Noble organs of five fallen women? The killings in London. That's what the wombs were for.

Sweet God, she was going to be sick. She sucked in a deep breath through her mouth, fighting to keep the bile at bay. Choking to death on a mixture of vomit and her own blood was not going to help Temple.

"What about me?" she asked. Oddly enough

she felt no fear for herself. She thought only of Temple, and of Olivia and Reign and their unborn child. She would kill Villiers herself before she allowed anything to happen to Temple or that baby. "Are you going to 'sacrifice' me as well?"

The hand that touched her cheek was gentle, almost fatherly. The gleam in his eyes could only be termed loving as he gazed down at her with such terrifying pride.

"Of course not. You're my Chosen, Vivian."

"Chosen how?"

Another of those damned smiles. " 'A woman of her blood will give the Mother flesh.' When Lilith rises she's going to need a body to inhabit. I'm going to give her yours."

Chapter 19

"The women should remain behind."

Temple laughed in Reign's face. They were sorting through the trunk of weapons Temple kept stashed in his cellar rooms. "You tell them that and see how far it gets you."

His friend obviously didn't share his humor. "I don't want Olivia in danger."

Laughter evaporating, Temple clapped a hand on the other man's shoulder. "I don't blame you, but do you really think she's going to let you go without her?"

An expression of defeat fell over Reign's face, but his gaze was proud as it fell upon his wife who sat on the other side of the room, clad in trousers and sharpening a wicked-looking blade. "No. She's determined to see this through and help save Vivian."

Temple was touched. "My thanks to both of you for that."

Reign shot him a narrow glance. "Did you think the lot of us would actually leave you to confront the Order on your own?"

He shrugged. "It would be the smart choice. You have Olivia and your child to think of. You all have wives. Why should all of you walk into a trap when I can do it on my own?"

His friend turned to him. "Because we've all been hurt by the Order in some way or another? Because we all want to see this end? Because no one wants to see you lose the woman you love? How about because we don't want to lose you?" His voice rose with every question. "Christ, Temple. Tell me you're not truly that stupid."

Did he laugh or punch his friend in the mouth? "I never said I loved her," he replied. The words caught around his tongue as he spoke.

"You don't have to. It's obvious to everyone but you."

A frown was the only reply Temple had a chance to make before Chapel joined them.

"Frank should stay here," he said, referring to Father Molyneux.

"Of course. Do you want me to talk to him?" How easy it was for him to fall into the roll of leader even after all these years.

Chapel replied that yes he would, and Temple left to complete the task. It wasn't difficult convincing the priest to remain behind. He wasn't well and he knew it, and he had enough reason to know that he would be more of a hindrance than a help.

The plan was fairly simple. Marcus would sneak in under cover of darkness, inserting himself into Villiers's compound. Hopefully no one would notice him, and if they did, he had the signet to back up his claim to be a member of the Order.

Payen and Violet were going to hang back while Temple and the others went inside. While Violet was eager to have her revenge on Villiers, she realized that it was smarter for them to remain out of sight, should the others need their help. Their presence might make Villiers do something rash.

"I'd like to say a prayer before you leave," Molyneux announced to the room when they were ready to leave.

Temple didn't know how much good God could do in this situation, but it certainly couldn't hurt to ask. He nodded his acquiescence and gestured for the others to come forward. They stood in a circle, holding hands, their heads bowed as the priest asked God to bless and protect them. He hadn't been one for religion in many years, but Temple felt a swelling in his heart when Molyneux added a prayer for Vivian as well.

After the prayer, they allowed Marcus a few minutes to say farewell to Shannon. She was obviously scared for her lover, but good Irish lass that she was, she bore it well. If Marcus managed to survive this assault—which Temple was going to do his damnedest to ensure—the two of them would probably make a future for themselves.

One more reason to get this night over with quickly. The sooner Villiers was dead and the Order crushed, the sooner they could all get on with their lives.

Living. That was a concept he hadn't had the luxury of indulging for quite some time. Always duty and responsibility. No one had asked him to do it, he simple assumed the mantle all by himself. It made it easier to be alone.

When this was over someone else could have the responsibility of the Blood Grail. Or perhaps they'd keep the pieces separate so everyone could share the burden. It would be nice not having to hide all the time. He could be lazy for once.

He looked forward to being lazy. Maybe he'd travel, do all the things he hadn't allowed himself to do for the past few centuries.

Would Vivian come with him? Or would she decide that her heart was better given to a man who could appreciate it? She would be happier, no doubt, but the idea of Vivian with another man made him want to rip someone's face off. Preferably the face of that other man.

With the farewells said and the plans all made, there was nothing left to do but depart. Marcus would fly with Temple since he was the only one in the party without said ability. Flight would make them harder to detect, although Villiers no doubt expected them to arrive by air. Flight was also faster than the ferry, and time was something they could not afford to waste any more of.

"We need to leave," he announced, gathering the group.

They left from the roof of the school, the added elevation making take off that much easier. Marcus climbed onto Temple's back so he could see better and not interfere with Temple's movement. It wasn't easy to fly with someone in your arms, or hanging off your neck.

Temple leaped off the roof first, taking point with Marcus while the others followed. They flew west toward the mainland, veering slightly toward Villiers's location. Temple had to rely strongly on Marcus's memory for details and landmarks, as it was difficult for the young man to see in the dark, especially at such a height. Temple however, could see perfectly, and thankfully Marcus's memory was impeccable. He directed the murder of vampires to exactly the right spot.

They touched down on the roof. There weren't any guards positioned there, not that Temple was surprised. Villiers didn't want to prevent them from coming inside. He welcomed them with open arms.

At the edge of the roof, Temple stopped and turned to address his companions. "I want you all to know how much it means to me that you came with me tonight."

No one moved. In fact, they all looked rather put out with him. Saint gave him a particularly filthy look. "Do you honestly think we'd let you do this alone? Don't be an arse. This is as much our fight as it is yours."

Temple grinned at the darker man. "Then let's give Villiers a fight." It was as good as any other war cry he'd ever uttered. Though slightly less forceful, it was no less bloodthirsty.

"Good luck," Payen said, clapping Temple on the shoulder. "We'll be there when you need us."

Temple thanked him and was surprised when the other vampire walked away, but his wife remained behind. Violet looked at him with an uncomfortable but sincere gaze. "I hope Vivian's all right," she said.

"So do I," he replied with a faint smile, and then watched as she went to join her husband.

Payen and Violet took cover in the boughs of a nearby oak that faced the back of the building. There, they could listen and watch for signs of trouble, yet hide from prying eyes. They were close enough to the landing spot that their scent would not be easily detected by a nosferatu— if Villiers had one under his command. Temple hoped he didn't. Nosferatu were bastards to fight and even harder to kill.

They jumped from the roof in the back of the

building where the light was dimmer and shadows thicker to a landing below. There, Saint pried open a casement on the ground floor for Marcus to slip through. He was on his own now.

"Be careful," Prudence advised her friend.

Marcus grinned at her. "I always am." But Temple could see a flicker of fear in the mortal's eyes. He'd be foolish not to be at least a little frightened. If this went badly they could all die tonight.

The vampires watched until he was all the way inside, and then watched a little bit longer to make sure he wasn't detected. When he saw the light from a door opening inside, Temple allowed himself a little relief. So far, so good.

The remaining nine of them dropped to the ground.

"Think the front door is open?" Bishop asked with a grin, his teeth flashing white and sharp in the moonlight.

Temple returned the smile with a grim one of his own. "If it's not, it soon will be."

Of course the door was unlocked. Villiers really wanted to make this ridiculously simple for them. He should have left it locked, at least then he'd know they'd arrived by the sound of solid oak being ripped off its hinges.

Inside the building was quiet. Temple strained his ears and heard the unmistakable sound of Villiers's voice far below. "They're in the cellar."

"I suppose they wouldn't want the lot of us frying in the sun before they were done with us," Saint remarked.

The others slowly turned to stare at him in disbelief. "What?" Saint gave them a look that clearly said they were being foolish. "It makes sense."

Unfortunately, he was no doubt correct. It made sense to choose the part of this building no sunlight could permeate.

They moved onward, down the many flights of stairs, moving as slightly as possible. Temple caught Marcus's scent. The young man had come this way, and he had been alone. That was good.

There was only one entrance to the cellar, where the sound of voices was louder now. Temple heard Vivian, and his heart leapt in response. She was safe. She was alive.

The latch on the door was broken, as though it had been busted from the inside. Temple smiled, knowing without a doubt that Vivian had tried to escape—and almost succeeded.

He didn't bother to think, or hesitate. Hesitation got people killed, lost opportunities. He simply grabbed the handle and ripped the door right off its hinges. Then he tossed it toward the center of the room as he walked inside, followed by his own little army.

"Hello, Rupert."

He took stock of everything at once—the guards suddenly closing in, the restraints on the wall—

and Vivian. She was shackled to an altar in the center of the room with Villiers's standing beside her, looking so very pleased with himself.

"My dear, Mr. Temple. How lovely to see you again." Then he looked past them. "Gentlemen, our guests have arrived."

Temple turned and saw that more guards had come into the room behind them, along with several well-dressed gentlemen whom he guessed to be the upper echelon of the Silver Palm.

It only took seconds for violence to break out, but it seemed much longer. He was highly aware of everything, all of his senses on high alert.

He picked a guard up by the throat and threw him, ignoring the pain of a silver blade slicing his arm. Another he backhanded across the cellar. Marika kicked one of them in the chest and the air crackled with the sound of snapping bone.

"Enough!" Villiers shouted.

The smell of familiar blood filled his nostrils and Temple whipped around with a snarl that was feral even in his own ears.

Vivian.

Villiers had cut her—marred the perfection of her ivory skin with a thin slice along the fragile skin of her cheek. She shook her head at him, and he noticed that her nose was swollen and bruised as well. Broken. Temple faced his enemy, body braced to pounce. He was going to kill this bastard.

Villiers smiled. "So very predictable, Mr. Temple. I knew you'd rush here to save Vivian."

"I'd be too late if I tried to save Kimberly, wouldn't I?" Temple replied calmly. "Or did you not kill her this morning?"

The other man tilted his head thoughtfully. "Did you have someone spying on me, Temple? How smart of you. Did you think of that yourself?"

Behind him, Reign growled low in his throat at the condescending tone, but Temple gave no reaction. Villiers was trying to bait them. He enjoyed thinking he had power over them.

And in reality, he had all the power. The others might be willing to risk Vivian's life, but Temple wasn't. And Villiers knew that now.

"You're not going to survive this, Villiers," he promised.

Rupert ignored that. "This would be over so much quicker if the nine of you would simply step into those restraints on the wall there." Villiers pointed with a trembling hand. "Otherwise I might be forced to cut my dear Vivian again."

The guards closed in with silver-tipped bayonets. Villiers's lieutenants joined him near the altar, smiling smugly.

Temple took a step toward the restraints, only to be seized by Chapel. "Don't do this."

He smiled thinly at his friend. "I have to. You asked me if I loved her, and I believe now I have your answer." With that soft confession, he resumed his course and walked up to the first set of shackles.

He did not mind giving up his own life for Vivian's. What plagued him was that she would never know that he did indeed love her, so very much. It weighed upon his heart.

Villiers dragged the blade along the line of Vivian's smooth throat, not opening the flesh, but applying just enough pressure to leave a mark. "Now the rest of you, or I'll kill her."

He wasn't bluffing, and the others knew it. Whatever he needed Vivian for it was obvious that he didn't need her alive—or not completely.

"We're not doing this because you say to," Reign informed him, stepping forward only to have a bayonet waved in his face. "We're doing this for Temple."

Villiers made a face. "How very touching. Please stop talking and get into the restraints."

The weight in Temple's chest grew as one by one, his friends followed him into the shackles. They were sacrificing themselves for him. For Vivian.

Bishop glanced at him as he walked by. "I hope you know what you're doing."

He did—try to survive whatever came next and save Vivian.

Once they were in place, guards came along to fasten the shackles. It only took one breath for Temple to identify his guard, even though the man wore a hooded cloak. Bright blue eyes met his from beneath the lip of the wool hood. It was Marcus. He brought the silver-lined restraints around Temple's ankles, thighs, chest, and arms. The silver burned him, but only when he touched it. Marcus had left the shackles loose enough that he could avoid the pain.

Loose enough that they would be that much easier to break free of.

On the altar, Vivian watched the vampires give themselves up. She knew that it was for her as well as Temple—she could see it in the eyes of Olivia, Pru, Ivy, and Marika. They were doing this because they cared about her, and because they knew she loved Temple. Tears sprang to her eyes and spilled over in hot, shameful streams. How could they? And yet, as painful as it was, her heart swelled with love for each of them. For the first time in years she felt like she was part of a family, and she would gladly die to protect each and every one of them.

She struggled against the iron holding her to the altar, but it wouldn't budge. For the first time in her life she felt weak and powerless. As frustration dried her tears she saw Temple watching her and her breath caught in her throat, paralyzing her. There was love in his gaze. She didn't know when it first touched them, or what she had done to deserve it, but it was there.

This was *not* going to be the end, damn it.

"Excellent," Villiers crowed. "Now we can begin." He gave her a pat on the head, like he used to when she was younger and he wanted to reassure her. Bastard.

"Gentlemen, your assistance please."

She could only lay there, helpless as Villiers and his cronies set five silver bowls on the altar, one at each hand and foot and the other near the top of her head. Into these bowls they placed the contents of the jars from the table. Bile bittered the back of Vivian's throat at the sight of the bloody wombs.

She caught sight of Marcus, dressed like one of the acolytes in a dark robe. If he was free then Temple must have a plan. Payen and Violet had to be out there, waiting to spring.

"Now for the amulets," Villiers commanded.

Five men came forward and removed the amulets from the necks of Temple, Reign, Saint, Bishop, and Chapel. Why had they worn them? Without every component of the ritual, Rupert couldn't indulge his insanity. One look at their faces and she knew it had been part of Temple's plan. The hooded men brought the amulets to the altar and placed one in each of the bowls. Villiers smiled gleefully, his eyes shining with a terrifying madness, because he didn't realize he was mad at all. To him, this was about power.

"And now for the blood."

This time four more guards joined the previous

five. Each was armed with a long, slightly curved silver dagger.

"No!" Vivian cried. Straining, she turned her head to look at Villiers, to plead with the man who had been so like a father to her. "Please don't do this."

Rupert's hand settled on her brow, cool and dry. "I'm doing this for us, Vivian. You'll thank me when it's over."

She wouldn't be herself when this was over. Perhaps that was a blessing. The pain of losing Temple wouldn't be as sharp if someone else possessed her body and mind.

"Now!" Villiers cried.

The blades raised, flashed in the brilliant glare of the candles and lamps. And then blood began to trickle from the vampires' necks. The guards had sliced their throats with silver so the wounds wouldn't heal as quickly.

Strange relief washed over Vivian. Loss of blood couldn't kill a vampire—she remembered that. The wounds would eventually heal, and Temple and the others would reach a feral state that would enable them to break the shackles—and anything else—if Rupert allowed them to lose too much blood. This was not going to kill them, only weaken them if Rupert did it right, and she had no doubt he knew exactly what he was doing.

There was still a chance Temple and the others would survive, thank God!

Rupert's minions caught the flow of vampiric blood in silver goblets. The blood hissed and spattered as it struck the metal. The guards ignored it just as they ignored the pain on their victims' faces. Tears leaked out of Vivian's eyes once more, but she refused to shut them or look away.

Above her, Rupert began to chant in a strange language. It wasn't Latin. It sounded like old Gaelic. The harder Vivian listened, the more the words began to make sense. This was the language of Lilith—and she understood it.

Rupert begged the goddess to awake from her slumber, to accept his sacrifice to her and rise once more, joining with him. The guards came forward now, bringing their cups of blood to the altar. Rupert dipped his finger in the first—Temple's blood—and traced a line of hot wetness across Vivian's forehead. He crossed the line with the blood from another cup, drawing a pattern on her skin that she could not identify, but that each line was made up of a different vampire's blood. All the while he kept chanting, asking Lilith to come forth.

She recognized the words again—he was talking now about the offering of "noble organs" and then the part about a woman of Lilith's blood providing the body. He offered Vivian to the goddess for possession as he emptied each goblet of blood into the bowls surrounding her.

A hush fell over the room, as though all sound

had been taken away. The altar trembled beneath her and Vivian couldn't stop an exclamation of fear. It was working. Oh dear God, whatever Rupert had done, it was working!

Her gaze went to Temple, who strained against his restraints like an animal. The wound in his neck was still bleeding and he was pale and damp with perspiration. The metal around his wrists snapped. He was going to break free!

A mist began to swirl in the bowls at her feet. The same thing began in the bowls by her hands, and she could only assume that a similar phenomenon brewed in above her head. The mist rose like a sweet-smelling smoke, filling Vivian's lungs and clutching at her heart.

This was it. Lilith was coming for her. It didn't matter how she struggled, or if Temple broke free of his restraints. In a moment, she would no longer exist.

And then the fingers around her heart eased, and it felt like something was withdrawing from her, easing out of her and taking a little bit of her with it.

At the foot of the altar the mist thickened, took shape. The candles flickered and then she was there.

Lilith. Naked and shameless. Beautiful and terrible. It was like looking in a strange mirror, the features were so much like her own, but very different as well.

And Lilith's eyes weren't merely the color of a storm—they raged like one. Her glorious hair spilled over her shoulders, past her waist and her skin glowed with a pearlescent shimmer no human could ever hope to reproduce.

She stared at Vivian. Vivian stared back, unable to look away, pinned by her ancestor's power. She wasn't afraid, and as recognition flared within Lilith's eyes, followed by a maelstrom of rage, Vivian knew she wasn't the one who should be afraid.

Villiers, however, seemed oblivious. "It worked!" His laughter rang through the cellar as he raised his arms in triumph. "The power of Lilith is mine!"

Lilith turned her head and saw the vampires shackled and bleeding against the wall. Then her gaze came back to Vivian before lifting to assess Villiers and the men behind him.

"How dare you," she said. Her voice was night itself, dark and deep and full of stars. "You harm my children and presume to have command over me?"

Villiers blinked. "My lady?" He swallowed. "I offer myself as your consort."

The goddess sneered at him, her face becoming all the paler and more terrible. "As if I would accept you."

Villiers went white. His wild gaze fell upon Vivian, still shackled and helpless on the altar.

"She's supposed to be in you," he whispered. His face contorted. "You ruined everything, you slut!"

Pain tore through Vivian's chest as the dagger plunged into it. She arched with a scream and fell back on the hard stone.

And then there was nothing as her life flickered and sputtered out.

Chapter 20

Temple roared as he watched Villiers stab the woman he loved. He threw himself forward, finally snapping the chains that bound him. Marcus rushed forth to help free the others as the guards ran for their lives—or their deaths. Reign was freed first then the others, but Temple paid them no heed as they threw themselves into the fray, ripping through guards like the men were made of tissue paper. He rushed for the altar and the woman bleeding to death on it.

"Vivian!" Temple screamed, stumbling toward her. But it was too late. He knew it with a glance. She was too still, too pale. Villiers's blade had pierced her heart.

He collapsed upon the altar, weak and half crazed. Tears of blood streamed down his face as his hands caressed the body of his beloved. He couldn't save her. She was already dead when he gathered her into his arms.

There came a great roar from the foot of the

altar, so full of anguish that it matched his own, and Temple raised his head to look at the woman who made it. The mother of them all lifted her gaze from Vivian's still body and settled it upon Villiers with terrible fury.

At that moment, Villiers seemed to realize just how much danger he was in. He ran.

And Temple, crazed with grief, and frenzied by loss of blood, set the corpse of the woman he loved back on the altar and tore after the man who had killed her.

"Get him!" Villiers screamed as he ran past his men. "Save me, you fools!"

They actually listened. Two guards tried to intercept Temple. They weren't much of a threat, but they bought Villiers a little time. Bastard. What kind of leader put himself before his men?

Temple didn't bother with fangs. He simply grabbed both men by the back of the head and smashed their skulls together. They crumpled to the floor at his feet, their stillness strange when juxtaposed with all the carnage and noise around them. He didn't know if they were dead. He didn't care.

He stepped over them and continued after Villiers. One after another, members of the Silver Palm tried to block his path and he broke them like eggshells. Out of the corner of his eye he saw Bishop and Marika descend upon one of the well-dressed gentlemen, snarling, their fangs out.

From the look on Marika's face it was personal, and Temple realized the man had been part of the Silver Palm the two of them faced in Romania.

With the deaths of these men, the Order of the Silver Palm would fall. That didn't give him nearly the satisfaction it would if Vivian were alive.

He ran up the cellar stairs. The slice in his neck was healing, and the rage inside him numbed the discomfort of it. He'd been hurt far worse in the long course of his life. But he'd never, never wanted blood as much as he wanted it right now.

Villiers wasn't far ahead. The scent of terror clung to him like a whore's perfume. Its stink filled Temple's nostrils and pushed his fangs free of his gums. He could overpower the man right now, but he let him run on a little farther. Let him think he could escape.

His prey ran outside, and Temple followed. When he burst into the night air, he saw Villiers dangling helplessly, his feet well above the grass, Violet Carr's hand around his throat, holding him above her head.

"Drop him," Temple growled.

Violet hissed at him. "He's mine! He tried to kill Payen."

Temple was not going to argue with her. "He killed Vivian."

A stricken expression replaced the bloodlust on the female vampire's face. Behind her, her husband laid a gentle hand on her shoulder. Slowly,

Villiers was lowered to the ground. Temple moved forward and seized the man by the arms.

Villiers was trembling, but he had yet to piss himself. His courage would be admirable in any other man.

"Ruined everything," he gasped, looking up at Temple. "It's all ruined."

Temple glared at him. They had suffered so much because of this man. His friends had faced so much danger, risked so much. And yet, they'd found the women they loved. Temple had found the woman he loved.

And because of Villiers he'd lost her. There wasn't a hell dark enough for him. No pain deep enough.

But nothing Temple could do—no torture he could inflict would ever bring Vivian back. Nothing could change the fact that she was gone forever. There would be no satisfaction in killing the bastard.

Temple thrust Villiers at Violet. "Make it slow," he commanded. "Make it hurt." And then, he turned and walked away, Villiers's whimpers—and then his screams—ringing in his ears.

He returned to the cellar, where the fight had begun to wind down. Only a few of the Order were still standing, trying to fend off the vampires, Marcus and Lilith. Lilith tore them apart like rag dolls.

Temple didn't bother joining in. He went straight to the altar, where Vivian still lay. Her skin white, her body still. Her chest was stained with so much blood her shirt looked black. He sat down on the smooth stone beside her, reaching out with numb fingers to touch her cheek as his throat squeezed so tight he could scarce draw breath.

He hurt. Hurt so deep he didn't know how he could ever come back from it. It was as though a part of him had been ripped away, never to be returned.

A scalding tear slipped down his cheek, followed by another.

It hadn't been just her blood. He didn't know what it was—her strength maybe. Her loyalty. The way she made him feel. The way she could make him smile. Or perhaps the way he felt that he didn't have to be the best with her. He didn't have to be the leader. He didn't have to always be strong. He could just be himself.

Whatever it was, it had made him love her. And now she was gone without ever knowing that.

His friends joined him. Around them the sight and smell of death hung thick upon the air and yet the group of them stayed where they were, somber with mourning near Vivian's lifeless form.

Their hands touched him, settling on his back and shoulders, trying to comfort him, but it didn't work. There was no comfort for him. The world was a bleak, dark place and he did not want to be part of it any longer.

He unfastened the shackles that held her wrists

and ankles and gathered Vivian into his arms. He was weak, but not so weak that he couldn't hold her. Not so drained that he couldn't weep over her with all the tears his breaking heart could afford.

He was scarcely aware when the room fell silent save but for a few whimpers. Strong fingers came down on his head, stroking his hair with a mother's love. He looked up, eyes dry and burning, into the warm and compassionate gaze of Lilith.

"I saved some of them for you," she said in that dark voice, waving a hand toward several men still alive, cowering on the floor. "Feed and regain your strength. Leave the child with me."

She meant Vivian. Temple shook his head, violently, clutching the still warm body to his chest. "No. I won't leave her."

Smiling serenely, Lilith reached down and pulled the dagger from Vivian's chest. Then, she took Vivian from him as though he was a helpless child with a doll. "Go feed, my son," she instructed, slicing her wrist with the blade. "I will take care of your love."

Temple backed away, but it took another compulsion from her inhuman eyes to make him turn away from Vivian. He left her with Lilith, who sat naked and streaked with blood upon the altar, cradling Vivian in her arms.

He didn't want to feed. Didn't care to feed, but there was some satisfaction in draining one of the men who had witnessed Vivian's death, and he relished it like a wolf relished a rabbit, joining his companions in the feast.

"Boy," came that dark voice from behind him.

Temple turned, as did his companions, all of whom had regained the better part of their strength. Marcus was of course the worse for wear, but at least he hadn't had his throat slit. Lilith stood in the middle of the room, holding Vivian in her arms as though she was no more than an infant.

Of course to a being such as Lilith, they were all children.

"She is ready for you," Lilith said, holding Vivian toward him like a gift.

Temple came forward. That Lilith was taller didn't bother him. That she was so strong that she reeked of power didn't matter, nor did the fact that she was naked. It was her face he couldn't look at—that face that looked so much like Vivian's, but so otherworldly at the same time.

He looked at Vivian instead and frowned. Was that color in her cheeks? Was she actually breathing, or did his eyes deceive him? He took her from Lilith, and as he felt her sweet weight settle in his arms, he could feel the warmth of her through his sleeves. Her eyelashes fluttered. She was alive.

His gaze jerked to the goddess before him. She smiled at him and it was so beautiful it hurt to look at. "I have given my daughter the gift of immortality," Lilith said, her voice filling the room like rays of moonlight. "You will spend it with her, yes?"

Temple nodded, his eyes filling with hot tears once more, but this time they were tears of joy. "Yes," he replied.

Lilith actually clapped. "And now, we leave this place." And with that announcement, flames sprung up in all corners of the room, leaving a path for them to depart. Temple carried Vivian and, along with the others, followed the naked goddess out into the night.

Villiers's compound burnt to the ground, and with it went everything that remained of the Order of the Silver Palm. Even if any members remained, they would never again be able to cause the damage Villiers had. Now that Lilith was free, there was no reason for them to continue.

Lilith, who was much easier to look at when she was scrubbed free of blood and wearing clothing, was welcomed at the Garden Academy with all the adulation an ancient deity might expect. Two of the ladies even fainted. And when she heard that the school no longer had a head mistress because of Kimberly's misguided betrayal, she volunteered to take over the role.

"I've spent the centuries listening and learning about this world," she told the humans and vampires gathered around her. "But there is still much I wish to learn. The women here can teach me, and I can teach them."

Of course, she would probably tire of Clare, but for now it was the perfect place for Lilith to become reacquainted with the world before setting off in it. She would have to learn to present as a human to protect herself—not that there was much chance of anyone ever harming her.

"And you," she said to Marcus. "You are a smart man. You will stay here as well and help me find Sammael."

Marcus's brows rose, but he knew better than to refuse. Besides, staying at the school meant staying with Shannon, and that didn't bother him in the least.

And then there was Vivian. By the time the sun set the night after her "death" she was as good as new. Lilith's blood had made her a vampire, but a vampire unlike any other. Her strength and abilities rivaled Temple's because she shared a link with Lilith that the others didn't. And she had a few mystical abilities that no one could explain—such as the ability to "sense" Olivia's child, and communicate with her to an extent.

"Her?" Reign's face lit up. "It's a girl?"

Vivian nodded. "I'm sure of it." Then she gave the expectant parents a broad smile. "And she's going to be perfect, don't you worry."

They hugged her, kissed her on both cheeks, and then said their farewells to Temple. Everyone was leaving them now that the ordeal was over, eager to get on with the new lives they'd started.

"Let's get together soon," Olivia suggested as she and her husband prepared to take their leave. "You'll all come when the baby is born, won't you?"

And everyone said they would.

Payen and Violet followed on their heels, after inviting Temple and Vivian to visit them sometime at their home in Brussels. Vivian took the invitation as an offer of friendship and accepted, despite not knowing what the future held for herself and Temple. At this point she was simply glad to be alive.

And she didn't miss the look that passed between Violet and Temple. She knew Violet had been the one to kill Rupert, and she was glad Temple hadn't done it, even though her former mentor got exactly what he deserved.

Bishop and Marika were the next to leave. They made plans to meet up with Saint and Ivy in Paris in a few weeks, but even still, the way Saint held his "daughter" as they said good-bye brought tears to Vivian's eyes.

Saint and Ivy left shortly after that, and then Chapel, Pru, and Molyneux. Their departure was perhaps the saddest for Vivian.

"I don't expect we'll see Father Molyneux again," she murmured once they were alone.

Temple frowned at her. "Is that a suspicion or a feeling?"

She took his hand in hers. "A feeling. He's not long for this world."

He didn't say anything, he simply hugged her. She loved that he accepted her for what she was, even with these new changes.

She loved him.

That night he took her to the village to feed and taught her the proper way to do it. He needn't have worried. She didn't have the frenzy or lack of finesse of a new vampire. It was as though she had been reborn an ancient.

They returned to the school fed and silent, both knowing that now they were going to have to discuss what had happened, and what had yet to take place.

"Are you truly all right?" he asked once they were in the privacy of their room.

Vivian nodded. "Yes." And it was true. "I feel alive. I feel strong and powerful. For the first time in my life I know what I truly am and I'm not ashamed of it."

He smiled. "The blood of a goddess will do that to you."

Wrapping her arms loosely around his neck, she leaned back and gazed up at his beautiful, rugged face. "It's not Lilith's blood that makes me feel this way. I've felt this way since the first time you looked at me."

"From my cage?" he teased.

She grinned. "Yes. Perhaps it was the fact

that you were drugged, but I thought we had a connection."

He laughed as well and pulled her close. Then his grip on her tightened and his laughter faded. "I lost you. I thought you were gone forever when Villiers stabbed you."

She pressed her lips against his neck. "I'm never leaving you again—not unless you want me to."

He pulled back enough to meet her gaze. "I want you with me. I can't imagine forever without you in it."

Tears prickled her eyes. "You love me."

A sweet, crooked smile curved his lips. "I do. I don't know when it happened or how, but I do. I have for a while."

That was news. She pulled back a bit to better look at him. "You never said anything."

"Because I was an idiot. I didn't know then what I know now. You're the most important thing in my life. I realized that when Villiers tried to take you from me."

When Villiers stabbed her in the heart. There was irony in his trying to destroy the very organ Temple demanded. It still hurt to think of the man she had once thought so much of wanting her dead. But she wasn't going to think of him anymore. Not now. "I love you."

His gaze locked with hers. "I love you too."

Vivian laughed. "After all we've been through, that seemed to be remarkably easy."

Temple chuckled as well. "It was."

And then they stopped talking and stopped chuckling. They undressed each other slowly, savoring the fact that they were finally alone with no intrigue or agendas hanging over them, no mistrust or questions.

When they were both naked, he took her to the bed, and knelt between her splayed thighs. His loving gaze roamed over her, bringing a wonderful flush to her skin, making her tingle all over.

"I'm forever grateful to Lilith for giving you back to me," he said thickly. "If things hadn't gone as they had I'm not sure I could have ever brought myself to try to change you and risk you ending up like Lucinda."

"I think you would have, if you wanted to badly enough." She smiled. "Do you think you can put up with me for eternity?"

Temple grinned, flashing his big white teeth at her. "I do."

Then he bent down and flicked the tip of his tongue over one of her nipples. Vivian gasped. "Oh! That's nice." Becoming vampire had heightened *all* of her senses and the feel of Temple's mouth on her was the most exquisite pleasure she'd ever experienced.

And that was only the beginning.

He licked and bit until her flesh puckered and ached. He teased her other breast with his fingers, pinching that nipple tenderly, with just enough pressure to dampen her thighs and make her arch against him.

Then Temple slid his warm, slightly rough fingers down over her ribs, along her quivering belly, to the damp valley between her thighs. Her body jumped as his fingers parted the curls there, rubbing her with insistent tenderness. Vivian clutched at his hair, clenching her jaw to keep from crying out and begging him to take her right at that moment.

She wanted to make this last as long as she could.

As he continued to torture her breast with his mouth, one of his fingers eased between the slick folds of her flesh, searching out and easily finding the knot of flesh that ached and tensed for his touch. Need flared deep inside her, driving her to move against his hand.

Lifting his head from her heated, saliva-slick flesh, Temple watched his fingers stroke the wetness between Vivian's thighs. He parted the lips of her sex and gazed hungrily at the exposed, delicate part of her. Vivian shivered at the desire on his face, and she reached down, wrapping her own fingers around the thick length of him and squeezed gently, moving her hand up and down.

"Do you want me?" he demanded, arching his hips against her fingers.

Vivian nodded. "Yes. Now."

Temple couldn't even chuckle, his throat was so dry. He kept his gaze fastened on Vivian's as he guided his cock to the entrance of her slick cleft. She spread her thighs even wider, lifting his hips to invite him in.

He hesitated, then let go of himself. "If you want me, take me. Put me inside you."

Color blossomed in her smooth cheeks, but her eyes were bright, glittering with want in the candlelight. She was so beautiful, so breathtaking, his Amazon. All blood-flushed and damp heat, she was sweet enough to eat, which he intended to do later.

"Put my cock inside you, Vivian." It was a command and a plea at the same time. He didn't care if she was practically a goddess herself, or that she was probably more powerful than he was. In his arms, she was his and he was hers, and there was no imbalance of power between them.

Raising her gaze to his, his seductress reached down and took him in her hand once more, bringing him flush against the wet opening to her body, holding him as she lifted her hips to take the head inside.

She felt so frigging good.

"Now you," she whispered in a tone echoing the one he had used. "Fill me."

He did. Slowly, he pushed, easing the aching stiffness of his cock into her tight heat, shivering as her body parted easily, accepting him like a slick, silken glove. Vivian gasped, raising her legs to take him as deep as possible.

Each thrust was deeper and more insistent than

the last. He held himself over her as her calves slipped around him. She was so tight. So sweet.

Vivian clung to him, her body pliant and eager under his. "I want to taste you," he growled.

She shivered and he felt it as though it was his own. "I want to taste you too."

Now it was Temple who trembled. He'd been bitten before, but it hadn't affected him like this. Excitement overpowered his uncertainty and he lowered his body toward hers, slipping one arm beneath her back to lift her shoulders so that his mouth was at her throat and hers at his.

His fangs distended, gums tingling in anticipation. He pierced her skin a second before she pierced his and he was unprepared for the sheer jolt of ecstasy that slammed into him, bringing him to an explosive climax with absolutely no warning. Stars danced behind his eyes as Vivian's wet heat flooded his mouth and his cock. She cried out against his neck, her body shuddering and convulsing as she too was hit by orgasm.

They collapsed together in a boneless heap, lying together silent and incapable of thought for several minutes.

"If I didn't love you before," Temple joked. "I do now."

Vivian laughed. "Same here." She turned her head toward him, flashing him the superior smile of a woman who recovered well before her man. "What do you want to do now?"

Chuckling, he drew her into his arms, holding her against his chest. He could spend forever holding her like this.

"I'd like to take you to Paris," he said. "And maybe Russia. Would you like that?"

She was all wide-eyed and mock innocence. "Tonight?"

He grinned. "No, but soon. Tonight you'll be lucky if I'm able to walk let alone travel."

She snuggled closer. "I'd love to go to France and to Russia. I've never been to either country."

"We have eternity," he reminded her softly, liking the way that sounded. "We can go anywhere you want and do anything you want."

"Anything?" she challenged.

"Within reason. No more falling down pits, that's just silly."

Laughing, she rolled on top of him, her eyes sparkling with so much love his throat tightened at the sight. "I'm so glad I chased you," she murmured as she lowered her head toward his.

Temple smiled, stroking the hair back from her face. "I'm glad I let you catch me."

And then she kissed him and Temple realized that out of all the choices he had ever made, all the consequences he had ever faced, loving Vivian was the best.

Epilogue

New York City, 2009

"**S**even hundred and thirty years old." Temple shook his head with a smile as he raised his glass of champagne. "And sometimes I feel every one of them."

Across the table from him, at the posh private table in an equally posh French restaurant, Reign raised his glass as well. "Here's to another seven hundred. Happy birthday, my friend."

They were all together, the ten of them for the first time since Christmas the year before. Ever since defeating the Order of the Silver Palm over a century earlier they'd made the effort to get together more often, allowing that if they had kept in touch more in the past, perhaps the Order wouldn't have been able to sneak up on them as it had.

After a chorus of agreement, they all drank. How odd it was, Temple reflected, to sit here with them in this modern place, the men dressed in suits while the women sported chic hairstyles and expensive dresses. They all looked as they had one hundred years earlier, but still different, as only time and fashion could command. Even his Vivian, who still favored trousers, was dressed in an elegant black dress that displayed the creaminess of her skin and set off the amazing red of her hair.

There were two other women in the restaurant with hair as red, but neither was naturally that shade. And there were many women equal in height to his wife now as well. In fact, in this city her statuesque form, full lips, and stormy eyes weren't considered a defect, but rather something to be revered. She thrived in this relatively new century, and had blossomed into a wonderfully confident woman before his very eyes.

If possible, he loved her more now than he had the day Lilith gave her back to him.

Speaking of the goddess . . . "Has anyone heard from Lilith?" he asked, taking another sip of champagne.

"She's in Greece last I heard," Saint replied, his arm slung casually over the back of Ivy's chair. "I believe someone claimed to have seen Sammael there."

Bishop shook his head. "I feel sorry for him if she finds him." He was seated on the same side of the table as Saint, with Marika positioned between them. Although there was great affection on her part for Saint, it was obvious that her heart belonged to Bishop from the smile on her face. And if that didn't do the trick, the roundness of her belly certainly would. The two of them were expecting their first child, having jumped on the bandwagon started by Reign and Olivia over a century earlier.

Their daughter, Dreux, named for one of their brethren who had taken his own life six centuries earlier, was in England, attending night classes at university for the fifth time in the last fifty years. Temple had no idea what she was studying this time, or why Olivia and Reign continued to indulge her when she was obviously old enough to go out on her own. She rented a flat with Olivia's nephew James and the two of them got on quite well, even though people often mistook Dreux for James's older sister when the boy was twenty years her senior. James had been changed at twenty while Dreux's body seemed to stop aging once she hit her mid-twenties and her vampire genes fully came into maturation.

It had been fascinating to watch from a distance, but the stories he heard from Reign made Temple think twice about becoming a father himself.

Apparently Saint shared his reservations as he and Ivy had yet to reproduce. Chapel and Pru, however, had two. A girl named Francis after their long departed friend Father Molyneux, and a boy named Marcus. Both of their children were off somewhere else as well, finding their own way in the world at ages ninety and seventy-five respectively.

Temple raised his glass. "Another toast. To Molyneux and Grey, two of the best men I've ever known."

There were sad smiles around the table as glass after glass joined his. Molyneux had succumbed to illness shortly after defeating the Silver Palm. He had been able to return to his beloved France and died in his own bed, as peacefully as any man could wish.

Marcus Grey had died a year after his wife Shannon in 1970 at the age of ninety-eight. He had been at an archaeological dig in northern England, excavating Norman ruins when his heart finally gave out. He was buried beside Shannon on the Island of Clare. All five of their children were still alive, as well as their grandchildren and great grandchildren, all of them having been blessed by the same longevity given to their parents.

"To life," Chapel said. "May it always be measured in experience rather than years."

"To life," Temple repeated in unison with the others. He took Vivian's hand in his as he lifted his glass. "And to love, the one experience that makes all the years worthwhile."

The others cheered and teased him for being sentimental, but as Vivian leaned over and kissed him, Temple didn't mind the ribbing. He was simply glad for the woman beside him and the friends gathered around him—and all the experiences—and years—that involved them.

And all the adventures that were yet to come.